THE
PSYCHOLOGY
❧ OF ❧
TIME
TRAVEL

Kate Mascarenhas is a part-Irish, part-
Seychellois midlander. She has worked as a
copywriter, a psychologist, and a bookbinder.
She lives with her husband in a small terraced
house which she is slowly filling with Sindy
dolls. This is her first novel.

THE
PSYCHOLOGY
⚓ OF ⚓
TIME
TRAVEL

KATE
MASCARENHAS

HEAD
ᵒᶠZEUS

First published by Head of Zeus in 2018

975312468

A catalogue record for this book is available from the British Library.

ISBN (HB): 9781788540100
ISBN (TPB): 9781788540117
ISBN (E): 9781786699152

Printed and bound by CPI Group (UK) Ltd, Croydon, CR0 4YY

Head of Zeus Ltd
First Floor East
5–8 Hardwick Street
London EC1R 4RG

WWW.HEADOFZEUS.COM

For Matthew Murtagh

1

Barbara

The laboratory, in Cumbria, was home to four young scientists. Margaret was a baroness turned cosmologist. Lucille had come from the Toxteth slums to make radio waves travel faster than light. Grace – who never gave the same account of her history twice – was an expert in the behaviour of matter. And the last was Barbara: the baby of the group, hair so fair it was nearly white, ruddy-cheeked and naively wholesome. She specialised in nuclear fission. All four women were combining their knowledge in a new, and unique, project.

They did so in near isolation. The lab overlooked the Lakeland Fells. Some nights, when Barbara's head was too full of equations, she would run outside with Grace and yell at the darkness because they liked to hear the echo. There were no neighbours close enough to complain. No one visited by day either – not even the postman. Each month Barbara collected mail from the village five miles away: bills for Margaret, the latest *Paris Match* for Grace, and letters from Lucille's grandmother in Montego Bay.

But one spring afternoon, a van stopped outside the lab with a delivery for them all. The driver jumped out and pulled open the rear doors. He unloaded a hutch full of rabbits.

When he left, the women carried the hutch to the workroom, and peered inside. The rabbits had crammed themselves into the darkest corner. Their ears and limbs lay flat against their bodies. Each hair trembled. The rabbits were watchful and chary of their new owners. They were right to be.

Barbara snapped on a pair of latex gloves. She opened the wire door and reached for the nearest rabbit. His fur was brown and his eyes black. He struggled for a moment then settled in her arms. Through her lab coat Barbara could feel the warmth of his body.

'Shall we give him a name?' she asked the others.

'Yes,' Margaret said. 'For the history books!'

'He's a scruffy fellow,' Grace said. 'His name should be scruffy too.'

'Call him Patrick Troughton,' Lucille suggested.

Everyone laughed.

'Patrick it is,' said Barbara. 'Shall we capture this on film?'

They all agreed, and Barbara fetched the camera. Through the viewfinder she watched her colleagues pose: Lucille, coiffed like Aretha Franklin with NHS glasses perched at the tip of her nose; blue-eyed Grace, her petite features framed by a dark pixie cut; and finally Margaret, smiling imperiously and smoothing her steel-blonde bob.

Barbara set the timer and ran to stand at Lucille's side. This was a special occasion. The women erupted in laughter, from shared excitement, as the camera clicked.

'Right then, ladies,' Margaret said. 'Let's put Patrick to work.'

At the far end of the workroom was a hollow steel machine, about the size of a hatbox. The women had spent two years on its design and construction. It could propel a marble up to thirty seconds through time. On most attempts the marble arrived intact.

Today, Patrick would become the first living time traveller – just as long as he, too, remained intact.

Barbara weighed the rabbit. On examination, his mouth and nose were clean, and his feet were free of abscesses. His nails were recently clipped. She shone a torch into his ears to check they were clear. He appeared to be in excellent health. Finally she checked his respiration and heart rate, and wrote the figures down.

'Normal range,' she told the others.

'Mine isn't,' Grace replied.

More laughter; nervous this time. The team needed a successful animal trial. Without it, they'd never get funding to develop human time travel.

'We're all set,' Barbara said, and placed the rabbit in the time machine. She adjusted the dials. Now she must join Margaret and Grace and Lucille as spectators. There was nothing to do but wait.

At the machine's whine Patrick's ears twitched. He shuffled and sniffed the metal walls, but they were too smooth for him to climb.

'Three... two... one...' Barbara counted down.

Patrick's fur was fading to fawn, like a coat lightened by years of wear. He grew steadily paler, towards translucency, until he resembled only a ghost of himself. He slipped out of existence. The dematerialisation was complete. The steel cavity shone with afternoon sunlight.

Please come back, Patrick, Barbara prayed. *Come back safely.*

The women edged closer to each other. Grace gave Barbara's arm a reassuring squeeze.

And as surely as he'd disappeared, the rabbit returned. Whole. With an understandable expression of surprise.

'Oh thank God,' said Lucille.

'Respiration and heart rate?' Margaret prompted.

Barbara took the measurements. Patrick was so solid in her hands. He felt *real* – and he made their work, thus far theoretical, feel real too. To Barbara's relief, his heart and breathing – though faster than before – were still in a normal range.

'We've done it,' Barbara said. 'You bloody brilliant women. We've *done* it.'

They hugged, their voices mingling as they spoke over each other, and Barbara's vision blurred with tears. She was so grateful – for Lucille's superluminal research, and Grace's thermodynamics, and Margaret's utter, unshakeable conviction that they would succeed. The team were pioneers. They were going to be the first people to travel through time.

'This occasion calls for cigars!' Lucille said. 'What's on the menu this evening?'

Barbara wiped her eyes. 'I'm afraid all that's in the larder is sardines and baked beans. With evaporated milk and tinned peaches for dessert.'

'All lovingly decanted,' said Grace.

'Speaking of feasts,' Margaret said, 'we should give Patrick a last supper. Check his digestion's shipshape before dissection.'

'No!' Barbara exclaimed involuntarily.

'No?' Margaret repeated. 'Why shouldn't we feed him?'

'Feed him – but don't dissect him.'

'We must, darling,' said Grace. 'The sooner we check for internal injuries, the sooner we can plan human trials.'

Grace was right, and Barbara struggled to reply because

she was embarrassed by her own sentimentality. She'd conducted her share of dissections over the years. However, none of those animals had achieved anything as wondrous as this rather dim, rumpled rabbit: he was the first living creature to ever travel through time. A summary execution horrified her.

'We have all the other rabbits for replication experiments,' Barbara said when she found her words. 'There's going to be lots of dissections to choose from. Patrick doesn't need to be one of them.'

'Actually,' Margaret said, 'I *can* see the benefits to keeping him alive. The press will be interested in the first rabbit time traveller. You know how gaga the public go over animals.'

Press coverage would make it easier to attract funding. Up till now they had got by on a few small grants. They had been helped, too, by Margaret's wealth. But they would require much greater investment to continue. Clearly Margaret thought Patrick could play a small part in winning the money they needed.

'I suppose he'd make a sweet lab mascot,' Grace said.

'So Patrick lives,' Lucille concluded.

Patrick swiftly became Barbara's pet. She took responsibility for feeding and watering him, and for changing his bedding. He came to recognise her voice. His personality turned out to be a playful and affectionate one. He'd even sit on her lap if called, which gave her quiet satisfaction. Everyone recognised that Patrick belonged to Barbara. But when she was forced to leave the lab – before the completion of their project – she was not allowed to take Patrick with her.

*

All four of the pioneers were still working together when the military agreed to subsidise tests with humans. Most of the money that flowed through was spent on fuel. The pioneers' small prototype machine had minimised fuel requirements by using existing wormholes, but this cheap, crude technology was only suited to small inanimate objects – or expendable travellers like Patrick – because the risks of malformation were high. Safe time travel was more energy intensive.

Money was also allocated to labour. Transporting people through time required a machine the size of a tennis court. A fleet of engineers came to the Fells to assist with the build. They sheltered in a circle of caravans, while the pioneers continued to sleep in the lab. One of the engineers mentioned to Barbara that down in the village, the locals were convinced the time travel project was a ruse: the engineers were building a nuclear weapons site, and the secrecy was meant to prevent demonstrations. The idea of a functioning time machine seemed too absurd to believe. Barbara was faintly amused by this, but didn't dwell on it, because the villagers seemed so remote from her day-to-day work. All the world seemed distanced from her. She knew Margaret cared a great deal about public perceptions, and was driven, in part, by a need to make her mark before everyone. Whereas Barbara was excited by the prospect of time travel itself, and loved her colleagues because they were going to help her achieve it. Her life had shrunk to the size of the lab, but she felt it was about to grow – grow as far as the time machine allowed her to travel. It was easy then, to throw herself into the complex, grinding mathematical work the team needed to make their project succeed. It was easy to forget to rest, or to eat, until the others made her. Three in the morning would roll round and she would still be at her desk. Grace would pad across the workroom, her satin eye mask high on her head – the one Lucille had adorned with curly eyelashes in permanent ink – and she would implore:

'Come to *bed*, Bee.'

'In a minute.'

There was always another minute needed, so Grace would have to drag her by the arm into the dorm. There were four iron beds, but once the frosts started and their breath misted indoors as well as out, the women doubled up for warmth like babes in the wood. Often Bee didn't sleep even once she was under the covers because her mind raced with her work. But it was comforting to feel Lucille's arm slung over her in slumber, or to hear Grace's soft breath.

In waking hours the others were as diligent as Barbara. She concentrated on minimising the amount of fuel they would require; Lucille perfected the warping of wormholes to maximise the speed of travel; and Grace carefully tested the composition of objects that passed through the time machine for any changes that might pose a safety risk. Their endurance paid off. The time machine was completed by the first week of December. Rather than switching it on, the pioneers announced the machine would be activated in the New Year. Margaret told the engineers this was because most journalists were already thinking about their holidays and it would be easier to get their attention in January. Barbara wondered whether they believed her. The invention of time travel, surely, would be a big story for any journalist, however demob happy they were. Privately, Margaret had said that they should proceed with a December date for their inaugural trip, but she didn't want an audience. If anything went wrong she wanted full control over who knew.

All the engineers accepted Margaret's instruction to take leave. They were eager to see their families, and loath to spend more time in poorly heated caravans, no matter how cheerfully adorned with tinsel and red baubles. Barbara knew that her parents would expect her in Cornwall – that Margaret would be expected in Windermere by her aunt, and that Lucille would be expected in Liverpool by her mother. Grace would have been welcome at any of the pioneers' homes. But by consensus the pioneers stayed in the lab instead; now that their work was nearly complete, none of them wished to leave. They were going to change the world.

*

On Christmas morning the pioneers donned their boiler suits and trod the brittle white grass to the time machine. Barbara set it to transport them one hour into the future. The women held hands. They stepped, in unison, through the machine entrance, and heard the doors slide shut on the present. Barbara's eyes did not adjust to the darkness. She smelt ozone and heard steel parts screech against each other. Her ears rang as the machine fell quiet. Behind her the doors slid open again – she could feel winter sunshine on her neck, and see her own shadow on the smooth grey floor. The pioneers dropped each other's hands and turned to face the light.

At the entrance to the time machine, the women's future selves stood on the grass. They looked as gleeful as the hosts of a surprise party. The future Grace hopped on the spot in excitement.

Barbara's gaze was drawn to her own twin.

Your face is the wrong way round, Barbara thought. *You've been burning the midnight oil – that's why you're pale. You are trembling – you are blinking over and over. Has the hard work been worth it? You can remember my feelings. But I don't know what you're feeling at all.*

Barbara tentatively extended a hand in greeting.

Her older self laughed and crushed her in a hug.

'Isn't it funny?' the elder Barbara whispered. 'I feel *protective* of you.'

Barbara laughed too then. What could she do but laugh? It was absurd, to embrace one's self. She was still laughing when the pioneers stepped back into the machine to go home. She was still laughing when they arrived in their own time. The world she returned to seemed brighter and more deeply coloured than before. Wasn't it wonderful, she thought, that time travel had granted her a new joy in her surroundings?

'Are you hearing things differently?' she asked the other pioneers. 'Your voices sound musical to me.'

Her friends exchanged puzzled glances.

'Someone's had too much excitement,' Grace told Barbara fondly. 'What's for Christmas dinner?'

'Tinned turkey,' Barbara said. 'And baked beans. Lovingly decanted.'

*

On Boxing Day they made their second trip into the future – in fact, they made numerous trips, returning to Boxing Day in between each one without stopping to rest. The effect was dizzying. If the pioneers left their home timeline at noon, they might arrive in the next late at night, and the transition felt instant. Their daylight hours shortened and lengthened drastically.

'Enough,' Lucille said when they returned home for the fifteenth time. 'I need sleep.'

'I don't,' Barbara sang. 'I don't. I don't.'

'You oddball,' Grace said. 'We always have to wrangle you like a toddler at bedtime.'

Margaret appraised Barbara. 'I think we should all get some rest.'

Barbara obliged by getting into her camp bed but as soon as the others slept, she intended to use the time machine again on her own. Once the others were breathing deeply she extricated herself from Lucille's embrace. Clean boiler suits, ready for the next day, hung on the wardrobe door. Barbara stepped into one of them, taking care to be quiet. As she left the bedroom, Barbara thought Margaret's eyes opened and fixed on her, but she turned over without comment.

The time machines ran on pellets of atroposium, encased in a lead briquette to minimise the handler's exposure to radiation. Barbara went to the fuel stores, which were in a separate building, to collect a couple of briquettes. She slipped them into her pocket. But then she was distracted. Instead of proceeding to the time machine she was transfixed by the storeroom's overhead light. How beautiful the glow was! The bulb's reflection on the concrete floor was astonishing – as if Barbara had broken through to a deeper level of sensory awareness. The transcendental nature of time travel had opened up this new world for her. She knelt on the ground, as if she could lap up the reflection like a dog at the waterside.

The following day she was woken by Margaret. Barbara lifted her head from the floor, disorientated. Her thoughts were racing, and they had taken on an unusual quality: she could *hear* them. They were as loud and indistinct as a rioting crowd. Margaret's voice competed for her attention.

'I've been looking for you everywhere,' Margaret was saying. 'What are you doing in here?'

'I don't remember.' Barbara's jaw ached. She must have been grinding her teeth in the night. The inside of her cheek was raw, as if she had been chewing it.

'Never mind, we haven't the time. I contacted the BBC this morning, to tell them the good news. They're sending a crew now.'

'That's good.'

'Are you sure you're quite well?' Margaret said. 'You seemed feverish yesterday. If you're coming down with something I can manage the interview with Lucille and Grace. It's absolutely vital we make a good impression.'

'I'm fine,' Barbara said, although there were black arabesques writing at the edge of her vision. 'Will we know the questions in advance?'

'We can rely on them to ask about paradoxes. They'll almost certainly raise that hoary canard about killing your grandfather before he grows up.'

'I think I can handle that.'

'Good. Wash your face and comb your hair, dear, we need to be presentable. Everyone in Britain is going to see your face! Everyone in the *world*.'

Barbara did as she was told then kept quiet while the others talked and laughed. The BBC crew arrived shortly, which was the cue for everyone to congregate outside the time machine. Barbara didn't like the influx of the camera and sound men. Over the past months she'd grown used to seeing only faces that she knew. For reassurance she looked again at her friends, and realised for the first time that Margaret was holding Patrick. He didn't much like to be held. Rabbits generally prefer to have all four feet on the ground. It was only Barbara's lap he could ever relax on.

'Why isn't he in his hutch?' Barbara asked.

'Patrick's our mascot! He should be here, of course.'

'Can't *I* hold him?' Barbara would benefit as much as Patrick. His warmth might calm her. She could still hear the rioting crowd of voices in her head.

'You can't be jealous of me holding your rabbit!' Margaret said in surprise. 'Come on, that newsman's beckoning us.'

They spent a few minutes rehearsing the interview, so that the questions and answers would flow convincingly. The lights were tremendously hot and bright. Barbara kept staring at them, and the newscaster reminded her to look at him. He was a grey-besuited man with a salmon pink pate. Then the real interview was under way.

The questions began benignly.

'So which period of history are you going to visit first?' the reporter asked. 'Tudors and Stuarts? The Roman Empire?'

'Sadly, we won't be shaking hands with Henry VIII,' Grace said. 'Time travel requires a particular infrastructure. You can't go back to any period before the machine's invention.'

'Which is no bad thing!' Lucille exclaimed. 'For some of us in particular, history would be a dangerous place.'

'Are there limits on travelling into the future, too?' the reporter asked. 'Can you tell me if I have a pools win on the horizon?'

'At the moment we're making trips of a short duration,' Grace explained. 'But the distance is getting longer all the time. We've already met some of our future selves.'

'How does that work?' the reporter asked.

Margaret took the lead. 'Well, for our first excursion, we activated the time machine at ten a.m. on Christmas Day. It transported us, instantaneously, to eleven o'clock of the same morning. At half past eleven we activated the time machine again, and travelled back to one minute past ten. What that means is between ten and ten-oh-one we didn't exist in the world at all. But between eleven and eleven thirty, there were twice as many of us – and we were able to meet!'

'I see. Isn't that rather risky?' asked the reporter. 'Everyone's seen *Doctor Who*. What if your future self accidentally killed you? What would happen *then*?'

The question was Barbara's cue to speak. She replied: 'That's called a paradox. A paradise, a paradigm, a patrick...'

'Say again, Dr Hereford?'

Barbara rubbed her fingers and thumbs in agitation. Her jaw was working up and down again. The crowd roaring in her head had reached a crescendo. 'Hereford is my name. People have names when they matter. We picked a name for our rabbit because he is pious, I mean a pioneer. I am a pioneer; and I *won't* be dissected, not for anyone! Not for you, Mr Salmon Pink Pate, Mr Cat Would Eat You All Up. I won't be dissected, or neglected, or resurrected!'

Lucille put a hand over the camera. 'The interview's over.'

'But, Dr Waters!' The newsreader grasped Lucille's wrist to loosen her grip on the lens. 'Our viewers will be very disturbed by this outburst. Don't you have an explanation?'

'She must be delirious,' Lucille said. 'Have you never seen a person with flu?'

'She's *clearly* unwell,' Grace said. 'Margaret, go ring the GP, fast as you can.'

Even in her disarray, Barbara saw Margaret's lips tighten.

Margaret rarely took orders, and Grace rarely gave them. But Margaret left to make the call, the rabbit still in her arms.

'No!' Barbara cried out. 'Leave Patrick with me!'

Grace brought her face close to Barbara's. 'My poor darling...'

The GP did not diagnose flu. Instead he suspected manic depression and sent Barbara immediately to the psychiatric hospital. It was in the ward that Barbara saw the footage of their interview, played over and over again on the news. Was she on drugs, the reporter speculated? Or had the process of time travelling, of which we understood so little, somehow destabilised her? The nurses switched the TV off when she shouted at the screen. She remained distressed, wondering what the other pioneers thought of her breakdown. Manic depression was a more frightening illness than influenza. She wished they would come to see her, or telephone her, so she could ask them if they were still her friends. Every visiting hour, she looked out, hopefully, for the arrival of Grace or Lucille or Margaret. She was sure they would come any day now. Any day.

2

Ruby

Ruby Rebello's grandmother was the time traveller who went mad.

Ruby had known this all her life. Granny Bee's meltdown had been broadcast to the nation and lingered in the popular memory for decades. Ruby's mother explained what had happened to Granny Bee when Ruby was quite small, but insisted that they mustn't mention it again. Well into adulthood, Ruby obeyed. A fascination with these family secrets led her to become a psychologist, yet she still refrained from asking Granny Bee about her past. She assumed this was what Granny Bee wanted.

And then, one afternoon, the past caught up with them.

They were in Bee's back garden, near St Ives bay. Bee was completing a crossword, while Ruby was changing the oil of her motorcycle; she had ridden from London the previous day. Breno, Bee's collie, was seeking refuge from the heat indoors. His staccato barking suddenly drowned out the drama playing on the radio.

'Must be someone at the front door,' Bee said, without looking up from her puzzle.

'Are you expecting visitors?' Ruby smeared oil across her flannel dress.

'Not a soul.'

Whoever caught Breno's attention had gone by the time Ruby reached the porch. The path was quite empty. There was only an origami rabbit, sitting at the centre of the doorstep. Ruby picked the rabbit up. Two words were inked in copperplate on his ear: *For Barbara*.

Ruby looked around once more – as if the messenger might be hiding behind a shrub or hedge, to watch her reaction. Breno sat panting happily. He could normally be relied upon to pester lurking guests; they must have passed out of his range.

Defeated, Ruby returned to the back garden.

'Look what I found by the door.' She placed the rabbit on the picnic table.

Barbara put down her pen, and ran her finger over the rabbit's ear.

'Do you know who it's from?' Ruby asked.

'Grace Taylor. She wrote her capital letters that way – all curls. A mystery present is just her style. She liked to keep everyone guessing.'

Like the other pioneers, Grace Taylor had become a household name. But Ruby had never heard Bee speak of her old colleagues. This breach of familial silence left Ruby unsure how to react. Instead of looking her grandmother in the eye, Ruby stared at the toes of her boots.

'D'you hear from Grace often?'

'No.'

'You didn't want to stay in touch?'

'She kept her distance, after I first went into hospital. All three of them did. I did try to contact Margaret several times, early on – there were issues over who owned what in the lab. But she wouldn't talk to me directly. It wasn't just my career that was over. It was our friendship.'

Ruby dared to look up. Bee was smiling sadly.

'Granny, that's awful,' Ruby said.

'In some ways it's just as well. Your mother doesn't like me to discuss that time of my life.' Bee's mouth pursed in a moue of anxiety. For years Ruby had thought Granny Bee's past was too painful for her to mention. Ruby hadn't known Bee's silence was imposed by Dinah.

'Why doesn't she like you to talk about it?' Ruby asked.

'The idea of time travel frightens her.'

'That's true for lots of people. It seems such an… *alien* thing to do.' Time travelling was an elite profession, out of reach for the average Joe or Josephine.

'Yes, but your mother's fear was very personal. She was scared of what it had done to me. And the one time she encountered some other time travellers… let's just say that didn't go well either.'

'You don't need to talk about time travelling with her.' Ruby took Granny Bee's hand. 'You can tell me what happened, instead.'

'Yes.' Bee smiled, squeezing Ruby's hand in return.

*

Back in the cottage, Bee pulled down shoeboxes from the top of her wardrobe, which were swollen with creased photos from the past. The box contained scenic pictures of the Fells where Barbara had worked; horizontal triptychs of mist and rippling earth and water. Others were technical shots, of machine components and test subjects, which Ruby assumed were a record of experiments. But she was most interested in the four women. She picked up a sun-bleached photo. There was Bee, her rosy face still recognisable; Lucille, who looked so full of wisdom and mischief; Grace, exuding all the cool of a French New Wave actress; and Margaret, her face already showing the determination that would make her one of the most powerful women in Britain. Such different women, and yet their laughter and uniforms suggested camaraderie. Bee didn't look mad. She looked like she belonged.

Bee pointed at the photograph.

'That rabbit in my arms was the first time traveller. He was my pet.'

'Is that why Grace sent you a paper rabbit?'

'Maybe.' Granny Bee took the origami from the pocket of her pinafore. She unfolded it into a small square of paper. 'Hm. That's interesting.'

'What is?'

'There's information printed on the back. It's notice of an inquest. From Southwark Coroner's Court.'

Ruby craned forward to look. The inquest was to be held in February 2018, and concerned the death of a woman in her eighties. The space where the victim's name should be read *Undisclosed*. But the most intriguing information was the date of death: 6 January 2018. This woman wouldn't die for another five months.

'This is from the future?' Ruby asked.

'Looks like it.'

'Why would Grace send this?' The most obvious explanation was that the body belonged to Grace herself. Or – Ruby's throat tightened – it belonged to Bee. 'It isn't a *warning*, is it?'

'What melodrama! I think it's a memento mori.'

'A what?'

'Dear me, Ruby. Fancy a woman of your education not knowing that. A memento mori is a symbol, to remind you life is transient. We all need a spur to action now and then.' Bee's eyes were bright, and she fingered the grey paper eagerly. 'I think often about how I should spend the life I have left. And I've decided. I'm determined to time travel again. Just once would do – just once before I die. Grace is back in touch – that's a good sign she's willing to listen to me now. And I've got a plan to make Margaret listen too. Margaret was always very pragmatic. She may have seen me as a liability. But that's not true any more. If I can make a new scientific discovery – something Margaret *wants* – she'll let me back in. I know she will.'

'Oh, Granny. I don't think this is a good idea. The last time you time travelled you were so ill.' Ruby had looked up the old news reports of Bee's breakdown. It had sounded dreadful. To see Bee return to that state would be unbearable.

'Life's better with a few risks than a lot of regrets,' Bee said.

Fear made Ruby curt.

'If Margaret has any sense, she'll turn you away.'

'Dear heart,' Bee said. 'We can forget we had this conversation. I need never mention it to you again, if that means you'll be less anxious. But I'm still determined to make one last time travel trip, with or without your support. I won't stop trying, Ruby – please don't ask me to.'

It was tempting to pretend Bee had never raised the topic. Wilful ignorance was one way to manage the stress of her wilful recklessness. Then Ruby considered how, all her adult life, she'd maintained the silence around Bee's past. Was it right to return Bee to that isolation by refusing to support her? In spite of all Ruby's misgivings, she didn't want Bee to enter danger alone.

'All right,' Ruby said to her grandmother. 'I'll help you.'

She watched Bee refold the coroner's announcement. Their implicit deadline – the date of death, 6 January – was concealed once more.

3

Odette

The toy museum relied on voluntary labour to keep afloat, and the newest volunteer was a young archaeology student called Odette Sophola. A shortage of hands meant that on Odette's first day, she would be responsible for opening the building.

It was Epiphany: the sixth of January. Odette walked up the museum steps at two o'clock, key ready. Her toes were numb despite the sheepskin lining her boots. The sky over the museum was as pale as porcelain and the chill hurt her teeth. But her eagerness to get into the warm was short-lived; for when she unlocked the doors, the reek of sulphur was waiting.

Odette clapped a hand to her nose. She stepped back from the doorway, as though, if she moved aside, the smell would leave politely like a patron. Was it a gas leak? She thought not; the stench was too stomach-turning, too *organic*. Until she found the source, opening to the public was out of the question. Rearranging her scarf into a makeshift mask, and wincing as a tassel caught her braids, she entered the foyer.

Her soles squeaked on the Minton floor. The peeling radiator ticked. Nothing was obviously out of place. It was the first time the museum had opened since Christmas. Maybe, in the meantime, a rat had died in the walls. Or a soil pipe had burst. Odette walked to the exhibition hall and considered her options. Strictly speaking, she should telephone the museum's manager, Sally. But Odette was new. She wished to make a good impression by solving the problem herself.

A steel crook, for opening the high windows, rested against a cabinet of Roman dolls. Odette picked it up and hooked it through each window latch. Blessed ventilation. If the air cleared, she might be able to tell where the reek originated. Crook still in hand, she zigzagged across the hall. At the back of the room the pungency made her cough. It was worst by the door to the basement stairs. She was drawing closer.

Sally hadn't included the basement when she'd shown Odette round. 'Nothing's in there but the boiler room,' she'd said, 'and some toy storage.' Odette walked downstairs now, holding the scarf tighter to her face. The passageway below was narrow and dark. She flipped a Bakelite switch. The pale yellow bulb flickered and made her blink. Cracked subway tiles lined the walls. The entrance to the boiler room read *Staff Only*. Paint, or some other dark liquid, had leaked under the doorway and left a maroon stain on the lino. Not quite maroon. Noir rouge. Like a slice of agate; like her mother's nail polish.

Was now the time to ring Sally? Or possibly – the police?

Odette warned herself not to overreact. The stain may look like blood, but was that likely? Might there not be a more sensible, everyday explanation? Her imagination sometimes leapt to the wildest scenarios, and she had learnt to counteract them with level-headed questions. Better to be sure what was in that room, before she rang anyone.

She turned the handle, but the boiler room door didn't budge. Puzzling. It couldn't be locked, because there was no keyhole. She tried again, then leant her full weight against it. When it gave way she nearly lost her balance.

Her eyes watered, and she gagged on the putrid air. Something crunched underfoot – little white polygons of bone in blood. By the light of the corridor, Odette could see the door had been bolted. The brass fitting swung underneath the handle. Her shove had been enough to loosen the screws. But – if the door had been locked from the *inside*...

'Hello?' Odette gasped. 'Is anyone there?'

The boiler groaned and Odette heard the buzzing of flies. One of them flew from the shadows. It stopped to feed in a puddle on the floor, inches away from an abandoned pistol. Odette swivelled, searching for the gun's owner, and cried out. A tumble of limbs and cloth was slumped against the wall. Part of the woman's head was missing. The skin that remained was marbled – *like a piece of jade*, Odette thought.

Her hands shook. She needed to call the police, but she couldn't look away from the corpse. During her archaeology degree she'd handled human skeletons. That hadn't prepared her for the violence of this death. The rotting flesh reminded her, as dry bones could not, that she too was made from fat and lymph and sinew. Humanity was reduced to nothing more than briefly animated meat. Odette stared and stared at the broken body. How could anyone wreak such damage? Until she understood their reasons, the world would feel broken too.

*

Her confusion deepened once the police arrived. The small museum was overrun with strangers in uniforms and hazmat suits, creating boundaries with tape. An officer told her to sit in the foyer. Someone gave her a cup of tea but she only drank a sip because it was bitter.

She had expected to see Sally, or some other representative of the museum. No one came. Odette soon realised that the police weren't admitting anyone past the crime scene barrier at the front steps of the museum. The only reason Odette was on the police side was because she'd been first on the scene. She was part of the evidence that they needed to collect and analyse. Presumably Sally was being questioned outside – or at the station, or even on the phone. Odette preferred to think she was somewhere nearby. It made her feel less isolated.

A short round woman with a shining face carried a table into the foyer. The wood was splintering. The woman sat on a folding chair and said she'd take Odette's statement. Her voice was too loud. She used words of one syllable, as if she were speaking to a child. Except you'd smile at a child, and this woman wasn't smiling.

'Where are you from?' she said.

'I'm staying with my parents in Hounslow. Just for the Christmas holidays – normally I'm in halls in Cambridge. I'm a student.'

The woman didn't write the response down. She repeated: 'Hounslow?'

Odette sensed the underlying sentiment: if you were brown you didn't belong. She allowed a brief silence to elapse, before giving the answer the woman wanted. 'I've lived in England since I was a child. I was born in Seychelles.'

She watched the woman write THE SEYCHELLES in her notebook.

'And you've just started cleaning here?' the police officer said.

'Not cleaning – volunteering, to get some work experience before I graduate.'

They went on to the morning's events. Odette gave the details with detachment. She listened to herself and wondered how she was speaking so calmly, when there was a woman who, below their feet, had once been alive but wasn't any longer. Her words dried mid-sentence. The woman repeated the preceding question.

After the statement Odette had to stay in the foyer, in case there were any further questions for her that day. No one took the table away. Another bitter tea was handed to her, and this time she drank it, not knowing how long it would be before she could have a drink at home. The question about her origins had disquieted her. It said the police saw her as out-of-place, and it was a short step from 'out-of-place' to 'suspicious'. The afternoon edged closer to evening. She was moved from one side of the foyer to the other because she was by the doorframe, and the police needed to verify it hadn't been forced. Finally, the round shining officer returned, this time to take her fingerprints.

'I didn't touch anything apart from the door,' Odette said.

The officer ignored that comment. When the prints were complete, she said, 'You can go. We have everything we need from you for today.'

'Thank you.' Odette's shoulders slumped.

It had long turned dark outside. Odette walked past the police officers still scattered round the barrier.

A woman, dressed in leathers and a helmet, leant on a motorcycle at the side of the road. She beckoned Odette to her.

Odette took a few steps closer. 'Hello?'

The woman raised her visor to reveal brown eyes, almost russet, beneath the street lamps.

'I have something for you,' she said. In her hand was a small card. 'Victim support. In case you need someone to talk to.'

The card had the name and contact details of a psychologist. *Dr Ruby Rebello.*

'Are you with the police?' Odette asked, confused. During the interview no one had mentioned victim support.

'No, I run a private clinic, but I work with a lot of victims of crime. I treat trauma.'

Odette tucked the card in her coat pocket.

'Thank you,' she said, to be polite. She wasn't the victim of this crime. Once she was at home, in her own bed, the world would surely start to make sense again. She wouldn't be plagued with questions of how this death had occurred. She wouldn't constantly be wondering *why*. It was the year of her final examinations. Soon she'd forget that poor dead woman. In the stress of revision and looking for a job, Odette would hardly ever think about her at all.

But no matter how sternly Odette repeated this, she knew it wasn't true.

4

Margaret

Following Barbara's breakdown, Margaret was determined to prevent a similar incident ever arising again. She contacted a woman at the British space programme, who specialised in the biological hazards faced by astronauts. Margaret hoped there were sufficient parallels between the two fields to shed light on the health risks of time travel. The specialist's name was Angharad Mills, and Margaret sent her a confidential account of the pioneers' working conditions.

The following week they met in Angharad's office. Before training in bioastronautics, Angharad had been a well-known ballerina. Two worn satin slippers hung on her wall in a teak frame. She poured Margaret a coffee.

'Time travel's still in its infancy,' Margaret said. 'It's hard to predict what the effects on body and mind might be. Before we embarked on human trials we did explore risks to physical health, but I'll admit we didn't really consider how our behaviour could be affected. I wish we had.'

'Barbara's breakdown probably did have a physical component,' Angharad said. 'But I don't believe it was caused by the conditions of time travel per se.'

'How do you mean?' Margaret asked.

'We have bodily cycles that respond to daylight. According to the description you sent, your team's exposure to daylight was very disrupted during your first fifteen trips. That's enough to trigger a manic episode in a predisposed person – psychiatrists see similar symptoms in manic depressive patients who work shifts or travel internationally. If Barbara were an air hostess, the same health issues may have arisen.'

'She had a bad case of jet lag.'

'Your phrasing is a little reductive but – yes.'

'I'm very sympathetic to Barbara's situation.' Margaret gazed through the window. On the lawn, Angharad's colleagues were building a snowman. 'There's no one more sympathetic than me. But she *did* cause our team considerable public embarrassment. I'd be greatly reassured if I knew how to avoid more travellers falling ill. That must be my focus now.'

'The "jet lag" problem has a simple solution. Just dispatch travellers to a time of day that matches when they left their own timeline.'

'I'm afraid we need schedules to be flexible.' If, as Margaret planned, time travel became a tool for espionage, restricting arrival times would be impractical.

'In that case...' Angharad took an unusually large watch from her desk drawer and passed it to Margaret. 'Astronauts use these to monitor waking hours and exposure to daylight. Issue them to any time travellers you recruit, and make it a disciplinary offence to travel without one. Then they can make the trips they need, and only stop if the watch shows their bodily cycles are under too much strain. Our suppliers could design you a suitable timepiece from scratch. One that matches your requirements.'

The watch was a handsome object made from brushed steel. Ghostly numbers hovered above its surface.

'An excellent idea,' Margaret said.

'One last thought. The strongest predictor of mental breakdown is a previous breakdown. Twenty per cent of people have experience of psychological distress. They'd be the ones most at risk of an episode like Barbara's. To be safe, you might want to bar them from the profession.'

'Bar them? How would I identify them – medical records?'

'Yes. You can also make psychometric tests a standard part of your selection process.'

Margaret found that idea very appealing. 'Would tests eliminate everyone with Barbara's disposition?'

'No,' Angharad replied. 'That's impossible. But the chance of problems arising would be greatly diminished.'

Which was a worthwhile goal, in Margaret's eyes. The time travel programme couldn't have any more damaging attention from the press. 'Thank you, Dr Mills. You've been more than helpful. If there is anything I can do in exchange...'

'I'm glad that you asked.'

'Oh?'

'If you need a medical engineer, please keep me in mind. I'm quite fascinated with your project.'

'Another excellent idea.' Margaret drained her coffee cup. 'We're yet to establish our headquarters, but as soon as this brouhaha with Barbara settles down, I'm sure we'd benefit from your expertise.'

*

At the lab, Margaret relayed Angharad's advice to Lucille and Grace. They sat around the rabbit hutch, feeding strips of carrots to Patrick through the mesh.

'The watches sound very sensible,' Lucille said.

'If we buy one for Barbara, can she come back to work?' Grace asked. 'As soon as she's out of hospital, I mean.'

Margaret couldn't tell if Grace was being obtuse, or provocative. 'Barbara won't be coming back.'

'But that's ludicrous! She's one of us.'

Barbara *wasn't* one of them. Not any longer. She had forfeited her place by humiliating them all, in front of the entire country. The remaining pioneers needed to distance themselves from her if they weren't to become a laughing stock – but Margaret guessed neither Grace nor Lucille would be amenable to such an argument. She tried a different tack.

'You're not being fair to Barbara,' she said. 'Think how it must be for her. *If* her mania isn't a life sentence – and that's a big if – she may wish to forget the interview ever happened. She can't do that if she comes back to time travel, because she'll be in the public eye again. The world will always be watching and waiting for her to lose her grip. Why would you want that for her?'

'I don't!' Grace said.

'Have you been to see her? At the hospital?' Margaret asked.

Grace frowned. She shook her head.

'Why not?'

'Because,' Lucille said quietly, 'it would feel cruel. We'd just be reminding her of work, and work made her sick.'

Margaret snapped her fingers. 'Exactly. She doesn't need reminders of work.'

'Are you saying we shouldn't even see her socially?' Grace said.

Margaret believed Barbara should be cut off cleanly. Maintaining a friendship offered no advantages and could make it more difficult to forge new connections. The pioneers' remote workplace had deceived them into thinking they were self-sufficient. They must now look to the wider world – and sever historical loyalties, if they were no longer of use.

'Whether you pursue a friendship with Barbara is at your discretion,' Margaret said. 'I know I'll be leaving her in peace. It's the kindest thing to do.'

Grudgingly, Lucille and Grace agreed to let Barbara be. Margaret resented having to manipulate them. She wished they'd simply appreciate her attempt to protect their careers. If Barbara jeopardised the pioneers' reputation, how did Lucille and Grace think they'd find work? Wasn't it difficult enough for Lucille already – a black woman, sending her wages home to help her parents? And God only knew what Grace's situation was. Her speech was wincingly non-U and Margaret assumed her position must be just as precarious.

Yes, Margaret was acting in all their interests. She was sure of it.

5

Ruby

Ruby's holiday with Bee drew to a close, and against her better instincts, she returned to Dalston. The origami rabbit still worried her. She wanted to know why Grace had sent Bee the inquest details, and the only way to find out was to ask Grace herself. Bee's earlier attempts at contact had been unsuccessful, which suggested any meeting would be on Grace's terms. Deciding how to approach her would take care.

First Ruby needed to do her research. She already knew a little about each of the pioneers because they were high-profile figures. Margaret Norton was the most conventionally ambitious. In 1968 she had founded the Time Travel Conclave, an elite quango with responsibility for all time travel missions, and almost immediately had assumed the role of director. Five decades on she showed no signs of retiring. Lucille Waters and Grace Taylor worked at the Conclave too; Lucille managed exchanges of information between different time periods, while Grace continued to be an active researcher. She specialised in the study of acausal matter, whatever that was.

Grace had also taken a surprising detour into conceptual art. Some of her work was on show at Tate Modern. The day after Ruby came back from Cornwall, she decided to visit the gallery and see the installations at close range. When she arrived she hopped on the escalator to the third floor, and wove her way through the tourists and students. The downpour outside had made them a sorry crowd: they all smelt slightly dank. Ruby's hair was plastered to her forehead and the tip of her nose was pink. By the time she found the right room she felt clammy and wretched. It was crowded in there, too – a guide was leading a special tour for blind visitors, who had permission to touch selected exhibits.

Ruby stood by a man who was running his fingers over an embroidered piece of linen. It looked like a sampler, of the kind that normally commemorates a birth. The name stitched in the cloth was *Grace Evangeline Taylor*. Chains of flowers, rattles and other baby paraphernalia were sewn round the borders. They looked especially quaint because the date in the centre was decidedly futuristic: *29 April 2027.*

'I can't tell what I'm feeling,' the man said, which struck Ruby as an unexpectedly intimate comment. He was, however, speaking literally. 'I can feel the cloth, and I can see a blue shape, but I'm buggered if I know what it's a picture of.'

'That bit's a flower,' said his guide.

'A forget-me-not,' Ruby added.

'Ah,' the blind man said. 'Thanks.'

The guide explained that the sampler dated back to the thirties. Grace had modified it. Originally it displayed her birth date – *10 October 1937* – but she'd unpicked those stitches and reused the strands of silk to sew the date of her death. Ruby suppressed a nervous laugh. It seemed so incongruous to foretell one's passing at ninety with the twee symbols of babyhood. Perhaps Grace liked to indulge in a little gallows humour.

Ruby moved on to the second artwork, which looked more traditional. It comprised a self-portrait in oils. Grace was shown in profile, reading a book. Her hair was white. Half-moon glasses sat on her nose. According to the blurb on the wall, the novelty of the piece lay in its construction rather than its style. The painting had been created in reverse order. Grace had travelled twenty-four hours into the future, where a near-complete painting awaited her final touches. She then travelled an hour closer to the present, twenty-three hours in the future, to undertake the preceding brush strokes. She kept travelling back towards the present, until finally the canvas was blank, and she had to paint the first line. She made this first line with a fresh, directly experienced memory of how the final painting would look. At no point in the process did she feel the image was of her choosing; she was always responding to what was already on the canvas, or what she had seen in the future.

The final installation was Ruby's favourite of the three. Grace had placed a chartreuse pencil upon a velvet cushion. She had travelled fifty years into the future and collected the pencil, which she brought back to the present day to lie beside its younger twin. They were the *same* pencil, and yet occupied different spaces. Ruby forgot, for a moment, the dampness of her jeans against her calves, and the tickling cough that was forming in her throat. Here was an astonishing object: proof, that you could reach out and touch, of the ability to move through time.

Tentatively, Ruby ran her fingers over the exhibit. The original pencil was smooth and the future version had gained a patina. She glanced, guiltily, around the room to see if anyone had noticed her touch the exhibit. Maybe it didn't matter; she could be one of the blind visitors, after all.

Ruby bypassed the other collections, intending to go home. When she reached the ground floor she saw the rain had started again. Another soaking didn't appeal. Her umbrella was hanging on the hat stand in her tiny Dalston flat because she'd been foolish enough to expect sunshine. But the gift shop probably stocked umbrellas – and if not, the storm might subside while Ruby browsed.

She flicked through a coffee table book or two, and dawdled towards some souvenirs at the back of the shop. A few bits and pieces were related to time travel, including a slim tome of time travellers' slang by someone called Sushila Pardesi. Miniature copies of Grace's pencil installation were also on sale. They quite charmed Ruby.

She took the phrase book and miniature pencils to the till. The cashier was scanning them when Ruby's eyes settled on a woman by the entrance. Ruby stared. It was Grace herself, examining a rack of scarves. She wasn't the white-haired septuagenarian of her oil painting. *This* Grace looked only a little older than Ruby; late thirties, at a guess. She, too, had been caught in the rain. The water made her hair shine blackly like an otter's. She wore a cornflower blue trenchcoat and a black polo neck. Her mouth was as bright as a split cherry.

She picked up one of the silk scarves, folded it, and slipped it into her coat pocket. Ruby felt Grace was putting on a show – and sure enough, Grace *looked* at Ruby, grinned, and raised a finger to her lips. The burnished metal of a time traveller's watch was fastened round her wrist.

She sauntered through the exit.

'Are you paying by card?' the assistant prompted.

Ruby nodded dumbly.

As soon as the transaction was through she ran out into the drizzle. She pushed through the crowds at the riverside, searching vainly for a flash of blue, fearful that Grace was long gone.

'Ruby!' a woman shouted. '*Ruby!*'

The voice came from above. Ruby lifted her head to the skyline. Grace was standing on the footbridge over the Thames. And she knew Ruby's name. Should Ruby have been surprised? Time travellers are privy to all kinds of information we're yet to provide.

'Send my love to Barbara!' Grace called.

Ruby made her way to the bridge steps. But by the time she reached the top Grace had slipped back into the crowds. How unnerving that she knew who Ruby was.

Grace had left the stolen scarf behind – it was knotted round one of the railings, and the tapered ends were snapping like pennants in the wind. Did Grace remember that Bee liked scarves? Ruby untied it. The silk, which had turned translucent with moisture, was printed with a reproduction of Grace's sampler. Something about it made Ruby uneasy.

She looked at that date again: 2027.

Oh God. She'd been so *slow*.

If Grace knew she was going to die in 2027 – if she was telling the truth about that – then they wouldn't hold an inquest into her death in 2018. Ruby felt sick. If Grace's own death didn't drive her interest in the case, Granny Bee must be the one who was in danger.

6

Odette

Odette was required at the inquest, to give witness testimony. She allowed so much time for her journey she was half an hour early. An arts market lined the street outside the coroner's court and she occupied herself by looking at paintings and pots. She stopped at a second-hand bookstall. The bookseller was completing a crossword.

'Back again?' he said to Odette. His false teeth were a little too large.

She smiled politely. He had confused her with somebody else.

One of the book trays contained foreign language novels. She rifled through the French section, looking for something her mother, Claire, might like to read. Her fingers halted at a tattered paperback, the cover striped in green and cream bands, like an old Penguin crime. *La revanche de Peredur.* She pulled it out. In the corner, someone had written what looked like O/S in faint pencil. She supposed it could be a zero and a five – a price tag, in old money. She turned the pages. The novel was presented as a parallel text. Half in French. Half in Kreol.

'How much for this?' she asked.

*

The inquest room was plainer than Odette had expected. She'd never been to court, and legal dramas had led her to imagine a panelled chamber, rather than magnolia walls and stackable conference chairs. A dozen people were already waiting, scattered like counters on a battleships board. Odette sat at the end of a row. Her nearest neighbour was a man of thirty or so, who was slight, with dark curls. He held a tablet and was frowning at whatever was typed there.

A side door opened to admit the coroner. Earlier in the month Odette had met him for a brief conversation. His name was Stuart Yelland; he was in his sixties, likeable, and he screwed up his left eye when he thought of a question. He took his place behind the table and said a few words about the process to follow.

'You will have noticed,' he said, 'that the inquest announcement didn't include the deceased's name. Although DNA, dental and fingerprint profiles were gathered, she could not be matched to a missing person record. Nor were there identifying documents on her person.'

In Odette's row, the curly haired man sighed and shook his head.

The first person Yelland called to speak was the police officer who had taken statements at the museum. She recounted the police's initial impressions of the scene, and the body.

'The deceased was in a basement room, with only one entry point, which had been bolted from the inside. The bolt had been wrenched from the wall, allegedly by the first person on the scene.'

She stared hard at Odette. The memory of the bolt, swinging in the half light, flashed through Odette's brain. She raised a hand to her mouth.

Returning her gaze to the coroner, the policewoman continued. 'The deceased was white, female, and of advanced age – in her seventies or a well preserved eighties. At the base of her neck she had a laceration scar, ten centimetres in length, which predated the occasion of her death. She had four fresh gunshot wounds in her stomach, one in her left hand, and one in her head.'

Each detail that the police officer provided made the pictures before Odette's eyes a little more vivid. Odette's palms were damp. Her breathing was shallow.

'The bullets were embedded in the wall behind, indicating she had been shot at the scene. The number of gunshot wounds raises the probability of homicide.'

'How so?' Yelland asked.

'It's hard to shoot yourself more than once.'

'Hard – but not impossible?' Yelland prompted. 'I'm trying to reconcile how she could have been murdered, then locked the door after her killer's departure.'

'Shooting yourself more than once might be possible, but it's improbable. And in my professional experience, gunshot wounds to the hand are defence injuries.'

To Odette's relief, that drew the police officer's testimony to a close. Revisiting the details of the crime scene made Odette nauseous. How on earth was she going to give her own account, if she struggled to hear the police officer's?

The coroner called the pathologist as the next witness. She enumerated, in slow Yorkshire vowels, the weights and lengths of internal organs, which took some time. Eventually she moved on to the deceased woman's injuries.

'Swabs from the wounds revealed some evidence of bacteraemia,' the pathologist said. 'The culture was somewhat... unusual.'

'Unusual how?'

'We identified two types of bacteria. *Deinococcus radiodurans*, and a nasty little pathogen called *alkalibacterium macromonas*. They're both bacteria that thrive in radioactive environments. Previously I've only encountered them in high concentrations at nuclear power stations. My conjecture is that either the deceased had recently visited such a site, or the bullets had been stored in radioactive conditions. The bullets may then have introduced the bacteria to her bloodstream at the point of impact.'

'Might this woman have died from an infection?'

'No. Macromonas works quickly, but not as fast as a bullet to the brain.'

Odette twisted the fabric of her skirt between her fingers. She focused and defocused on the dots in the cotton. Anything to root her in the here and now, to prevent her from flying back into that room in the museum cellar.

But she had to return there. Her time to speak arrived.

There was a jug of water waiting, when she took her place at the front. Gratefully, she poured herself a glass and took a sip.

'Please take us through the events as you experienced them,' the coroner asked.

'It was two o'clock in the afternoon,' Odette began. 'I know it was dead on two, because it was my first day volunteering, and I kept checking the time. The main door was locked. I let myself in, and there was the most awful, rotting smell.'

She paused.

'Take your time,' the coroner said. But Odette had only ever heard that phrase from people who wish you to continue. She took another sip of water, and blinked slowly.

'I opened the windows. The smell was coming from the back of the room, and down the stairs.'

'Was there any evidence of disturbance?'

'Nothing but the smell. Everything looked… normal. But I had only been there once before. Everything looked normal till I reached the boiler room door.'

She remembered the maroon stain across the floor.

'Miss Sophola?'

'Something had… collected… in a pool… It was reddish, and clotted. I thought my imagination might be running away with me.' She looked at the coroner fearfully. 'That's why I didn't call the police straight away. I tried the door. It was locked.'

'Miss Sophola, this is a very important point. The evidence points to an assailant who must have escaped the room somehow. Are you quite certain that the door was locked on your arrival?'

'Absolutely. When I forced the door, I wrenched the bolt off – I saw it swinging – I saw it—'

Her lip trembled. The discovery behind the bolted door was present and vivid and filled her senses. Stuart Yelland was asking another question, but Odette barely made out the words: she was hearing, again, the boiler ignite in the basement. She could smell the corpse. She was standing in its blood. Without thinking she covered her face with her hands, as if she might still block out the stench.

'Miss Sophola?' Stuart Yelland's voice sounded so far away. 'I'm going to call a short break.'

Odette felt a hand on her shoulder. It was the coroner's

assistant – a stocky woman in a grey suit. She smiled reassuringly at Odette as she led her to the next room.

*

No further questions were required of Odette once she had collected herself. She was unsure whether to stay for the rest of the inquest. Her desire to understand the case repeatedly collided with the fear she would lose her grip again. In the end she reached the compromise of sitting in the corridor until the close of day.

The attendees eventually filed from the inquest. Stuart Yelland was the last of them. She stood up and caught his attention with a wave.

'Can I ask how it went?' she asked, when he approached her.

'I reached an open verdict.' He paused. 'I'm glad I have this opportunity to talk with you. I wanted to recommend that you seek some emotional support, if you haven't done so already.'

Odette remembered the psychologist who had offered victim support. Maybe she had been rash to refuse her help. Since then, the dead woman had been much in Odette's thoughts. So much that she sometimes felt, as she had during testimony, that she had never left the crime scene at all. Was a sympathetic ear what she needed?

She didn't think so. Surely she was struggling to move on because the death made no sense. No one had offered a convincing explanation for how the woman died, and violent acts without explanation were terrifying. If Odette worked out what had occurred in the basement, surely she would feel able to let it go?

'I don't need help,' she insisted. 'I need to know what happened. Then I can draw a line under it.'

'But, Miss Sophola, we can't establish what happened. You must accept that. Please, take my advice. Finding the deceased could have a lasting emotional impact on you. Don't try to manage it on your own.'

He patted her kindly on the arm and bid her goodbye, leaving her to contemplate what he'd said. That evening she would be catching the train back to Cambridge. Her course books would await her, with her revision notes, and the clear, tangible arguments she was preparing for her exams – a set of discrete, manageable mysteries, to distract her from the bigger mystery threatening to overwhelm her.

7

MAY 1969

Lucille

B y the spring of 1969, the new Conclave headquarters – an assemblage of marble buildings close to St Paul's Cathedral – were complete. The small team of pioneers grew into an elite profession for a few hundred people. And as soon as the new machines were operational, time travellers arrived from the future, too.

Broadly speaking, there were three types of time traveller. The first group were experimental physicists. Of the pioneers, Grace fell into this category. They studied the effect of time travel on physical matter, the creation of causal loops, and the conditions that could prevent time travel. The time machines wouldn't transport anyone further than three hundred years into the future, and the experimental physicists tried to understand why. It was almost as if the supporting infrastructure disappeared in 2267.

The second group of time travellers used the machines as a means to an end. This group included the spies and military personnel who gathered intelligence from different time periods to inform strategic decisions. There were salesmen, too, open to the new commercial opportunities time travel might bring. The sales team identified products which could be traded between eras, primarily for luxury markets, to secure a revenue stream for the Conclave. And there were also scholars – anthropologists, conservationists and geographers, to name but a few, who studied new eras as they might study an unfamiliar land.

The third and final group of time travellers provided internal services. Administrators and maintenance staff kept the Conclave running. Medics and psychologists monitored the health of everyone who used the time machines. A specialist legal department was established; despite its geographical location in London, the Conclave's justice arrangements were quite separate from the English judicial system. This was partly necessary because time travellers can move easily between different eras of English legislation. Similarly, if a Conclave employee committed a crime with the help of time travel, the English police force lacked the means to pursue them. As a result, the Conclave had its own criminal investigative team.

Lucille belonged to the internal services division. Her role was Head of Knowledge, and she oversaw the communication and exchange of information between different time periods. It filled her with delight to see the Conclave expand and thrive. But she grew regretful, too, that among the new faces there was no place for Barbara. Long after conceding that they should leave Barbara alone, Lucille continued to hope there was a use for her skills. Accordingly, once everyone had settled in the new headquarters, she devised a proposal, which she brought to Margaret during a routine progress meeting.

'The engineers have had some success receiving radio transmissions through wormholes,' Lucille said. 'It won't be long until we can set up a Conclave-wide radio communications system. Like the time machines, they won't be able to contact periods earlier than their own invention. But we'll be able to chat to people in the year 2260 without leaving the comfort of our armchair.'

'Go on,' Margaret urged.

'We're finalising a very simple design – the receivers will resemble telephones. The user will speak to an operator who tunes you in to the correct year. When we can call each other across the decades, we'll drastically cut down on the number of trips we need to take.'

'Excellent news,' Margaret said. 'Radio communication will improve efficiency no end. But I'd query whether it should be *Conclave-wide*. That sounds rather... uncontrolled. Usage should be a privilege, held by the most senior employees, and sparingly extended to their subordinates. Then we can keep a tighter rein on the flow of information.'

'If that's what you want. We'll need to hire operators. They won't need to time travel, but they will need to be proficient in time travel technology – and ideally they should be up to speed in superluminal research. I think we should offer one of the roles to Barbara.'

Margaret closed her eyes. 'We agreed not to contact Barbara. Didn't we all feel that it would be cruel?'

'Yes – when she was in no position to work with us. But if we were offering her a way back – an interesting, novel opportunity that would make good use of her skills – that wouldn't be cruel at all. Don't you see? Working with radios needn't aggravate her symptoms at all. Her problem's with circadian rhythm, and such – isn't that what Angharad said?'

Shifting in her seat, Margaret replied, 'I'm not sure it's so simple. We don't know whether Barbara has recovered enough to work *anywhere*. And if she has, she could still fall ill again.'

'But surely—'

'Honestly, Lucille, you haven't thought this through. In the very best case scenario, she would be the topic of Conclave gossip. I won't have her subjected to that. In the worst scenario, we would have to let her go again at some unspecified point, putting her through the same anguish. You know I'm right about this. Is she ever on staff when you travel into the future?'

She wasn't. Lucille still wanted to offer Barbara a job. Barbara was free to turn them down; at least she would have the opportunity. Making the decision for her seemed wrong. 'Barbara is one of the reasons why we were successful. Wouldn't this be a good way to honour that? To show she's still appreciated?'

'Ah! You want to make a *gesture*.' Margaret smiled broadly. 'I have the very thing. Name your radio system *Beeline*.'

'Name... the radio system?' Disappointment crept into Lucille's voice.

'I think that's a fine tribute. Now. Shall we discuss the budget you'll need?'

*

'Margaret wouldn't even consider giving Barbara a job,' Lucille said to her fiancé George. She was visiting him in Liverpool; they were in the kitchen of his parents' two-up two-down, adjusting his crystal radio set.

'I'm not surprised,' said George. 'That one hates to be shown up.'

'You don't think she's doing what's best for Bee?' Lucille leant on his shoulder. His overalls smelt of car paint; he'd been working at the plant in Speke.

'Only by accident,' George said. 'Bee's better off without her help.'

'I don't believe that.'

'Because then you'd have to admit Margaret's no good for you either.'

'You wish I'd leave?'

'You should work wherever you damn please. Just watch out for that Margaret. Never trust the aristocracy.'

'She's only got a minor title. Baronesses are one step up from commoners.'

'She's below you, queen.' He donned the earphones and passed her a cigarette. They had played with radio sets since they were children.

'What can you hear?' she asked.

'Storms. Singing. Footsteps. Someone singing in another language.'

'Give over them earphones,' Lucille said. 'You have them to yourself all the other nights.'

'It's no fun without you. Besides, I get scared. You mock, but I do. Some of the voices are spooky. Like a ghostly voice's calling my name. *George! George!* Hey! Get your ghosty hands off me!' He protested as she wrested the earphones from him.

She snapped them onto her own head. 'I can only hear whispering.'

Electronic noise drowned the words. The noise ceased. As clear as a tuning fork, she heard a Cornish voice say: *Tinned sardines and fruit with evaporated milk. Lovingly decanted.* Bee's voice; Bee's words.

'What is it, queen?' George was at once serious. He cupped Lucille's face, wiping a tear from her cheek with his thumb. 'What did you hear? Tell me.'

'I was imagining things,' she said. 'Do you ever do that? Convince yourself you've heard something in the static?'

'All the time.'

'I just feel so guilty,' Lucille confessed. 'Bee's going to be left behind. And I'll still be carrying on there, year in year out.'

'I *do* wish you'd leave,' George said. 'But we both know you won't. Do you know what that means?'

'What?'

'You have to make the Conclave better, from the inside.'

She laughed. 'How do I do that? The place never bloody changes. It can't.'

He lit another cigarette. 'You'll have to think of something.'

8

Ruby

Ruby still wanted to talk to Grace directly, to hear it confirmed that the dead woman was Granny Bee. Without much hope, she contacted the Conclave. She requested a meeting with Grace 'to follow up on their recent conversation'. The Conclave said they'd get back to her. At least it wasn't an outright refusal, although there was no guarantee Grace would comply. Now there was nothing to do but wait. Ruby did all of this without Bee's knowledge. Bee didn't want to contact Grace until she had a new discovery to offer the Conclave. But Ruby couldn't wait that long to hear if Bee was in danger.

A week passed, and Ruby's anxiety about Bee's safety didn't wane. It affected her sleep. She spent too long each night googling Grace on her phone. A pirated set of video installations, made by Grace some years ago, caught Ruby's attention because of the title: *Death and the Time Traveller*. Ruby clicked on the first of the series, which yielded an interview with a newly recruited barrister in 2030, yet to take her first trip. She was filmed in black and white, perching at the edge of a slouchy leather sofa. At her side was a pot of aloe vera. Other than that the room was featureless. Grace, unseen behind the camera, asked Fay what she was looking forward to about time travel. Fay responded that she would meet her father for the first time since his death.

> I want to give him books, ones he'd like, that were written after he'd gone. I want to show him photographs of the people he wouldn't get to meet, and the events he wouldn't get to witness. I want to ask his opinion on current affairs. I want to give him family gossip. I want to compare failings, because now I'm an adult I know what my failings are, and perhaps we could find common ground.

Her wistfulness touched Ruby, who had the strange sensation of recognising Fay's face, but not being able to place where from. She discarded the thought. In 2017 this woman must still be a child; Ruby could only be confusing her with someone else.

The video cut to a later interview, after Fay had taken her first few trips, and been reunited with her father. She spoke rapidly, half laughing.

> It was so good. I thought I was starting to forget what he looked like. But as soon as I saw him I realised the memories were inside me, waiting to come back. I talked till I went hoarse and the best thing was how happy he was to hear it all. We planed wood. In the garden, listening to Radio 4. He was a furniture restorer, did I tell you that? No? When I got home I burst into tears. My hands kept trembling. I've been back to see him a couple of times, and I'll stay whenever I'm in his timeline. The funny thing is, the other time travellers – I'm thinking of

Teddy Avedon in particular, he's been showing me the ropes – they keep telling me that it's *green* to be so excited. They mean I'm being gauche. Teddy says I'll get used to seeing dead people. But I think he's wrong. Whenever I visit my father, the trees in his garden are young again, and so is he. I will *never* take that for granted.

The screen cut to black. Grace spoke through the darkness, pointing out that Fay may have an interesting perspective on death. As a specialist in time travel law, over which the Conclave had sole jurisdiction, Fay would be defending clients against the death penalty. Fay reappeared, in the same chair.

In the twenty-first century, where I come from, the English legal and judicial systems value fairness. But Conclave justice is different. It has more in common with medieval Europe, or colonial America, or twenty-fourth century Britain – because it values divine judgement more than fairness. They implement something called *trial of ordeal*. This is a very ancient, religious ritual, where the accused has to take a painful or difficult test. If they pass, the judge takes it as a sign from a higher power that the accused person is innocent. But if they fail, then that's a sign they are guilty. For time travellers, the higher power is fate. All time travellers have experienced trying, and failing, to change a course of events at some point in their career. So their faith in fate is very strong.

I don't present any evidence as part of the trial. But if the defendant is found guilty, I'll use both the evidence from the initial investigation and the defendant's own testimony to negotiate their sentence. The judge doesn't award any custodial sentences. The guilty party pays a fine to the injured party, or if the victim's dead, the family can dispense a corporal punishment. Anything from head shaving up to execution. Most time travel legislation derives from the twenty-fourth century, which is pretty bloodthirsty, I can tell you. That's why the Conclave thinks blood revenge is a mitigating factor in sentencing for murder.

The film then jumped forward to an older Fay, recently returned from maternity leave. Her eyes were ringed. Through yawns she said she was happy to be back at work.

Being a lawyer sounds like a desk job, but my caseload covers a full three centuries, so I have to skip about from decade to decade to get everything done. During my maternity leave I really missed travelling. I suppose it's like having wanderlust? Time lust. It feels weird now if I don't have that flexibility of where and when I go. I have friends and family in other timelines that I don't have here, so… yeah. While I was with the baby I couldn't see those people. *(Grace asks a question, inaudible to the viewer.)* No, I never doubted they still existed. It was more like we were in separate lives. With the next baby my partner's going to take leave instead. I don't want to be away from my job that long again.

Grace cut to another Fay, with pepper and salt hair, and lines bracketing her mouth. She spoke animatedly of collecting thistles during her last field trip into the past.

The petals were golden, like lions' manes. And they grew on every English lawn, but I picked them less than a mile from my mother's primary school. She was probably in lessons. I really felt I was gathering something precious. As soon as I got back to my timeline, I took them to the Conclave garden. My mother had died of a stroke while I was away, so I'd said I'd visit my sister at some point to talk through funeral arrangements, but I started chatting with one of the horticulturists about a trip he'd just made to Japan, and I lost track of time. It was quite late when I arrived at my sister's. She kept going on about how we're orphans now. *(Long pause.)* It's not that I don't know how she feels. I know she believes Mum's gone for ever. But I don't want to be reminded of feeling upset in that way. It doesn't seem very... relevant... any more. Not to my life. I hate admitting this, but I wished my sister would shut the hell up.

The fourth Fay was thinner – almost gaunt – and subdued. Ruby could see, on the timeline along the base of the video, that several minutes of footage remained.

When you're a time traveller, the people you love die, and you carry on seeing them, so their death stops making a difference to you. The only death that will ever change things is your own.

Ruby hit the pause symbol. She let the phone go dark, wishing she'd never started down this particular rabbit hole. Until the meeting with Grace, the last thing she should be doing was dwelling on death. She really should be trying to distract herself.

One distraction was a woman named Ginger Hayes, who worked in a nearby brain injury unit. Technically, Ruby was single. But Ginger made an appearance at her flat once a month or so, for sex, and to drain Ruby's reserves of red wine. Ruby had never been to Ginger's house – which was apparently in Tring – and this exclusion from her everyday life made Ruby suspect she was married.

Later that same week, Ginger lay naked on Ruby's bed, with flakes of mascara haloing her eyes. While Ruby was in Cornwall visiting Bee, Ginger had been in Brittany. Her skin was dense with freckles: a gift from the Breton sunshine. Ruby traced the constellations that adorned Ginger's chest. Cassiopeia. The Seven Sisters. Had Ruby believed in astrology, she would have read their future from the patterns on Ginger's body.

'I assessed a new client this afternoon,' Ginger said. 'She was injured on her bike. A motorist opened his car door in her path, and she was thrown into the road. Now she's aphasic. When she tries to talk, nothing comes out but a stream of swear words.'

Romantic pillow talk, by any measure.

'Can you do anything for aphasics?' Ruby asked.

'This woman will probably benefit from speech therapy. She's still young, which is in her favour. But her family want her to be the way she was before, and she won't be.'

'How old is she?'

'Twenty-seven. Mother to a toddler.'

Ginger's comments were downbeat, but Ruby appreciated the importance of Ginger's job. They shared stressful working lives. Rarely did they discuss anything other than their clients.

Ruby's arms circled Ginger's waist and they kissed. Ginger's lips were tannic. All week Ruby had fretted over the origami rabbit, how the body might be connected to Barbara, and what Grace could possibly be playing at. It felt so comforting, now, to be held. The closeness tricked her into an admission.

'I'm sleeping badly,' she said. 'I keep worrying about my grandmother.'

'Oh.' Ginger fell back on her pillow. 'Is she ill, then?'

'No,' Ruby said. 'I mean – yes; she has bipolar disorder.'

'Hm,' Ginger said.

Ruby's urge to confide in her ebbed. Had she overshared? By the usual constraints of their relationship, yes. She knew nothing of Ginger's family. Ginger didn't speak of her interests or where she was from. The secrets she shared were her patients' rather than her own. Telling Ruby where she'd been on holiday was the most intimate detail she'd ever revealed. Picking up Ginger's left hand, Ruby looked for a white circle among the freckles on her ring finger. The evidence was inconclusive.

Ginger pulled Ruby's hand to her mouth, and kissed the inside of Ruby's wrist. Maybe Ginger was right to shy away from personal revelations. Hadn't Ruby wanted her for a distraction?

So Ruby let Ginger distract her. Afterwards, she fell asleep swiftly – for the first time that week.

*

The next morning Ruby heard Ginger in the kitchenette, opening and closing cabinet doors. Normally she would have left before dawn. Perhaps trouble at home had kept her here.

Ruby got out of bed and crossed the little hall to the kitchen doorway. Ginger was wearing Ruby's dressing gown. Her hair was bright as marigolds against the green fabric. She filled the kettle.

'I'll make you breakfast,' she said. 'If there *is* anything for breakfast. D'you know what's in your cupboards? A torn bag of rice and a very sticky bottle of Worcestershire sauce.'

'There are eggs in that ceramic chicken.'

'Perfect.' Ginger busied herself with frying pans and butter. 'I don't have any clinics today. I'm giving a presentation on neural plasticity, but that's not till noon.'

So they were to talk of work again. 'Who's the presentation for?'

'Some new rehab workers. They always love the London cab example. You know, where the drivers memorise so many routes it physically restructures their brains?'

Ruby nodded. Her own day would include two clients with depression, and a third with PTSD. According to the usual pattern of her conversations with Ginger, she should volunteer that information now. But her new impulse to make personal admissions was back. Her previous attempt to discuss Bee had failed, and Ruby was not quite brave enough to talk of her explicitly again. She found herself drawn to a halfway position: couching personal concerns in professional interest.

'There's something I've been thinking over lately. Do you know if time travel changes the brain?' Ruby had plausible grounds for ignorance. She only knew the basics of brain anatomy; she specialised in talking therapies.

'Time travel doesn't do much in the short term.' Ginger pushed a stray lock of hair behind her ear. Heat shimmered over the pan. 'But more experienced time travellers generally have a weird hippocampus.'

'No one wants a weird hippocampus,' Ruby said, wryly. 'What causes that?'

'One theory is that time travel places your recall abilities under unusual stress.' Ginger cracked two eggs into the spitting fat. 'Let's use your memories for comparison. Think of something that happened a long time ago.'

'OK. I remember my grandmother reading me *The Box of Delights*.'

'The Box of What?'

'*The Box of Delights*. It's my favourite book. It has puppeteers, and schoolgirls who love pistols, and a magic box that takes you to the past—'

'When *exactly* did she read you this?' Ginger interrupted.

'No earlier than 1990. I could read the words along with my grandmother, so I was old enough to be at school. We probably read it in the winter. I remember the wool of her smock on my cheek. That would make sense, because the story's set at Christmas.'

'Right. You don't automatically recall when the event occurred. You can piece a likely date together from hints and trifling details. A time traveller goes through the same process with events that she's witnessed in the future. Sometimes she gets the date wrong, and mistakenly places it in the past. She expects her friends and family to remember something that won't happen for years. If she works in intelligence, that kind of mistake can be dire. Have you got a fish slice?'

'Second drawer down on the left.'

Ginger found the slice, and slid an egg onto a plate.

'I didn't know you were so domesticated,' Ruby said.

'Don't expect me to make a habit of playing housewife.'

Ruby's mobile was ringing in the bedroom.

'Back in a tick,' she said.

By the time she reached it the call had gone to voicemail.

The number had been withheld. She dialled to hear the recording.

'This is a message for Dr Rebello.' The caller spoke with a quaint, mid-Atlantic accent. Ruby thought of Audrey Hepburn in *Breakfast at Tiffany's*. 'My name is Grace Taylor, and I'm calling to arrange an interview.'

She gave details of a hotel she would be staying at the following week, and instructed Ruby to meet her in the hotel restaurant at half eleven on Tuesday. The message ended there. Grace didn't provide any other contact details.

Granny Bee had said that Grace liked to keep people guessing: she was deliberately obscure. Having met Grace, Bee's explanation was convincing. Ruby remembered how Grace placed a finger to her lips in the gallery shop, as if they were co-conspirators. That kind of game troubled her, because she felt as though she were being manipulated. But now Ruby's conversation with Ginger made her wonder if another explanation lay behind Grace's behaviour. How much were future and past jumbled in Grace's mind? She'd travelled years into the future on multiple occasions. Maybe she was too dislocated from the events the rest of them lived through. Was she confused about what Ruby knew, and what she didn't?

Suddenly, Grace seemed a pitiable figure. Ruby didn't know, yet, whether to feel sorry for her or afraid of her. At least, in just a few days, she would get the chance to pin her down.

9

Odette

Having crammed successfully, Odette survived her final exams. She neglected celebrating with friends in Cambridge and instead went home for a family meal in Hounslow. The guest list was limited to three, because Odette's older sister, Ophélie, now lived in Mahé. Three was enough. The hawthorn was flowering in the garden. Her father Robert was playing the piano, and her mother Claire was making octopus curry.

'Can you do my laundry too, Maman?' Odette rested her head on the table in mock idleness. The waxed oak smelt like home. French exercise books were stacked in towers at the table's edge, to form a skyline of Maman's marking.

'Laundry and cooking don't mix.' Maman swooped to kiss Odette's head. 'Not unless you want underwear in your coconut sauce.'

Odette slunk like a child to the utility room, her holdall in hand. She crammed the machine with T-shirts and spring dresses that she hadn't had time to wash while she was revising. The softener bottle was cracked. Her hands slickened with soap. No matter; there was a sink. She ran the hot tap and the boiler audibly ignited.

The *whoosh* transported her back to the museum, where she could hear nothing but the basement boiler and breathe nothing but the stench of death. She believed the blood was on the floor again. She believed the body was slumped before her with its broken head and hand and heart. The world had been disturbed and made no sense.

Odette was oblivious to the water still running over her palm. The temperature rose, until her father – who had entered the room without her realising – snatched her hand from the stream.

'Midge,' he said quietly. 'Midge, come back.'

Her childhood nickname reached her. She stared at the red mark on her hand.

'Oh, God,' she groaned.

'I came to say don't use the softener.'

'Too late.'

'Is this happening to you a lot?'

'Laundry mishaps?'

'No. You… disappearing.'

'I knew what you meant. Sorry, Papi.' Odette breathed deeply. 'It's happening some of the time. Especially at night. It's the strangest thing – every so often I forget where I am and really believe I'm back in the museum basement. This time it was the sound of the boiler that set me off. It reminded me too much of the museum boiler, I think. You won't tell Maman, will you? You know how anxious she gets.'

'I'll keep quiet on one condition. You need someone to talk to.'

Odette was tiring of people telling her she needed support. The psychologist; Stuart Yelland; her father. And now Papi had her in a corner – either she must find someone to talk to, or worry her mother unduly.

'So you're giving me an ultimatum?' she checked.

'Yes. Now let me put you in touch with a professional.' Papi was a GP.

'No. I don't want to see one of your friends. Maman might still find out if you do that and I really don't want to worry her.'

'Odette…'

'I'll find my own counsellor… I promise. You don't need to arrange it.'

Papi nodded, grudgingly.

They went back upstairs. Maman was uncorking Prosecco in the kitchen.

'Let's watch the sunset while we eat,' she said.

Odette accepted a glass gratefully. They dined outside, on the decking, while the clouds turned the colour of Odette's scalded palm. Enough time passed for her wine to dull the sting. Sunsets were always so slow in England. That was one of the things Odette remembered about Seychelles; the way the sun went instantly, like the flicking of a switch, at the end of the day.

*

For months Dr Rebello's number had lain undisturbed behind a bank card in Odette's purse. But with Papi's threat hanging over her, Odette knew she had to ring. She hoped there would be a long waiting list. That might be enough to get her off the hook with Papi; she could at least say she tried. Unfortunately her telephone call was answered within three rings and an appointment was available the following day.

She turned up as arranged. The clinic was in a Victorian townhouse; Odette could picture it as the workplace of a gruff Austrian, dispensing treatments for neurosis and hysteria. She peered at the panel of buttons on the intercom and pressed the one labelled *Dr Ruby Rebello.*

'My name's Odette,' she said to the speaker. 'I have an appointment with—'

The intercom buzzed before she had completed her sentence. Odette stepped into a plain corridor with a stairway. She was about to knock on the nearest door when it swung open – to reveal the young, dark-haired woman Odette had met on the motorbike. Dr Rebello.

'Come in, Odette.' Dr Rebello smiled. She was olive-skinned and quiet-voiced, with a diamond nose-stud, a lumberjack shirt, and twelve-hole Docs.

She led Odette into a room with white walls and a beige carpet. Two chairs were arranged opposite each other. A coffee table, bearing a cactus and a box of tissues, was placed between them.

Dr Rebello sat down, and placed a notebook on her knee. She gestured to the other seat and invited Odette to explain why she'd come.

'Back in January – when you gave me your card – I'd just discovered a body in the toy museum. I suppose the police told you that much?'

Dr Rebello made a note. She hesitated, then said: 'Let's concentrate on what *you* have to say, shall we? We needn't concern ourselves with the police's account right now.'

This comment reassured Odette. She had found the police subtly discrediting. They had implied she was lying or mistaken about the basement being locked from the inside. The officer's focus on her birthplace told her they thought she didn't belong there – in their eyes she was out of place, and because of this she might be unreliable or even suspect.

To hear that Dr Rebello was more interested in Odette's own version of events made her more willing to open up.

'Since January, I've been having flashbacks,' she said.

'What kind of flashbacks?'

'Vivid. I feel like I'm *there*.' Odette described her experience at the coroner's court, and her parents' house, and all the other occasions in between when she had lost track of her real surroundings. Dr Rebello asked questions at intervals, continuing to take notes until Odette had finished, then put down her pen.

'During a traumatic event, memories aren't recorded normally,' Dr Rebello remarked. 'One theory for why this happens is that stress suppresses the hippocampus. I think you may have been traumatised – and that's affected how you're recalling the event. You're *re-experiencing* the moment that you found the body, rather than remembering it. To your mind, finding the corpse isn't something that happened in the past. You keep reliving it.'

'So what do I do?'

'We're going to construct a narrative of what happened when you found the body. As we do that, you'll probably feel you're slipping back in time, but I'll keep you in this room by asking questions about what you notice in the here and now. Piecing together your story will allow you to lay down proper memories, so that you can recollect the incident without panicking you're still there.'

This sounded a sensible course of action. Dr Rebello's calmness was what Odette needed. If Odette had confided in Maman, nobody would have stayed calm. Despite Odette's resistance, Papi had been right to say she should talk to a professional.

Yet one thing troubled her.

'I can't tell a story of what happened,' she said. 'Because I don't know *why* it happened.'

Dr Rebello put aside her notebook and studied Odette before speaking.

'Explain to me what you mean,' she asked.

'I *want* to think this woman killed herself,' Odette said. 'It's terrible, but it's better than the alternative. Because if it was homicide – if someone murdered her – the killer escaped an underground room without unlocking the door, and they're still free. How does that story make any sense? I have so many questions. About what happened. About *why*.'

Dr Rebello picked up her notebook again and wrote something down.

'The *why* doesn't matter,' she said quietly, without looking Odette in the eye.

And Odette thought: *she doesn't believe that. She's lying. She doesn't believe that at all.*

10

Angharad and Barbara

Angharad Mills, the medical engineer who had advised Margaret, was still working for the space programme. But there were no other senior women on staff, and she was tiring of her employers' chauvinism. She was therefore intrigued when she received an invitation to the Conclave. At their previous meeting, Margaret had hinted that a job might be available. Angharad didn't hesitate before accepting the invitation.

When the day came she arrived in the Conclave foyer and paused before approaching reception, to read the great directory sign displayed by the entrance. The departments were listed by floor. The basement was home to medical clinics and a series of laboratories – which included pathology and forensic sciences, as well as the physics labs which were so central to the Conclave's work. At ground level, there appeared to be a visitors' shop; the workers' bar and social area; the hall of time machines; the gardens; and a rear exit leading to the time travellers' accommodation. On the floor above, there was a range of offices shared by commercial services, public relations, administration and personnel. The legal, criminal investigation, justice and intelligence departments were on the second floor. A library, archives, Beeline's radio operators, and a lecture hall were on the third floor, along with Lucille Waters' office, which she occupied as Head of Knowledge. And finally, Margaret Norton oversaw the running of the Conclave from her rooms at the very top of the building.

As soon as Angharad reported to reception, Margaret's secretary came to greet her. They took the lift, which was lined with mirrors and red suede, to the fourth floor. The secretary led Angharad into Margaret's office: a high-ceilinged round room with heavy velvet curtains. Margaret sat at a dark oak desk. She had back-combed her hair into smooth immobility, and wore a string of pearls over a cashmere top. She looked presidential.

'Welcome, Angharad,' she said. 'Do take a pew. What do you think of the Conclave's new home?'

'It's very impressive,' Angharad said truthfully. 'How's time travelling treating you?'

'You might say I've hung up my boiler suit. My main priority now is to be the best leader to the Conclave that I can – and making strategic decisions is considerably easier from a fixed vantage point.'

'You're not time travelling at all?'

'No, it muddies the mind... all that toing and froing hither and yon. I have a clarity, a *linearity*, of thought that active time travellers can struggle to maintain. Lucille does the donkey work of compiling dispatches from the future. Bless her heart, whatever information I want from the future she fetches it.'

'I look forward to meeting her.' Angharad was hopeful that Margaret's renewed contact was paving the way for a job offer, and was keen to demonstrate her willingness to fit in.

'You'll meet Lucille, and Grace, in good time, I'm sure. Perhaps there'll even be an opportunity before you leave today. But in the meantime, I'd like your perspective on a matter of policy.' Margaret took a file from her desk drawer and splayed it open on the blotter.

Angharad leant forward to read the contents. The uppermost page appeared to be a psychometric questionnaire, for measuring anxiety levels. It wasn't a test that Angharad had seen before, and some of the questions were decidedly eccentric.

'The tests in this folder are a monitoring tool,' Margaret said. 'We use them to capture signs of anxiety and depression in time travellers. They won't be developed until the middle of the twenty-first century, but a psychologist of that period has placed them at my disposal for us to check on employees' mental health after every time-travelling trip. Might I ask you your initial impressions?'

Turning the pages, Angharad said, 'They contain a lot of questions about death – and the fear of death.'

'Yes. Time travellers are constantly encountering people who are alive in one timeline and dead in another. According to the psychologist – her name is Dr Joyce – death usually stops being tangible to them. Most time travellers adjust by developing a… casual disregard… for their own and others' mortality. It's quite a healthy adaptation, in my opinion, because it allows them to do their work. A minority of time travellers never learn to cope with this movement between the living and the dead, and can be quite incapacitated by it.'

'I see.'

'So during the hiring process I would like to detect which candidates show the most anxiety about death – and rule them out. These tests can play a part in that, but I wondered if you might have some supplementary strategies.'

'You want employees who don't care about their own mortality?' To Angharad, this sounded like a fast track to hiring risk-takers and nihilists. But Margaret wasn't inviting criticism. She wanted solutions. And if a Conclave job was in the offering, Angharad would provide solutions. 'You have two options. The first is to administer a more nuanced test at the recruitment stage. If the questionnaires aren't sufficient, people may be lying in their responses. They might not admit their true feelings about death, because it's a personal topic. So I'd suggest something more… physiological… than a questionnaire.'

'Go on.' Margaret picked up a fountain pen and filled it with ink.

'Play a showreel of images relating to death, along with more neutral pictures. You can determine if the candidate finds the death images more distressing by tracking physiological data, like pupil dilation – or brainwaves, if you want to use EEG technology. That kind of test is much harder for candidates to fake their responses.'

Margaret wrote down Angharad's suggestion. 'You mentioned a second option.'

'Yes.' Angharad hesitated, for her next proposal was a controversial one. 'You could recruit people irrespective of their death anxiety results, but then condition them to care less about death.'

'*Condition* them.' Margaret paused in her note taking, and pursed her lips. 'Do you mean brutalise, Dr Mills?'

'I'm thinking of a more informal process. You might call it hazing.' Angharad had seen plenty of hazing during the space programme, and before that, in the ballet. The dancers would march new girls to the laundry rooms, make them strip, sit on a washing machine in full throttle, and then draw circles round any flab that shook. Angharad reasoned that it was briefly humiliating, but not brutal. 'Hazing takes the form of games and dares and pranks. In your case, you'd need games which desensitise the players to a risk of death. If an employee doesn't respond, you can offer them an ultimatum. Leave the Conclave, or cooperate with further, intensified conditioning.'

'Thank you, Dr Mills. I won't rush to implement anything but it's good to have these options on the table.' Margaret smiled. 'How would you fare, if you were on the receiving end of this hazing?'

'I'd cope. Working at the Conclave would be worth some initial unpleasantness.'

'You think so?'

'I want to study the human body in unprecedented physical conditions. Monitoring time travellers will give me that opportunity. And there's nowhere else in the world I can do that – not until other countries start building time machines.'

'That won't happen for decades,' Margaret said. 'We have the monopoly on fuel.'

'Well – there you are, then. The Conclave stands alone.'

'We'd be happy to have you, Dr Mills. As we're in agreement, I'll ask my secretary to prepare a contract. Now, your very first assignment will be to travel to 1973 – there's a serious staff health issue in that year and your silver selves will need your help.'

Angharad's answers must have satisfied Margaret. The

much anticipated job offer had been made. They shook hands, and Margaret walked Angharad to the door.

＊

Nearly three hundred miles away, in St Ives, Barbara was also considering her career prospects. Her recuperation had taken eighteen months and her parents had been patient but she felt ready to regain some independence. She had just been to the local vet's, as they were seeking a receptionist. They told her the job was hers if she wanted it.

She took the long way home, along the Hellesveor path to the coast, to consider this change in her circumstances. The vet was a trusted friend of the family and, for an animal lover like Barbara, the job would have its perks. But it wasn't the academic work she had trained long and hard for. It wasn't time travel. Her heart had cracked a little when she said that yes, she would start the following Monday.

The wind was high and rapidly loosening Barbara's blonde up-do. It was when she paused, for the third time, to tuck her hair behind her ears that she saw a man flying a kite on the beach ahead. Not any man; a man she knew. Or had met, at any rate. He was Mr Rebello, the young Indian chemist from Porthmeor Pharmacy. She smiled at his attire. He was not dressed for the beach but in the trim brown suit he would have worn to work.

'Hello!' she called out.

She was a little breathless when she reached him. He smiled, with his eyes crinkled against the glare of the sun. His black hair was cut long in the fringe, and his face reminded her of the golden ratio illustrations she'd seen in art books. This immediately struck her as a ridiculously soppy thought. She knew she was blushing.

'What are you doing out here, during opening hours?' she asked.

'I'm flying a kite, Dr Hereford. My lunchtime is now my own; I've hired an assistant to sell Chupa lollies and cough syrup in my absence.'

'I wish I'd known you were seeking help. I've been looking for work, but it doesn't matter now – you have your assistant, and I'm going to help at the vet's.'

He looked at her with curiosity. 'That is indeed a missed opportunity. I confess, I never imagined you'd join my little firm.'

'What job *would* you imagine me in?' The question was dangerous. Across St Ives – across Britain – everyone knew what job Barbara had done, and why she left. Yet she had asked the question anyway, lest it gave some clue to his thoughts about her. Would he think less of her, because of her public humiliation? If he did, better to know that now, before her soppy thoughts escaped her control.

As if sensing a potential trap, Mr Rebello paused to watch the kite twist and jerk in the air. Eventually, he said: 'A job requiring bravery – and intimidating skill. Possibly a job yet to be invented.'

'Invent one for me now.'

'I'm in need of a kite-tamer. This beast is quite determined to escape me, or lift me off my feet.'

'What would be the payment?'

'A cinema ticket – as my guest – this Saturday night—' The kite jerked again.

'If we go to Redruth we can see *Stolen Kisses*.'

'Ah, now we're negotiating.' He laughed.

With a jolt, the wind snatched the spool from his grip. Barbara leapt into the air to catch the escaping kite.

'See,' Mr Rebello said. 'I knew you'd be perfect.'

'What's your name? Your first name, I mean?' Barbara asked.

'Antonio,' he said.

'Antonio,' she repeated, and the kite string pulled on her fist, as if she were growing lighter every minute. The lightest she could remember in a long time.

11

Ruby

The day after Ginger's visit, one of Ruby's clients' cancelled at short notice, giving Ruby the chance to catch up on email correspondence. She did so in the white-walled therapy room, enjoying the tranquillity of her surroundings. Granny Bee had sent an email. She always wrote her messages with the same care and attention she would give to a letter.

Dear Ruby,

The weather in St Ives has taken a turn for the worse. Mrs Cusack next door lost some slates from her roof. One of them landed in my fish pond. I'm only thankful it didn't hit Breno.

Since you left I have not been sitting on my hands. I moved my old lab equipment down from the loft and the pieces are in good working order. And I've been conducting a literature review, to get myself back up to speed. All the Conclave's scientists have access to future results, so they spend most of their time trying to understand how you reach a given conclusion, rather than making novel discoveries. But there are some curious gaps in their research topics. I think I've spotted a way to reuse spent fuel, which could make immense financial savings for the Conclave. It's strange to me that they're not using it already.

The Conclave are canny about money ordinarily. You do know they used my doctoral research for commercial ventures? My word, they have their fingers in a lot of pies. They made a pretty penny from my early experiments, which I could take some pride in if I wasn't so indignant. I'll put some websites at the bottom of this page so you can see the merchandise for yourself.

Look after yourself. I spoke to your mother and she said she's forgotten what you look like. For God's sake pay her a visit.

Love
Granny Bee

Ruby read through the links Bee had supplied. The Conclave certainly seemed keen to exploit any possible revenue stream. The links all related to products manufactured and sold with Conclave branding. One in particular caught Ruby's attention. The Conclave's most popular product – launched in 1992 – was the Conjuror's Candybox.

*

Ruby was exactly the right age to remember Candyboxes from her own childhood.

She'd first seen one during the eighth birthday party of her classmate, Danielle Reeves. For the party Danielle wore a Laura Ashley dress in aqua taffeta: her ringlets just skimmed the tops of her puffed sleeves, and her net skirts flared whenever she spun on the spot – as she did repeatedly. She looked *beautiful*. Ruby was in love, to the full extent of her seven-year-old heart. The whole class sat in a circle on Danielle's living room floor as she opened her presents. The Conjuror's Candybox wasn't the biggest gift – the four-foot teddy bear was that – but it caused the most excitement. When Danielle removed the packaging everyone craned forward to get their first glimpse. They saw a box made from plastic, in primary colours, with a hole in the top. It was about the size of a Rubik's cube.

'Who wants to put their sweet in first?' asked Danielle.

They clamoured. *I do, I do.* Everyone had their party bags, which contained sherbet chews wrapped in wax paper. Danielle surveyed the party guests. Her eyes rested on Ruby.

'Give me yours,' Danielle said. The others groaned in disappointment. Ruby could have burst with pride. Danielle took the chew, which had softened in the heat of Ruby's hand.

Everybody watched as Danielle dropped the sweet into the Candybox. It immediately dematerialised on entry. The children fiddled with their shoe straps, plucked at the deep pile carpet, and kept checking that the hole was empty. Then the box beeped and – miraculously, to the onlookers – the sweet reassembled.

'Ruby gets to eat the chew,' Danielle said. 'It's her sweet.'

Ruby put the sweet in her mouth.

'How does it taste?' Danielle asked.

'*Good*,' Ruby slurred. The chew stuck to her teeth. She was eating a magical, vanishing sweet and it tasted all the more delicious because Danielle had picked her to christen the new toy.

*

The Conjuror's Candybox had been marketed as a party trick. Ruby had never wondered how it actually worked. Eyes down on the links Bee had provided, she learnt that the Candybox used time travel technology to transport sweets one minute into the future. Danielle and Ruby had been unwitting time travel experimenters.

According to Wikipedia, the Candybox was quite a money-spinner in its first year, but the Conclave ceased production in 1993 because of irresolvable design flaws. Frequently the box malfunctioned and the sweet, instead of disappearing, rebounded at high speed. Parents complained it was dangerous, and there were numerous reports of injury – usually caused by the shrapnel of a boiled sweet.

Ruby clicked on the last of Bee's links. It led to a thriving web community of Candybox modifiers. Nostalgia, and a geeky interest in repurposing old goods, had driven recent second-hand sales. Apparently, with manipulation, the Candybox could transport objects further into the future than the intended one minute. The longest distance achieved so far was about an hour. The people adjusting the Candyboxes weren't scientists. They were librarians and curators – the kind of women who write zines and collect retro toys. One of them had drawn a cute web comic about the life of Lucille Waters – her early years in fifties Toxteth, winning a place at university, and finally sending messages across time via radio. The artist also reconditioned Candyboxes for sale. Ruby was tempted to buy one, for the sake of nostalgia. She had just reached for her purse when the intercom rang out. Her next client had arrived; the Candybox would have to wait.

*

Heeding Bee's mild rebuke, Ruby arranged to see her mother, Dinah, the following evening. Dinah lived in Wembley. She was golden-skinned like Ruby but they did not otherwise look alike; Dinah had a mass of chestnut hair with a strange blonde streak that repeatedly fell over her right eye. For the past ten years she had lived in a mock-Tudor semi, which was bequeathed to her by a childless paternal aunt. She indicated that Ruby should regard the house as her home, too, if she wished. Although Ruby appreciated the gesture, weeks – sometimes months – could slip by between Ruby's visits. Their relationship was cordial, but they had never been close.

When Ruby arrived at the house, dinner preparations were already under way. Dinah subscribed to recipe boxes with pre-measured ingredients in little bags. This meant there was very little food preparation Ruby could assist with, and she sat on her hands at the dinner table until Dinah brought through two plates of sea-bass.

'I'm glad you were able to come,' Dinah said. 'There's something I've been meaning to tell you.'

'Oh?'

'I've met someone. A man. At church.'

'Oh. That's nice.'

'He's called Henry, and he's a widower. I've met his daughters. Obviously I've told him all about you. Only...'

'Yes?' Ruby speared a piece of fish, and raised it to her mouth. It tasted rather good.

'He was a little shocked I've never been married. And, well, I didn't want to overwhelm him further after that revelation, so I haven't mentioned how old you are. Or rather, how young I was when I had you.'

'I see,' Ruby replied drily. 'You should have just said we were sisters, Mum.'

'That would have caused problems,' Dinah said, impervious to Ruby's sarcasm. 'No, I didn't want to lie to him – just to delay giving him the full family history till we're better acquainted. He's rather old-fashioned in some ways – but traditional values can be nice in a man, can't they?'

Ruby poured her mother a glass of table water and decided to treat the question as rhetorical. She wasn't sure she wanted to meet Henry. If he had old-fashioned views about teenage single mothers, he probably didn't take too kindly to lesbians either. She wondered how he felt about mental health problems, too.

'Does he know about Granny Bee?' Ruby asked.

'Really, Ruby, of course he knows I have a mother.'

'I meant, does he know about her past? That she was a time traveller? And why she had to leave?'

Annoyance flashed over Dinah's face. 'No. Why do you have to bring that up?'

Ruby toyed with her saffron mash, her appetite waning while she considered the information Bee had recently given her: that Dinah had instigated their years of silence about Bee's former life, because of her own fear.

'While I was in Cornwall, I had a good chat with Granny Bee,' Ruby said.

'You two are always as thick as thieves.' Dinah laughed shortly. 'I might almost feel left out.'

'She reminisced about the lab. I can't believe you never let her talk about the pioneers. You pretended it would upset her! Remembering made her *happy*.'

Dinah threw her fork onto the plate with a clatter.

'Ruby,' she said, her voice quiet with frustration, 'when I was a child, conversations about the pioneers *always* made my mother happy – to begin with. But soon she'd start ruminating on how they cut her off. She'd endlessly question how she could win back their favour. She should have been angry with them, and instead she wanted to be friends with those bastards. Then after the rumination came the depression. Just as you'd think she was over the worst of that, she'd attempt suicide. *That's* why I don't like to bring up the pioneers. *That's* why I told you not to discuss them with her. Because yes, eventually, she *will* be upset.'

This perspective shook Ruby. She had spent some of her childhood in Bee's care, while Dinah finished her studies, and from what Ruby could recall, Granny Bee's mental health had always been stable. But maybe that was because Dinah wouldn't let her dwell on the past.

An uncomfortable silence followed while the food cooled between them.

'I think I should go,' Ruby said. She needed to think, on her own, what to do next.

'Stay,' Dinah said. 'There's mousse in the fridge.'

'I've ruined dinner. Look, I'll call you in the week, OK?'

Dinah gave a small nod. Ruby placed her napkin beside

her plate and left her mother sitting at the dinner table. Once she was outside she arranged an Uber, and began mentally rehearsing a phone call to her grandmother. She needed to say Bee should slow down: that her plan to time travel again might be unwise. Just as the car pulled up, Ruby dialled her grandmother's number.

'Granny Bee?' she said, as she got into the back seat.

'Is that you, Ruby, my love?'

'I've been thinking, about your plan to rejoin the pioneers...'

'Yes?'

'You could so easily reopen old wounds.' Ruby's voice was as high as a child's. 'If you keep on this path I'm worried you'll get ill and hurt yourself.'

'Dear heart.' Bee's voice was kind. 'You must stop worrying about me. I've had this illness since before you were born or thought of. You can't use it as an excuse to wrap me in cotton wool. Besides... I've already started limbering up. I've done some experiments and I'll be back working alongside the pioneers in no time.'

'You've done what?' Ruby asked in consternation.

'I bought a second-hand Candybox! Did you read about those collectors who adapt them? They try to extend their reach into the future. Oh, the science is pretty basic, but I want to give it a go. To break my duck, so to speak.'

'You're impossible,' Ruby groaned.

'Good grief. I'll be fine. A schoolgirl could adjust one of those boxes. If a schoolgirl's physics experiment is too much for me, you might as well bump me off now.'

'OK, OK,' Ruby relented. 'Experiment if you must. On one condition. You come and stay with me in London. I want to be able to keep a close eye on you.'

Ruby said goodbye. She still had nearly an hour's journey. Her head fell back against the seat and she closed her eyes, desperate to shut out her anxieties about Granny Bee.

12

Odette

Under Dr Rebello's guidance, Odette's symptoms improved. The flashbacks and nightmares dwindled, then finally stopped. She could now remember the day she found the corpse without feeling she was slipping back, bodily, to the basement.

'But the questions still bother me,' Odette told Dr Rebello.

'Questions?'

'Who was the dead woman? Who killed her? Why?'

'How would knowing the answers change your life?'

'The world would make sense again.'

'Are you sure? Whys tend to lead to more whys.'

This, Odette had to admit, was true to her experience.

'Maybe,' Dr Rebello said, 'we're better off accepting the past is what it is. If it can't be changed, does the *why* matter?'

'The *why* always matters.' Odette started to laugh.

Dr Rebello smiled. 'What's funny?'

'I was just thinking. When I was a little girl, my nickname was Midge. Because I was always buzzing about, asking questions, and my mother had to swat them aside like flies. One question after another.'

'Tell me more about that.'

'In Seychelles everybody knows your auntie and her dog. You have no private business. And the tourists who swan in and out aren't immune, either. My aunt had a guest house so we knew the secrets of the holidaymakers too. When I asked questions my parents thought I was gossiping.'

'Were you?'

'No. Gossip's about getting a thrill, isn't it? A vicarious thrill. I wanted to understand people. To solve their mysteries.'

'Give me an example.'

'OK... I remember something from when I was six years old. One morning seven women from Scotland came to the hotel. They looked related. All of them had green eyes, and their noses looked the same to me; sharp and pointy. They were fair, very fair. The Kreol phrase for them was *bla rose* – that means people with white-pink skin. My Kreol's rusty but I remember that.

'I wasn't sure how old they were. The youngest-looking one was probably twenty-something – about the same age as my sister. And I thought the eldest was a great-grandmother at the very least. They were all named Dr Niven, except the oldest lady, who was a professor.

'All week I watched them. These women barely spoke to each other, but they were inseparable. At mealtimes I remember laughing because they raised their spoons to their mouths in synchrony. After a few days, I was very used to them coming and going as a single block. So I was really amazed when Professor Niven came into the lobby alone. She must have crept away without the others' knowledge. She must have had a secret. I was pretending to be a detective, you know.

'I followed Professor Niven outside. She took the path

from the hotel, as far as a place called Trois Frères. I lost her for a bit, so I looked for millipedes – they're very fat in Seychelles, you should see them. The next time I saw the old woman she was under a cinnamon tree, with one shoe off. She was rubbing her heel. It was too late for me to hide so I ran towards her.

'I asked her, in English: "Why did you go out for a walk all alone?"'

'And she told me: "The others are preparing for my wedding. It's today, at noon."'

'This seemed hilarious because she was much too old to be getting married. I asked her why she wasn't there too, and she said, "I'm not going. I've been seven times already. Do you know about time travel?"'

Dr Rebello dropped her pen. Odette waited for her to pick it up.

'Are you all right? Am I... not making sense?' Odette asked, because Dr Rebello was frowning.

'You're making perfect sense.' This time Dr Rebello's smile looked strained.

'OK. Professor Niven explained that the other guests weren't her relatives. They were all *her* – the same person, at different times, having travelled to the same point to meet. I asked her whether all time travellers go back to their wedding day.

'She said: "A few. When they're trying to understand something."'

'And I didn't say anything but I thought, this woman is like me. She wants to understand why things happen too.'

'Did the conversation end there?' Dr Rebello asked.

'She asked me what I wanted to do when I grew up. I told her: solve mysteries.'

The psychologist was looking into the middle distance.

'Dr Rebello?' Odette asked. 'What are you thinking about?'

'I was reflecting on my advice to accept what can't be changed.' Dr Rebello closed her notebook. She stood up. 'It's in your nature to ask questions, Odette. Perhaps we can't change that either. The session's over for today.'

13

Angharad

As soon as Angharad completed her probationary period, she travelled from 1969 to 1973, where a health crisis was under way at the Conclave. The time machines were nuclear powered, and this meant radiation-resistant bacteria thrived and proliferated in the fuel core whenever the machines were used. One strain of bacteria, named macromonas, was pathogenic. Ordinarily it posed very little threat to the time travellers, because the fuel core was sealed. But in 1973 a time machine combusted. The seal was damaged, and the machine's components flew through the air, causing injury to a large number of staff. Many of the resulting wounds were infected with macromonas. Angharad arrived the following day to help with the aftermath. They needed all the medical expertise they could get. Over the next week she devised a treatment programme of antibiotics and, for the minority with radiation syndrome, the drug TP508. She also strengthened hygiene protocols to limit the spread of germs.

Once all the time travellers were in a stable condition, she decided to visit her future self, who was on maternity leave in 1973. Angharad was still awed by the novelty of visiting other time periods and ventured from the Conclave with some trepidation. Since 1969, the governing party had changed from Labour to Conservative, and the IRA would begin their attacks on mainland Britain. But the appreciable differences, from Angharad's perspective, were at street level. She noticed prices had gone up quite a bit, considering less than a decade had passed; and there had been a small uptick in the earth tones of clothing and cars. The world hadn't changed so much it was unrecognisable. It had altered just enough to seem uncanny to her. She was both at home, and a stranger.

She took a bus, and then a train, to her home town. The way to the maternity hospital was still familiar. Her siblings and their children had all been born there. Angharad was grateful for any continuity. The building was a single storey block, partitioned from the road by privet hedges. Inside, the corridors echoed with newborns crying. Angharad followed the sound into a long ward that smelt of sterilising fluid and milk. Iron beds alternated with cots. She passed the series of new mothers – all of them with the same drained pallors; all of them wearing prairie nightgowns, in embroidered muslin and floral lawns. At the very end of the room Angharad came to a woman she recognised, who cradled a child wrapped in pink wool.

'Hey,' Angharad called gently.

The woman looked up, her eyes widening slightly, then she smiled.

'Hello, you!' she said. 'Come and see our girl. This is Julie.'

She tilted the bundle towards Angharad. The sleeping baby's mouth, pale and soft as rose petals, had pursed to suckle at a dream breast. Angharad's heart ached.

'Labour was fucking horrible,' her older self said cheerfully. 'Thirty-six hours and eighteen stitches. But it helped to know for definite we'd both make it.'

'Well done you.'

'Do you want to hold her?'

Angharad nodded. She took the baby in her arms, and sat in the easy chair by the bed. Julie stirred, but didn't waken. Her fists were as red as radishes. Close to, Angharad recognised the blanket; her mother had knitted it when Angharad was still small. She had always hoped she'd wrest it from her siblings when her time came to have children. The baby gripped the shawl's silken corner.

When you're born I'll already know you, Angharad thought. *And then I'll know you for ever.* It was a queer kind of bliss, mingled with terror. Angharad was glad she wouldn't have responsibility for someone so utterly dependent on her just yet. She had four years to prepare. But she wished she could revisit and revisit this moment. How sad that she wouldn't. She knew she wouldn't come back, because only one of her future selves was present. A single reliving would have to do. The two women exchanged smiles.

'Have you had many visitors?' Angharad asked.

'Just family. Margaret sent a present, hot off the factory line.'

Three dolls, bearing a resemblance to the pioneers, stood on the bedside cabinet. Two of the dolls' torsos were just visible through the V-neck of their boiler suits, and Angharad could see that their upper bodies were decorated with a raised pattern. They were action figurines suited to a much older child than Julie – as if they'd been bought by someone unfamiliar, or unconcerned, with the capabilities of newborn babies.

'A little replica of Margaret,' Angharad said. 'I'm not sure I like that idea.'

'Me neither. But it's entirely typical, isn't it? Do you know anyone else who'd give a model of themselves as a gift? I mean, Margaret's not *vain*, but she's...'

'An individualist?' Angharad supplied.

They both laughed. And beneath the new mother's embroidered collar, a red speck enlarged like an ink blot, staining the white cotton.

'You're bleeding,' Angharad said.

'Damn... The dressing's leaked.' She dabbed at the mark.

For reasons she couldn't explain, Angharad didn't want to know how she'd cut herself. She was almost frightened of the prospect. The oddness of seeing her own future may have caught up with her. *I'm being irrational*, she thought, and she forced herself to ask:

'How'd you get that cut?'

'When the time machine broke, of course.'

'*You* were there? But you were on maternity leave.'

'No; it was my last day. I left straight after the accident. Everyone was wailing and screaming and I was desperate to get away. By the time you arrived I was already on the train out of London. Don't worry, the wound's quite clean – there's no infection.'

That strange feeling, of fear and oddness, grew more intense.

'Can you explain something to me?' Angharad whispered. 'You all knew the accident was going to happen. Why on earth did you get into the machine?'

'You wouldn't understand.' Her older self smiled. 'You're still very green.'

The answer was cryptic – and condescending. Angharad

wondered if she came across that way a lot. Many people disliked their own personal traits, she knew, but it was disconcerting to experience her flaws as a separate party. She let the question drop, and looked again at the baby. Julie provided their common ground.

'I'd do anything for her,' Angharad said softly. 'I'd die for her. I'd kill for her.'

'I know,' said the older Angharad. 'We both would.'

14

Ruby

On the final Saturday of July, Ruby gathered her post and saw that among the usual bills was an unmarked brown envelope – presumably hand delivered. She tore it open to find a solitaire ring. The gold band was engraved with a chain of numbers: *193920151939201
8*.

'What have you got there?' Bee was on her way to the kitchen in her pyjamas. She had arrived the night before, with Breno, the Candybox, and lab equipment in tow.

'Mystery gift.' Ruby assumed it was from Grace. Another little puzzle to work out. But Ruby couldn't mention that. As far as Bee was concerned, Grace didn't know who Ruby was.

Ruby tried the gift on each of her fingers. The only one it fitted comfortably was the ring finger of her left hand. Bee watched with amusement.

'Spill the beans,' she said. 'Who's sending you engagement rings?'

'You think it's an engagement ring?'

'That's what it looks like. You must know someone who'd send this to you?'

'I *hope* not.' It couldn't be Ginger, with her evasiveness

and her alcoholism and her probable wife. No keeper she. Ruby suppressed a snort of laughter, and followed Bee into the kitchen.

*

After breakfast, Bee and Ruby sat at the kitchen table with the Candybox. Ruby turned it on. Bee took a white paper bag from her pocket, and tipped a cobble beach of sugared almonds onto the table.

'I bought them yesterday. I like to have something sweet to eat on the train. Now... let's see... to send this into the future, I suppose I just put the sweet in here?'

'That's how I remember it,' said Ruby.

Bee dropped one of the almonds into the box. They watched it disappear.

'Why can't we adjust how long it takes to reappear?' Ruby asked.

'Because this technology is as simple as time travel gets, and in fairness it's well suited to children. They don't want to wait longer than a minute. Now, with the right modifications, and the right fuel, you could use the Candybox to send objects months into the future. But you'd need an arms' dealer's budget to pay for it.'

'What makes the fuel so expensive?'

'Sourcing costs. The main constituent is atroposium which has to be harvested from garnet rock. It's rarer and harder to mine than coal, or uranium. Fuel was by far our biggest expenditure in the early days. Margaret funded us until the military money came through.'

The Candybox's *beep* sounded.

'Aha!' Bee said, looking inside the box.

She tipped the almond out, picked it up and popped it into her granddaughter's mouth. Ruby bit it cautiously.

'That's definitely a sugared almond,' she said.

'A *time-travelling* sugared almond,' Barbara said. 'And *you've* eaten it.'

Ruby dropped a second almond into the machine. The almond began to dematerialise – but then stopped, and shot straight up out of the box, with enough force to shatter on the ceiling.

Ruby jumped. 'That's the design flaw that took it off the market.'

'You're lucky it didn't hit you in the eye,' Bee said.

She made a few adjustments to the Candybox that she said should improve the reliability, and then she attached various pieces to the side of the machine, taken from her apparatus. Ruby passed tools, periodically shooing Breno from under the table. He was scouting for crumbs and the pickings were rich due to Ruby's relaxed housekeeping.

'I'm probably going to sound dim,' Ruby said. 'But what exactly are you doing?'

'I'm making a fuel converter and connecting it to the Candybox,' Bee said.

'Why?'

'So we can run it on time machine fuel.'

'You said that was expensive.'

Bee gave Ruby a sideways glance. 'There's something you don't know.'

'What?'

'When I was talking about expensive fuel...' she whispered. 'I *have* some.'

'I don't understand. How did you afford it?'

'I stole it.'

'Granny!'

'Not deliberately. I had two briquettes in my pocket when I left the Fells. But I didn't return them.'

'Why not?'

'Keeping them made me feel better. I'd come away from the project with nothing, Ruby. No job, no friends. The pioneers even had my pet rabbit. So it felt satisfying to keep something that belonged to the lab. I know it sounds petty.'

'The other pioneers *must* have noticed the briquettes had gone.'

'Oh, they did. The police came round to my house, actually, and searched for them. I'd hidden one beneath a patio slab, and I hid another behind some loose bricks in the chimney stack. They only found the one under the slab.'

'Oh, Granny. You might have gone to prison.'

'There was some talk of pressing charges,' Barbara admitted. 'But I wasn't fit to stand trial.'

'You would be now, though. You could have returned the fuel after you recovered, but you kept it, and while you were in your right mind. How much is it worth?'

'About half a million, in today's money.'

Fucking hell. Even Breno stopped in his scavenging to look up at Barbara, no doubt sensing a change in emotional temperature.

'There must be a black market in fuel,' Barbara pondered. 'D'you think I should sell it instead of using it in the Candybox?'

'No. No I don't think you should sell it. What are you thinking? It'd be traced back to you. You can't just make half a million pounds without someone asking questions.'

'I suppose you're right. But, Ruby, it's been fifty years. A lot of the people who'd put two and two together are dead.'

For a mad second Ruby thought about what they could do with five hundred thousand pounds. Then she checked herself.

'No. Any risk of you being arrested is too much. And I won't be able to sleep until we've disposed of it.'

'Fine, my love,' said Bee. 'Let's use it in the Candybox. That'll burn up some of the briquette, and then I'll discard the remains, I promise. Although I wish you'd let me buy you a house instead.'

'Don't spend your ill-gotten gains on me! I'd never be able to relax. Let's use the fuel right away, if that's the quickest way to get it off your hands.'

With difficulty, Bee rose from the sofa and fetched the fuel briquette from the bedroom where she'd left her bags. The briquette was quite a mundane-looking thing, not unlike a tablet of charcoal, and was about the size of Bee's palm.

Bee sat back down and adjusted her spectacles. She slid the briquette into the Candybox through the fuel converter. Ruby watched the machine steam and vibrate. The steam smelt pleasant – rather like fresh laundry. But Ruby was apprehensive about having a nuclear-powered machine in her flat.

'It is definitely safe, isn't it?' she asked.

'Oh yes. I've lined the fuel converter with lead. So what should we send through time?'

The engagement ring was still on Ruby's finger. She slid it off.

'You can't send that,' Bee said. 'Somebody picked it out for you.'

Except Ruby didn't know why. Grace's tokens had perplexed her, and she was tired of feeling confused. It felt freeing to drop the ring in the machine and watch it vanish, albeit temporarily.

'When will it come back?' Ruby asked.

Bee pencilled some sums on a piece of scrap paper. 'Forty-eight days. I hope whoever picked the ring won't be hurt if it's damaged in transit. You're heartless, Ruby.'

'There's a swinging rock in my chest instead. Red and stony, like my name.'

Bee shook her head and sighed.

15

Odette

Some questions wouldn't leave Odette alone, no matter how diligently she followed Dr Rebello's advice. Odette asked herself again and again: how did the woman in the basement die? If the pattern of injuries couldn't be self-inflicted, how did the murderer escape a room locked from the inside? And who *was* she?

The very day that Odette completed her last session with Dr Rebello, she contacted the coroner's office. Inquest documents were available to researchers, and Odette requested copies so she could check the finer points. They arrived the following week. She stacked the documents neatly on her desk, in three piles. She read the reports several times, marking the pages of most interest to her with neon tabs.

Missing person records were also available to read online. Odette ran numerous searches for women in the right age range, with the right physical characteristics, and made a note of approximate matches, but none of the women had a scar below the neck as a distinguishing feature.

Claire, Odette's mother, was concerned. She regularly invaded Odette's room without knocking, and stood by the desk, shaking her head, picking up the nearest dog-eared page.

'This isn't healthy,' Claire said. 'You should have moved on from this by now, Odette. When are you going to start looking for a job?'

'I *am* looking for a job.' When Odette wasn't poring over post-mortem results, she'd been seeking a good graduate role, but nothing seemed right. The majority of schemes underwhelmed her. She thought she might enjoy crime investigation if she only trusted the police. When Odette first came to England she'd considered herself light-skinned, but here she was black, and she'd witnessed the police pull her father over more than once. So she didn't fancy applying for a job with them. Intelligence work – the only other field that appealed – was open solely to UK nationals. Odette was a Commonwealth citizen.

Claire pinched Odette's chin. 'Looking for a job isn't enough. You have to *apply* for them. As long as you have too much time on your hands your head will fill with nonsense.'

It was true that Odette had felt rudderless since graduation. She made a little money by placing internet orders for friends back in Seychelles; they didn't have credit cards, so they'd browse online, tell Odette what they wanted, and transfer the payment from their banks with some extra for her trouble. But that didn't give her a routine. So she began waiting tables at Le Petit Cadeau, a nearby restaurant, until she could find something more suitable. Although she was glad of a few shifts, she proved bad at waitressing. The manager would tell her to wipe tables and she'd start with a good will but then she'd abandon her flannel as her mind wandered back to the corpse and the bolted basement door. She'd stand before the table, arranging the pepper mill and soup spoons in a model of the crime scene. The body had lain *here*; the gun was *there*; *this* was the only exit. She moved the elements round like pieces on a chessboard and came no closer to understanding the dead woman's fate.

In frustration, Odette decided to telephone the coroner himself. There were still rocks she hadn't turned. The forensic photographs hadn't been made public, for instance, and Odette wanted to check over them.

The coroner's name, she remembered, was Stuart Yelland. Odette recalled his habit of screwing up his left eye whenever he thought over a question. She imagined him doing this when she dialled his number outside the restaurant. The only private spot was in a side alley, by the bins; and even that was overlooked by a kitchen window.

The coroner's secretary answered first, then put Odette through.

'Yes?' Yelland barked.

'This is Odette Sophola,' she said. 'I found the body at the toy museum? I wanted to ask—'

'Ah. I remember you,' Yelland said more gently. 'Forgive the curt welcome – my secretary didn't realise you were a witness. She thought you were a journalist.'

'What?'

'The journalist who covered that inquest was quite relentless – terrible pests, the media – but he's gone quiet lately, thank God. What can I do for you?'

'I'd like to see pictures of the crime scene.'

'They're not available to the public.'

'I know. But I thought maybe if I saw the body again... now I'm no longer in shock... I'd notice details I missed at the time.'

'Ms Sophola...'

'Some witnesses are allowed to examine evidence, aren't they? Properly Interested Persons?'

'Relatives, yes, and beneficiaries of the estate.'

'I found the body. Don't I count as a Properly Interested Person?'

'Potentially. That's at my discretion.'

'And if I were a Properly Interested Person, I'd be allowed to see the photographs?'

'I'm afraid I'm not going to permit that.'

'Why? I was *there*.'

'I have to balance your request against this woman's dignity. Let her rest in peace. It isn't right, to hand out pictures willy nilly. Don't you think it would be healthier to speak to someone about your feelings? Last time we spoke, you said you might seek counselling.'

I already have, Odette thought irritably. His swerve into her personal motivations was condescending – and possibly a deliberate distraction.

'You were first on the scene,' Stuart Yelland went on. 'Many people in your position suffer lasting distress. Do you really want to make it worse by poring over unpleasant pictures?'

Odette hung up. Yelland might be a nice old man, but he didn't understand. She needed to solve this. Until she did the unanswered questions would keep running round her head.

Her manager loomed at the window, tapped the glass and mouthed Odette's name.

'Just coming,' Odette called.

The phone call wasn't a complete waste of her time. Yelland had let one thing slip: he'd mentioned a journalist, which told Odette she wasn't the only person interested in tying up loose ends. That was reassuring because she was beginning to feel very isolated. She needed someone to talk to. But not a doctor, as the coroner suggested. She needed someone who could help her solve the mystery. Someone who wanted to solve the mystery as much as she did.

*

It was gone midnight when Odette got home, and she was too tired to do anything besides fall into bed. But first thing the next morning she searched newspaper websites for references to the inquest. She got a relevant hit when she tried *dead, inquest* and *toy museum*. This one brief item came from a local tabloid. It had been written in May by a man called Zach Callaghan. The write-up didn't refer to Odette by name; it said that *the dead body was discovered by a museum volunteer*. That may have been why it passed under her radar when it first went to print.

From Yelland's comment, she'd expected the piece to be longer. It didn't make sense that a journalist would badger Yelland for a few forgettable paragraphs. But Yelland had definitely said the journalist was persistent.

Odette telephoned the newspaper's editorial assistant and asked to speak to Zach Callaghan.

'He's a freelancer, not one of our staff writers,' the man said. 'If your query isn't something our regular team can handle it might be a while before he gets back to you.'

'Thanks,' Odette said. 'I'd just like him to contact me regarding an inquest that took place earlier this year.'

She left her name and number, and turned back to the internet. Maybe she could get a quicker response if she approached this man directly. Odette ran a search on the name Zach Callaghan. It wasn't super common, but it wasn't especially rare either. The top hit was for a painter, and the one below was for a head teacher who'd resigned in a scandal. Zach the journalist was number three. He had a personalised website with a *Contact Me* box which Odette filled out. From curiosity, she clicked on the page marked *Articles*.

Zach Callaghan hadn't written anything new in several months. His coverage of the hearing was the most recently dated link. Prior to that, his articles included: an in-depth analysis of Margaret Norton's alliances with arms' dealers; detailed investigations into the Conclave's tax arrangements; and an article on unexplained disappearances of time travellers. All three pieces had been published by national broadsheets, and there were others on similar themes going back years. He clearly wasn't a court journalist. He hadn't covered any other inquests.

Why would someone with a sustained interest in the Time Travel Conclave suddenly turn his attention to the body in the museum? Did this man, this Zach Callaghan, know of a connection between the two?

An envelope icon flashed in the corner of the screen, alerting Odette to a new email.

It was only one line long: *I no longer have any involvement with this story.* The message was unsigned, but came from Callaghan's address.

16

Barbara

Barbara stood alone in the toy store, deliberating over plush bears and raggedy clowns. Her baby's first birthday was approaching. Dinah liked monkeys but Barbara couldn't see one among the multiple soft toys. She circled the display, and came face to face not with monkeys, but with shelves of dolls: time traveller dolls.

They were meant for older children than Dinah. The bodies were made from hard plastic, and their clothes could be unbuttoned and changed. One looked like Margaret; another like Grace; a third like Lucille. All the pioneers but Barbara.

The dolls were idealised and hyper-real. Their eyes were as large as cherry drops and their cheeks were dimpled. Barbara could tell which doll was which from their hairstyles and the name labels on each breast pocket. Lucille was a different colour, of course. Each doll's décolletage was debossed with an ornamental pattern. Barbara picked Lucille up, to touch the decorative ridges along her neckline. Maybe the ridges were a mark to show belonging: like a sailor's tattoo.

In the years after Barbara's breakdown she'd responded

well to treatment, and appeared to get on with life. She'd married. She'd had a baby girl. But sadness at her lost career was always close to the surface. In secret, she read pulp novels about time travellers' adventures with a kind of horror. She found lunatics galore among the pages. They were Barbara's legacy. Unlike Margaret, in the early days she never thought of legacy at all. Her only thought was to travel through time, alongside her friends. Looking at the doll in her hand and the companion pieces on the shelf she felt sick with longing for that old dream.

She left the shop with a trio of dolls, her search for Dinah's present forgotten.

*

Barbara stood before her bathroom mirror, stripped to the waist with a razor in her hand. One of the dolls was propped against the toothbrush mug. Margaret. The ridged, curving pattern on the doll's neck and chest was clear. Barbara studied the pattern. She held the razor to her clavicle and tried to cut an arabesque into her skin. A line of blood ran down her breast. The cut didn't hurt, though she imagined it would sting later. She'd gouged a deep groove by the time Antonio, her husband, opened the bathroom door.

His eyes widened and his mouth made a dark O. He caught her wrist.

'Jesus, Bee,' he said. 'Look what you've *done*.'

'It isn't what you think,' she told him.

He stared at her, and didn't let go of her arm. She could feel his hand trembling.

'I didn't do it to harm myself,' she said.

'Bee.' His voice cracked.

'Look at this doll!' She pointed. 'See? She's a time traveller. Time traveller dolls have these marks. If I have them too, I'll match.'

'All right, Bee. All right.'

But he still held on to her arm, so she knew he was trying to mollify her. No matter how rationally she spoke, her illness made her explanations suspect to him. He would think that she was imagining signs where they didn't exist, because she was psychotic. Her eyes filled with tears. He'd never let her complete the arabesque.

She dropped the razor. Antonio pulled her towards him.

'I'll get blood on your suit,' she wept.

'It's all right,' he whispered to her. 'It's all right. We'll go to the hospital, and they'll take care of you.'

Nurses stitched her up, and the psychiatrist increased her medication. They all disregarded her explanation of why she cut herself. The psychiatrist told Tony she was a danger to herself. Eventually Barbara stopped disputing this. She'd tried to recapture the past, with a razor and some plastic imitations of friends. Perhaps, she allowed, that was lunacy.

17

Ruby

After they had tired of the Candybox, Ruby and Bee took Breno to Clissold Park. They kept him on the leash, because of the deer, but he was good-natured about it. Passers-by stopped to talk with him. Not only to him; Ruby reflected that London was a far friendlier place with a dog. Bee was deep in conversation with the owner of a labradoodle when Ruby felt the buzz of her mobile on her hip.

The name on the display said Ginger.

Ruby picked up. 'Hello?'

She heard laughter in response. A child's laughter; then two muffled voices.

'I can't hear you very clearly,' Ruby said. 'I'm outside.'

'A loser says what?' said the child, in an ersatz American accent. More laughter. Then footfall, and an adult voice – deep, Irish – scolding. Ruby thought he said: 'You're bad and bold.' The child kept laughing, then implored, 'Daddy, no, let *me* have it…'

'I'm sorry,' that Irish voice said. 'My daughter dialled your number. She keeps taking our phones.'

'That's OK,' Ruby said.

She listened to the dead line for a few seconds.

'Anything important?' Bee asked. The labradoodle woman had gone, without Ruby noticing.

'Just a prank call.'

They resumed their walk. Ruby could sense Bee's sideways glances.

With concern, Bee said, 'You look ever so shocked. It wasn't a smutty call, was it?'

'No... it was a little girl. Messing about.'

Ruby didn't want to give any more information than that. Despite her qualms about Ginger's relationship status, it was upsetting to have her suspicions confirmed. Hearing those voices was like discovering the people in a book were real. Till a few minutes ago, Ginger's partner had been Ruby's own intangible invention. The invention was never solid enough to sire children – or to have an accent.

Ruby wondered if he knew and consented to Ginger's involvement with other people. But the possibility felt fundamentally hollow. Ginger conducted herself like a cheater. They always went to Ruby's. Ginger never spoke of her home life. Ruby *felt* like a secret. And if Ginger was with a man, that might mean Ruby was a very particular sort of shameful secret.

Bee paused to look at a grazing deer, and Ruby stopped beside her.

'I don't believe you're upset over some prank call,' Bee said. 'Is someone treating you poorly, Ruby? I can always give them a piece of my mind.'

Ruby laughed weakly. 'I'm sure you would. Best I just forget about them, to be honest.'

'Well, the offer stands.'

'Thank you.' Ruby knelt to ruffle Breno's head. 'I need a pet. I'm done with relationships.'

'At your young age! Don't make lasting decisions while your heart's bruised.'

'Maybe I'll get a house cat. It'd be cruel to keep a dog in that flat.'

Breno barked, though whether in agreement or contradiction was unclear.

*

That night, as Bee slept in Ruby's bed, Ruby tried to get comfortable on the sofa. Despite her fatigue Ruby lay there for an hour, unable to relax because she kept thinking about Ginger's husband. She turned on the lamp and rifled through the paperbacks strewn across the coffee table for something to settle her thoughts. She settled on the book she'd bought at Tate Modern: the glossary of time travellers' phrases, by Sushila Pardesi.

Ruby had expected the phrase book to contain a certain amount of professional jargon – and it did; consistency principle, common chronology, topology change, et cetera. Many of the words described living life out of sequence. To live an incident you've already read about is called completion. Returning to an incident you've already experienced is called echoing. Feeling angry with someone for things they won't do wrong for years is called zeitigzorn.

But the real pleasure of the book was the slang. Quite a few of the colloquialisms defined members of in-groups and out-groups. Newly recruited time travellers are called wenches. People whose personal chronologies match well, because they belong to the same team, swim in the same cut. A time traveller may call their younger selves green-me, and older selves silver-me. And then there were terms for people who don't time travel. These people, the everyday people, were mostly defined by their march through a shared chronology, earning them the names plodders, or one-way travellers, or emus – who can't walk backwards.

Pardesi's short introduction explained that time travellers' slang is associated with the Conclave's communal areas – the dorms; the break rooms. These are the places where travellers wait to be debriefed. Their slang is immune to change, making it interesting to linguists. Introducing 'new' words is impossible in such a context. A word may be new to an individual time traveller, particularly if she's inexperienced in the field. But she'll take it back to her own period, which may pre- or post-date the period where she heard it, and it can no longer be associated with usage in a given year or decade or century. The opportunities for this to happen are multiplied many times over, because there have been hundreds of time travellers, hailing from different periods, congregating in the Conclave since the nineteen seventies.

Ruby's eyelids were now drooping. One final column of words caught her attention. It was the section on sex and romance. Sushila Pardesi noted that time travelling made it particularly easy to be unfaithful without detection. Adulterers had a term for their conquests in far-off decades: exotic material. Wishing she had closed the book ten seconds earlier, Ruby returned it to the coffee table, and turned off the lamp.

18

Odette

Despite Zach Callaghan's curt email, Odette didn't seriously consider giving up. There was no point going to the newspaper's offices if he was a freelancer, but with some further internet stalking she learnt that Zach taught on the journalism degree offered by a college in central London. Twice Odette went there in person, pretending to be a prospective student, only to be told Zach wasn't there that day. She was luckier on the third visit. The receptionist made her sign in, gave her a pass, and looked up the theatre where he was lecturing on high-risk reportage.

The lecture hadn't finished when Odette found the right room. She looked through the oblong of glass in the door and could see Zach speaking at the front. She remembered him now. He had sat in her row at the hearing – the man with the dark curls. When he'd finished his lecture, students swarmed past Odette into the corridor, and she slipped inside to join the few people with questions for Zach. Several times his eyes flickered in Odette's direction. *He recognises me too*, she thought.

Soon they were the only two people left in the room.

'Yes?' Zach prompted.

'My name's Odette Sophola. I want to talk to you about the inquest we both attended in the spring.'

'Don't you think it's presumptuous, tracking me down without an invitation?'

'Very. Have you never doorstepped anyone, in your line of work?'

'Are you saying you're a journalist too?' Zach unzipped his bag and placed his lecture notes inside.

'No,' Odette said. 'I'm just someone who knows that woman's death was suspicious. Like you do. Wouldn't you like to speak to me? I was *there*.'

Zach ran a hand through his hair. He wouldn't meet her eye. He was worried, scared, even, Odette realised – that was why he hadn't written anything in months. Something had happened to shut his mouth.

'Why did you stop calling the coroner, Mr Callaghan? Did someone threaten you?'

'No.' Zach slung his rucksack onto his shoulder and made for the door.

'Your family then?'

'I don't want to talk about my family.'

'Please – Mr Callaghan. I can help.'

'Oh? How?'

She thought rapidly. 'I can draw the attention away from you. Let me follow the story. Please. Just give me the information you have.'

He stared at her for a long moment, then shook his head.

'I must be out of my mind,' he said.

*

Zach insisted they walk to the nearest park; he could be sure they wouldn't be bugged there. They found an empty bench by the duck pond.

'I was looking into the Conclave's finances,' Zach began. 'The Conclave is subsidised by tax payers, but it isn't really held accountable to them – it's an arm's length organisation. The money's spent on military action, commercial development, a bit of academic research – all the kinds of things you'd expect. They also have labour costs. Do you know how time travellers get paid?'

Odette shook her head.

'They act as contractors. You can't really give them an annual salary because they might work much less, or much more, than twelve months in any given calendar year. It's more practical for them to negotiate their payment per mission, and self-assess their tax contributions. Which is all well and good, I've no objections there – I self-assess my own taxes – but it's very easy for a time traveller to exploit the tax system.'

'In what way?'

'Time travellers need money across multiple time periods, but the cost of goods inflates and the currency changes. To work round this the Conclave has its own currency, called the achronic pound, or achron for short. Workers are paid with achrons. Whatever the time period, workers can sell their achrons back to the Conclave, for pounds sterling or any of the British currencies that succeed it. The rate's set by the Conclave. Time travellers don't hold their funds in a central bank tied to a specific time and place. Rather, they carry their money with them. Whether they go back or forward in time, their personal ledger's stored in their wristwatches.

'So, in practice, a time traveller receives a lump sum as soon as they get a wristwatch, and this lasts them till they die. Grace Taylor, say, gets her first wristwatch in 1969, and it already contains a billion achrons. But for tax purposes, the Conclave may not have paid her those achrons in 1969. For the paperwork, she can ask to be paid in any year that she likes, on a mission-by-mission basis. A hundred thousand achrons in 1991, another five hundred thousand in 2137 – the date is completely immaterial to when she has access to the money.'

'How convenient.'

'Isn't it? Time travellers must declare their earnings to the tax man at least once in a twelve month period, but they can load their payments into the years where tax conditions are most favourable. They get paid with government money but can avoid paying their own share into the country's upkeep.'

'How's this connected to the body in the museum?'

'Hang on, I'm coming to that.' Zach waited until two runners had passed out of earshot. 'Someone sent me a database of time travellers' finances.'

'Who?'

'An anonymous source. Clearly someone with access to confidential data at the Conclave, but so far I haven't been able to identify them.'

'A source *within* the Conclave?' An employee on their side could be very useful. 'So what did their database tell you?'

'It contained banking transactions from all the time travellers' wristwatches. Ninety per cent of Conclave payments were officially made in 2097 to 2113. This makes sense if you know that no tax on earnings is collected in those years. I was most interested in the senior time travellers, because they were making the biggest money. There was something strange in Margaret Norton's transactions. Between 1969 and 2017 her investment habits were remarkably consistent. She had the kind of varied portfolio you'd expect for a woman of her background and income. But at the start of 2018, she sold multiple assets to the Conclave – including all her residential properties. And then she never withdrew another achron. Not a single penny. The database covers three centuries and she never made another transaction. What does that tell you?'

'She was expecting to need a lot of ready cash, but something happened to stop her spending it,' Odette said.

'Yep. It's the behaviour of someone in trouble. I wasn't sure what kind, although Norton does have some shady political associates. So all of last year I kept tabs on her whereabouts, in case there were any clues in the company she was keeping or any sign she wanted to relocate in a hurry. And I kept a close eye on the different coroners' courts. By the time you found the corpse in the museum, I was pretty primed to write about the violent death of a woman in her eighties. And then the coroner said he couldn't identify her!'

'You thought it was a cover-up?'

'I thought it *might* be. In February, a month after you found the body, the Conclave announced that Norton had retired, and a woman named Angharad Mills became interim director. Fair enough, perhaps, no one could begrudge someone in their eighties retiring. But there was no word of farewell from Norton herself, and it's not like her to miss a PR opportunity. So I put pressure on the coroner. Questioned him about whether he was in cahoots with the Conclave.'

Odette remembered how Yelland had spoken of journalists. 'He thought you were a pest.'

'I *was*. Somebody had to be. Then, one sunny morning, some disgusting pictures landed on my doormat. Pictures of my relatives, dead, lying in mortuaries. They could only have come from someone at the Conclave because all the people in the photos are alive and well *now*.'

'Photoshop?'

'Whether the pictures were real or doctored, they were a *threat*. If it had been a photograph of me, I'd have said screw it, I won't bow to pressure. But involving people I care about? I backed off.'

Conversation ceased while an old man threw crusts at the ducks a few feet away. Odette wondered how long Zach would keep watching people in this way – suspicious that they may be collecting information about him. After less than fifteen minutes, Odette felt paranoid herself. If she were wise, she would drop her pursuit of this mystery before the paranoia took permanent hold. But she thought it might already be too late for that. After months of revisiting the details of the case, she was ravenous for what Zach had given: a possible identity for the corpse. Odette wasn't going to abandon her own investigations now.

'Let me get this straight,' Odette said. 'Margaret Norton dropped off the face of the earth round about the same time I discovered the body in the museum. Then you pressed the coroner for more information but stopped because of the Conclave's intimidation?'

'That's about the size of it.'

'Your source, the one who sent you the directory. Can they tell you anything about Margaret's disappearance?'

'I emailed them. They've only ever made contact through encrypted messages, and they've never used the same address more than once. I emailed the last address they used, and asked whether Norton had any connection to the inquest. My message bounced back – the account had been closed.'

'We *need* someone on the inside.'

'Speak for yourself. I'm not touching this story again.'

'I understand,' Odette told Zach. 'Thank you for talking with me.'

*

Zach had given Odette a lead, and the only way to follow it was to get inside the Conclave. As soon as she got home, she looked up the Conclave's recruitment webpage, and dialled the number for their careers line.

'I'm a recent graduate,' Odette said. 'I'd like to make an application.'

'In which field?'

Odette scanned the webpage, which included a list of departments. Criminal investigation was third from the bottom. That made Odette smile.

'I want to be a detective,' she said.

The rep took her details, and explained the selection process to her. Odette didn't need an inside source to learn what was happening in the Conclave. She could find out on her own – as soon as she'd passed all the tests.

19

Margaret

Although many of the time travellers lived at the Conclave's central headquarters, Margaret did not. She had several homes across the country, including a substantial Georgian property just outside London. One evening, as the car approached this residence, she saw a man waiting by the front gate – an Indian, from the looks of him, in a suit that was fifteen years out of date.

He waved his trilby, as though to flag down the passing car. 'Dr Norton! Dr Norton!'

His voice was muffled by the glass. Margaret didn't have the faintest idea who he was.

'Don't stop,' she told the driver. They proceeded up the drive, and the gates closed on the Indian behind them.

Half an hour later he returned to her thoughts. She was in her drawing room, by the fire, unwrapping a parcel that had arrived from the royal taxidermist. Beneath the paper and string was Patrick. He'd died a month before, of quite natural causes, and left a healthy dynasty at Margaret's home in the Fells. Margaret was delighted with his new appearance. The taxidermist had captured

Patrick's shrewdness. The rabbit had always been wily, and she disciplined him accordingly. Margaret never coddled Patrick, as Barbara had done.

Thinking of Barbara gave Margaret a hunch. She was sure she remembered hearing Barbara married an Indian man. Called Ronny, or Danny, or some other not-very-Indian name. Might it have been him outside – perhaps to petition on Barbara's behalf, at her instigation? That would be just typical of Barbara. How irritating. Margaret positioned Patrick at the side of the fireplace – in his alert pose you might imagine he was ready to jump over the flames – and crossed to the telephone.

It was Lucille she contacted.

'Has Barbara's husband been bothering you?' Margaret asked.

'Not *bothering*,' Lucille said. 'He did get in touch. Barbara's in hospital and he was keen that we should visit.'

'Surely you didn't say you would?'

'No,' Lucille said, with audible reluctance.

'Whatever's the matter with her? The old trouble?'

'Yes. Some business with a razor. Lucky she didn't kill herself.'

An alarm sounded in Margaret's thoughts. If, one day, Barbara did do herself in, it would reawaken everyone's interest in her first, public breakdown. The Conclave should prepare for that eventuality, in case they needed to hush up the circumstances of Bee's death. Keeping things quiet would be in everyone's interests – not just the Conclave's. No doubt Danny, or Ronny, would want to grieve in peace. He should be grateful for the discretion.

'Lucille, could you obtain some documentation? I'd like to see Bee's eventual death certificate. In fact – obtain all our death certificates.' Might as well check whether there were any other surprises on the horizon.

*

The certificates were ready and waiting for Margaret when she arrived at work the next day. She perused them at her desk. Bee's was first: septicaemia, in several decades' time. Well, good. No scandal implied there. Lucille would die of cancer. Grace of a brain haemorrhage. And Margaret...

Margaret's death certificate had a blank space where the cause of death should be.

She picked up the phone and dialled Lucille's number.

'What can I do for you, Margaret?' Lucille asked.

'What's the meaning of this blank space?'

'It's the only certificate on record. I did check quite extensively.' Lucille sighed. 'The registrar told me a blank space is unusual, but not unheard of. It means something interrupted the certification process. The cause was contested for some reason.'

'For some reason?' Margaret was incredulous. 'You've been to the future, Lucille. Are you saying no one knows how I die?'

'There are rumours.' Lucille said. 'My own theory...'

'Yes?'

'Maybe your death arose during covert operations. It had to be kept a secret.'

Margaret rather liked the sound of that. A covert death. Most likely a noble one.

'At any rate,' Lucille went on, 'you live to a grand old age, don't you?'

Yes, Margaret said to herself; she had several good

decades ahead of her, and a likely death in the field. She felt a little better about the blank space now. But she locked the certificates in the bottom drawer of her desk, which was where everything went that she didn't want to see.

20

Barbara

On the third day of Bee's stay in London, Ruby said she had a conference to attend in Birmingham. Luckily Bee had plans of her own, and they included experiments.

As soon as Ruby left for her train, Bee set up her apparatus on the kitchen table. She'd been thinking about how to reuse spent fuel, and wanted to try out some ideas. From her reading she knew that the Conclave still used solid atroposium to power their time machines. In the sixties this made economic sense: the same material was already being produced for nuclear armament, and the pioneers were able to tap into the same supply chain. But there were limitations on this choice of fuel that had never been addressed.

The greatest problem was inefficiency. While a time machine's running, radiation causes damage to the fuel's structure, which means only a fraction of the fuel's potential energy can be used. Bee speculated that if the solid fuel waste were dissolved then some of the untapped energy could be harvested, because liquids are less susceptible than solids to radiation damage.

Bee intended to try this out for herself with the Candybox. When Ruby dispatched the engagement ring into the future, the Candybox had extracted all the energy it could from Bee's stolen fuel. Bee had estimated the ring would return after forty-eight days. If dissolving the briquette, and accessing its remaining energy, allowed the machine to run for longer, then the ring might travel even further into the future. Bee removed the spent briquette from the Candybox. She used her miniature lab kiln to melt the briquette in salt, at a temperature of around six hundred degrees Celsius. The kiln was connected to the Candybox via a ceramic attachment, so that the liquid fuel titrated directly into the machine. To Bee's delight, the Candybox quaked into life. She whooped in triumph – and Breno, who she'd left sleeping in the bedroom, barked in return. A few seconds later she heard his scratch at the kitchen door.

'Hold your water,' she called to him. It wasn't safe for Breno to be in there with all the equipment strewn about. She packed the pieces away, singing as she did so. Her experiment had a real, meaningful result. At the very least it showed that she still had a scientist's mind and was capable of innovations on the Conclave's behalf. By proposing this recycling method to the pioneers, she might open up a tiny crack of possibility, a slim chance of working alongside her old friends that she'd feared she'd never have again. And if she could work with them, she'd have access to proper time machines. Bee was a step closer to her real goal: experiencing the thrill of time travelling once more.

Who should she contact first? she wondered. Grace was the only one of the pioneers who'd been in touch. That made her the best starting point. Bee opened the kitchen door and picked Breno up on her way to the phone. She punched the Conclave's number from memory.

'All Grace Taylors are off site today,' the secretary told her, once Bee had been put through to the correct department.

'Is she in this period?' Bee asked.

'Yes, two of them are, but only until tomorrow morning.'

How inconvenient. Bee chewed her lip.

'Can I make an appointment to see Grace when she's back?' Bee asked.

'There's no availability in her diary for three months.'

Damn. Bee wanted to move faster than that. She had no time to waste; life was fleeting. That was the message Bee took from Grace's origami rabbit. She told the secretary she'd telephone back when she'd checked her own schedule. It was pointless asking to be put through to Margaret or Lucille – they'd refuse her call, if the past was any indication. What Bee needed was to see them face-to-face. It would be hard for the pioneers to turn her away if she was there in the flesh.

'Right,' she said to Breno. 'We'll have to put the back-up plan into action.'

21

Odette

Odette told her parents of her Conclave application, but not that she intended to spy on the other time travellers. As far as they were concerned, she had finally selected a graduate career. So, on the morning of the Conclave's recruitment tests, Maman was voluble, firing questions even as Odette put her jacket on to leave.

'How many other applicants will there be?' Maman fretted.

'I've no idea,' Odette said.

'I bet they've been preparing for months. Why didn't you apply earlier? You've had no time to revise.'

'It's not that kind of test, Maman. They want to know how I think. I don't have to remember any facts.'

'But if you'd only planned ahead instead of taking that silly job waiting tables—'

'We need to set off,' Papi interrupted. He was giving Odette a lift.

Odette kissed Maman on the cheek. 'Do I look smart?'

'Yes,' Maman said cautiously. 'But a tweed suit, Odette? Pinstripe would be more usual, no? Tweed is for academics... or... or... foxhunters.'

'She thinks she's Miss Marple,' Papi said flatly. 'We're going to be late.'

His tone troubled Odette. All week he had seemed distracted, and she wasn't sure why. They walked to the car and got in. Claire stood on the step to wave. She was still waving when they turned out of view.

'She really wants me to get this job,' Odette said.

'Your mother wants you to have a successful career,' Papi corrected. 'It doesn't have to be with the Conclave.'

The traffic halted at a red light. Rain speckled the windscreen and Papi turned on the wipers. They swept the glass three times.

'Why shouldn't I work for the Conclave?' Odette asked at last.

'I looked up their recruitment criteria. You don't meet it.'

'I'm not good enough?' Odette asked, dismayed.

'How could I think that? You're every bit good enough. But you need to have a clean bill of health to time travel.'

'I am healthy.'

'They include mental health. Only a few weeks ago you were in shock from finding that body.'

'Months, not weeks. I'm better now.'

A car behind beeped; the lights had changed. Robert swore and the line moved on again.

'I'm worried about you, Odette. Any episode of mental ill health is enough to rule you out,' Papi said. 'Surely the Conclave asked for your medical notes?'

'Yes. But my sessions with Dr Rebello aren't in my notes. She doesn't work for the NHS.' Odette looked out of the window to avoid eye contact with Robert. A pedestrian was struggling with an upturned umbrella.

'So you lied on your application,' Robert said.

'I didn't lie. I just… didn't volunteer extra information.'

'That's still a lie.' He shook his head. 'Rules exist for a reason.'

'Yes, to stigmatise people.'

'No. To stop them getting sick. What you're doing isn't safe. If you have an avoidable relapse, I'll never forgive myself.'

'So you're going to tell the Conclave I was traumatised?'

'I don't know, yet. But you can apply for other jobs, Midge.'

'Papi, I want to work at the Conclave. If you get in the way how will I ever trust you again?'

'Don't be melodramatic. It's my responsibility to protect you. Even if you disagree.'

Odette needed to buy time. If he would just let her get the job, and spend a few weeks in the post, she could learn what happened to the woman in the museum – and how the Conclave were involved. Then she could leave. Surely she could persuade her father to keep a secret for that long.

'We live in the same house,' Odette said. 'Watch me like a hawk. The second I show signs of a relapse, you tell the Conclave whatever you need to. But until then keep quiet. I mean it, Papi. If you don't give me this chance I'll have nothing to do with you.'

Papi grasped her hand and squeezed it. Despite this contact, Odette knew that in the task ahead, she was completely on her own.

22

Barbara and Fay

By lunchtime, the snowflakes were falling densely enough for the schools to announce an early finish. Barbara had a part-time secretarial job at Dinah's school and she went to Dinah's classroom to collect her.

'With any luck,' Barbara said, 'Daddy will have lit the fire already.'

Tony had stayed home that day, having woken with a stomach complaint.

'I'm not staying *inside*,' Dinah crowed. 'We're going to build an igloo in the garden.'

'Are we indeed?' asked Barbara.

The way home was quiet. They cut first through the high street – the shoppers had taken flight once the roads were threatened – and then through the side streets, until they reached the seafront. Barbara had no wish to dawdle, as she was keen to get them out of the cold. Dinah wore a tartan school coat and scarf. The tips of her ears were pink, under the inadequate protection of a felt bowler that kept slipping back on her head. Although a piece of elastic ran under Dinah's chin to keep the hat in place, these days it hung slack. Dinah and her friend Caroline played at being

Queen Victoria and Prince Albert, and Dinah would use her hat as a bustle. She'd step right into the elastic loop and pull it up to her waist so the hat was in position under her skirt. This improper usage had stretched the elastic beyond its expected limits.

Barbara pulled Dinah's hat back into position and quickened their pace. The sky was dark for the middle of the day, but there were only two more turnings before home. They took the first, which led onto a narrow, one-way lane, and Barbara stopped short. A man and a woman were standing right in the middle of the road. The man was in his twenties and had neon blue hair. He was smirking at Dinah. A punk, Barbara supposed, except she'd never seen a punk in a suit. The woman wore a beige coat and a cream sweater. Her hair was neat and fair; her expression impassive.

'Hello, Barbara.' The woman's words turned to mist on the air. 'My name's Fay.'

'Hello.' Barbara frowned. Was this woman, this Fay, a parent from the school? Or an acquaintance of Tony's? If they'd met before, Barbara didn't recognise her.

Barbara noticed then that the snow around Fay's boots was untouched. She must have been standing in the same spot for so long her footsteps were no longer visible.

Dinah was blowing on her fingers. The punk continued to leer at them.

'Bye then,' said Barbara, taking a step forward to resume her journey home.

Fay raised an arm to block Barbara's way, and revealed, in the process, a wide steel band encircling her wrist. She looked down at Dinah.

'Your daddy's about to die,' Fay whispered.

Dinah stumbled backwards, almost losing her footing.

The punk laughed. 'He's having a heart attack. Any minute now. Tick tock!'

'There's no need for that!' Fay said. She looked at the punk with disapproval – almost with accusation.

This couple were crazy, the sort of loonies who accosted you in the street with threats that made no sense. Who knew what else they might do? Barbara thought she should call for help – but her throat had gone dry.

The punk was watching Dinah intently – for a reaction, Barbara guessed; to see Dinah's fear. Dinah was ten and past the age of being carried but Barbara instinctively lifted her up, to transport her away, and pushed past the couple.

'Don't you have any questions for me?' Fay asked.

'Aren't you curious what we *are*?' the punk said.

Barbara half expected the woman to say she was the Angel of Death. Was that how she saw herself? A woman who announced tragedies? Who took pleasure in doing so?

'We're from the future,' Fay called to Barbara. 'That's how we know Tony's dying. I'm a time traveller. Just like you used to be.'

Barbara bolted up the lane, clutching Dinah tightly to her, not daring to check over her shoulder to see if the couple were following. All she could hear was her own heart and Dinah's breath and her feet crunching in the snow. She took the last turning before home. The car was in the drive but there were no lights at the windows, despite the dimness of the afternoon sky. Tony must have gone to bed. Barbara fished her keys from her pocket – every action seemed to take an age – and let herself in. Praia, the dog, padded out from the darkness.

She put Dinah down.

'Were they really time travellers?' Dinah asked. 'Why were they being horrible to us?'

'I don't know.' Barbara looked through the little pane of glass in their front door, to see if Fay was outside. The road was entirely empty.

'Did *you* do that when you were a time traveller?'

'No. Run into the kitchen and put the kettle on, sweetheart.'

Dinah left while Barbara took off her boots.

'Mum!' Dinah wailed when she reached the kitchen.

Barbara joined her. A saucepan lay on the flagstones at the foot of the cooker, leaking soup. Praia lapped at the puddle. Barbara shivered. This scene of abandonment, and Fay's threat in the road, filled her with foreboding.

'Stay here,' Barbara said to Dinah. 'Don't move until I say so.'

She crossed the kitchen, into the darkness of the conservatory. Tony lay on the rug by the table. His skin was waxen. Barbara touched his face. He was quite cold.

She swallowed a sob. Dinah would be terrified if she heard her crying. There were spare blankets on the wicker sofa. Barbara grabbed the top one to cover Tony. It was a memory patchwork. Each hexagon had been hand-sewn by Barbara, and each had a story attached. The broderie anglaise was from Dinah's communion dress. The blue silk was from the tie Tony had worn when he first travelled to London from Goa. The soft William Morris print was bought with Barbara's first wages. Bee recited these stories to herself silently, as she stroked the blanket covering her husband. She stayed in the dark conservatory until she knew she had to return to Dinah and explain her father was gone.

They never mentioned the couple in the lane again. Barbara suspected that day was too painful for Dinah to speak of. Time travellers would forever be tied with the death of her father. Because she loved her daughter, Barbara resolved not to mention time travel in her hearing, even if it would always be on Barbara's mind.

*

After telling Barbara that her husband was dead, Fay and Teddy fled from the lane, down to the store fronts by the sea. The snow flurries quickened until Fay could barely see a yard ahead of them.

'There's no point going to the station,' Teddy said. 'The trains won't get through this. Let's find somewhere warm to shelter.'

'Everywhere's closed.' Typical of small towns. London didn't shut up shop because of a snowstorm.

'Good. No inquisitive locals.' Teddy was looking in every doorway they passed. He stopped to examine an iron shoe scraper on one step. 'We can use that.'

He lifted it and swung it through the door pane. Fay jumped at the shattering of the glass. Bread-scented air engulfed her. They had vandalised a bakery. *This is madness*, Fay thought. *I'm a barrister, not a thug.* Teddy reached through the shards to open the door.

Fay followed him inside. No sooner had the door swung shut than he pushed her against the wall, flattening her with his weight, breathing hotly on her face. His tongue swiped the corner of her mouth as she turned her head from him.

'No,' she said. 'Please, get off.'

He backed away, his hands in the air. *Madness*, she thought again. *He's a mad man.* She looked longingly into the street, newly worried about being alone with Teddy. She barely knew him. It was tempting to dive back into the snow

– except he would only follow her, and there was nowhere for her to go.

'Sorry,' he said. 'Sorry. It's the adrenalin – forgive me.'

'I'm *married*.' This was true, but she mainly said it to soften the rejection, because she didn't want to anger him.

He laughed. 'You're not married in 1982. You're not even born.'

'That doesn't matter. I'm married in my personal chronology.'

'Wow, you're green. You'll feel differently when you've travelled more distantly. It feels like another life. Wait till you've checked out your husband's gravestone.' Teddy turned his attention to the rows of loaves. 'Your marriage is doomed anyway. It never works out between time travellers and emus. It's the power imbalance, you see. You're always going to know more than him about the future. And your values will change too. They always do.'

Fay said nothing. Teddy was venting from sour grapes. There wasn't any truth in what he was saying; no truth at all. He tossed her a floury roll, and she caught it automatically.

'I don't want this,' she said. 'I'm not a looter.'

'They probably bake it fresh every day. I bet anything unsold gets thrown out. Waste not, want not.'

Her stomach growling gave her away. She took a bite.

'You did well today,' Teddy said. 'You're definitely one of us now.'

'Won't Barbara Hereford suspect foul play? For all she knows we could be husband killers as well as street harassers.'

'The police wouldn't be interested if Barbara Hereford went to them. The Conclave has jurisdiction over crimes enabled by time travel.' Teddy yawned. 'But if you were worried, you shouldn't have told her your name.'

'I wasn't worried.' In fact, Fay almost wanted to be caught. Giving her name was self-sabotage. If she was going to do something unpleasant, she should be punished for it. Poor Dinah. Fay knew what it was like to lose a father.

She looked at the remaining bread in her hand, and imagined crumbling it in the snow, between here and the station. Like a trail to be followed: leading the police, or Barbara, or Dinah, straight to the guilty party.

23

Barbara

At eleven Barbara met Dinah for brunch. They ate at a crowded restaurant in King's Cross. Nerves kept Bee from mentioning her plan. She gathered her courage as they finished their eggs Benedict. The waitress stacked their plates.

'I wish I'd had the waffles,' Dinah said.

Barbara, preoccupied, ignored the statement. She took Dinah's hand across the table.

'There's something I have to do,' she said.

'That sounds ominous.'

Barbara pressed on. 'I've been conducting… science experiments. The first I've done in years. And I've hit on a way of recycling time machine fuel.'

Dinah's smile faded. 'I knew you were up to something. It was obvious when Ruby came round for dinner. What possible use could you have for time machine fuel?'

'None – except the Conclave could use my results. I could work for them again.'

'Oh, Mother, don't be ridiculous.'

'Ridiculous?'

'They won't let you back in. You know what they're like.

How cruel they are. Remember what they did to you – to *us*. Why kid yourself this will be any different?'

'You're right, of course. They'll turn me away. At first. Which is why I have a back-up plan. But you might not like it, and I won't go ahead without your permission.'

'Enlighten me.'

'I still get calls from journalists, Dinah. Even now. People still want to read about me. I always turn them away – because I thought digging up the bodies would distress you. But if Margaret thinks I might start giving interviews she'll be much more likely to listen. It would look bad to her funders, if her refusal to give me an audience was wasting money.'

'That's your back-up plan? Threaten to sell your story?'

'Yes.'

The waitress topped up their water glasses.

'Margaret Norton really hates bad press, doesn't she?' Dinah reflected.

'Yes. She does.'

'Then make your threats, Mum,' Dinah said. 'It's time you cut her down to size. Make that bitch squirm as much as possible.'

Barbara squeezed her daughter's hand before releasing it. 'I don't know where you got your vindictive streak! Not me, or your father.'

'It must be latent in you somewhere. Time you discovered it.' To the waitress, Dinah said, 'We'd like some waffles. With cream, I think.'

24

Odette

On arriving at the Conclave, Odette was taken upstairs to a waiting room. It was a plain room with a window overlooking the great reception hall. Three other hopefuls were waiting too: a man with an eyebrow ring, another man with a square jaw, and a woman in a tartan dress. They were comparing achievements in loud voices. Staking out their dominance early, Odette thought. For now she kept her own counsel. She was still subdued by her father's threat to call the Conclave and she needed to conserve her energy for the challenges ahead.

Through the glass, she watched the Conclave employees pass back and forth through the chilly granite foyer. Time travellers, Odette assumed. Not many of them were men. A young black woman, who was standing by the drinking fountain, caught Odette's eye, and they nodded at each other.

She heard the swish of the waiting room door slide open. A small, whiskered man with a kipper tie entered and greeted them.

'My name is Jim Plantagenet. I'll be talking you through the process for using the time machines this morning.'

The candidates exchanged glances. So they were to time travel as part of the assessment.

'First off we'll be giving you a quick medical. Nothing at all to worry about; weighing, checking your heart rate, taking blood and urine samples. All quite routine for a first time travel trip. We need to know you're in tip-top condition, otherwise it might not be safe to use the machines!'

'Can we refuse?' asked the man with the eyebrow ring.

'No,' said Jim. 'But you are free to withdraw your application without ill feeling on our part. The next requirement is also non-negotiable. We have strict hygiene protocols on exiting the machine. Do any of you know why?'

The candidates looked at each other blankly.

'Germs in the time machines,' Jim said. 'Or *alkalibacterium macromonas*, if we want to be precise. Macromonas can cause particularly nasty infections if it comes into contact with abraded or broken skin.'

'Why are there germs in the time machines?' asked the man with the square jaw.

'As I expect you're aware, time machines run on nuclear fuel. Macromonas is fairly unusual among bacteria because it thrives in a radioactive environment. I take a particular interest in it.' Jim went rosy with enthusiasm.

'Are we placing our health at risk?' the girl in tartan asked.

'Generally, macromonas is confined to the fuel core. However, we still exercise extreme caution. Conclave employees are encouraged to limit the spread of bacteria by following rigorous hygiene protocols whenever they've used the machines.'

'They're just limiting their liability,' said the man with the eyebrow ring, sounding a little bored.

'So no one's ever been hospitalised with a macromonas infection?' the tartan woman pressed. 'Or died from it?'

'Hospitalised, certainly. But I'm proud to say there have been no fatalities. The bottom line is, when the time machine stops, it will enter a special decontamination mode. Any macromonas within its four walls will be neutralised. Don't exit the time machine until that process is complete.'

The candidates digested this advice. Odette had remained silent throughout. She wasn't going to challenge any precaution the Conclave took on health grounds. If she did, they might scrutinise her medical history more closely.

'Now if you're ready, and have no further questions,' Jim said, 'I will lead you to your medicals. Our clinic is in the basement.'

Odette fell in line with the others. Papi might yet reveal her history of trauma, and stymie her attempts to solve the mystery, but for now she allowed herself a tingle of excitement. For this morning, at least, she would be a time traveller. How many people could say that?

25

Fay

It was late when Fay and Teddy finally arrived back at the Conclave. Though they were cold and tired, their journey wasn't over yet; they had several decades to travel across before they would reach their home.

'But what's the rush?' Teddy said. 'I've got something to show you, down in the basement.'

'Now?' Fay wanted to go to bed. Her own bed, in her own time, with her own husband.

'Come on.' Teddy walked backwards, his arms outstretched. 'It's not as though you'll be home any later.'

This was unarguable. Reluctantly, she followed him. They met no one in the corridors, nor on the stairs. The snow and the late hour must account for the quiet. She recalled Teddy's earlier attempt to kiss her, and felt uneasy. Hopefully there would be other people wherever he was taking her. She tried to remember, from the introductory tour, which teams worked in the basement.

'Are we going to biometrics, Teddy?'

'No. I've got another little game lined up for you.'

More initiations? Her heart sank. 'I thought we'd finished – in St Ives.'

'Just one more game. Then we're done.' He led her past several empty labs and through a door at the very end of the hall.

'But, Teddy, this is the morgue!'

If an employee died away from their home timeline, bodies were stored here while arrangements were made for their safe return. Occasionally an autopsy might be conducted, at the request of the Conclave's Criminal Investigation team.

Teddy grinned, and opened one of the cold chambers. Inside was the corpse of an elderly man. He was bearded, and the folds of his torso were tattooed. The pathologist must have cut him open, too, because there was a line of stitches running down the centre of the man's chest.

'Who is this?' Fay asked nervously.

'Does it matter?' Teddy asked.

'Of course. You want us to play a game with a dead body. I'll say it matters.'

'Oh ho, you're checking that we have consent? If that's what's bothering you, the body's mine.'

'So you have the same tattoos?'

'Not yet. He's got a few years on me.'

'This is a different man. You're a liar.'

Teddy stopped smiling. 'I'm trying to make the game easier for you. If you're going to be a bitch, what am I supposed to say? I'll have to tell the others you wouldn't play along. Old Maggie won't like that at all.'

This was the price of the job. Fay had come this far; she had played the Angel of Death game. That would be for nothing if she lost her job now.

'What do you want me to do?' Fay said.

'Can you juggle?'

Oh God. 'I guess.'

Teddy walked to a high double-doored refrigerator. When he opened it the light blanched his skin. He took a plastic pack of meat from the shelf, from among several, and checked the label.

'Here we are.' He returned, and Fay saw the bag was vacuum packed round a pair of kidneys. Large kidneys. Human sized.

'They belong to this guy?' Fay asked.

'To me. Yes.' Teddy tore open the packet. He proffered it to Fay. 'Now. Juggle.'

Gagging, she took a kidney from the bag. It was firm, cold, and leathery to the touch. She took out the second with her other hand, then stared at the kidneys that lay on her palms. If they did belong to Teddy then holding them was a morbid intimacy. She looked at his face.

'Go on,' he urged.

He wasn't disturbed at all. Was that because the body wasn't his? Or because it was?

Her soul seemed to detach itself. She felt far from her actions, as if she had floated above her body, and was now observing. One kidney arced through the air at the jerk of her hand. She caught it, and tossed the second kidney. Her palms were bloody.

'That's it,' Teddy said. 'Again.'

Another jerk. Another arc.

'Can I leave now?' she asked.

'Once more,' he said.

She half shuddered, half jolted the kidneys into the air, and caught them.

'I've had enough,' she said.

Teddy took the kidneys from her, and suddenly seemed subdued. 'All right. I'll tidy up here. You can get going.'

She stopped at the ladies' loos on the way to the time machines. The blood spiralled down the sink until her hands were white again. She wiped her face with paper towels. Before she left for home, she wanted the taint completely eradicated. But the taint was deep, and despite her efforts, Fay did not feel clean.

26

Ruby

While Bee ate brunch with Dinah, Ruby was in Birmingham, as she'd said, but not for a conference. She was there to meet Grace. Ruby was about to hear whether or not her grandmother had four months to live.

It didn't take long to find the hotel. The building was a conversion from a Victorian eye hospital, and grand if rather dark. On arrival Ruby asked the concierge where to find the restaurant. He informed her it was in the cellar; they were not yet serving lunch, but she could purchase a drink while she waited. She took the wrought iron lift downstairs. It was half eleven, but Grace was nowhere to be seen, so Ruby bought herself an orange juice and cracked open Sushila Pardesi's phrasebook.

Ruby was still halfway through the section on sexual slang. There were a few double entendres – she could have guessed the meanings of flux capacitor and quantum tunnelling, although Tipler cylinder required a bit more specialist knowledge. A number of terms had no application outside the context of time travelling. For instance – intercourse with one's future self was called forecasting.

Intercourse with one's past self was a legacy fuck. Infidelity committed with a past or future self was called me-timing. If colloquial usage was any indication, time travellers' proclivities were overwhelming autoerotic. But there were some interactions with other people alluded to, as well. A palmist was a time traveller who used her knowledge of a person's future to manipulate them into sex. That was a depressing insight into the Conclave's sexual politics. Occasionally there was a surprising detour into more romantic waters. A trip to see a lover for the last time before one's death was called a liebestod.

It was at that moment that Grace Taylor arrived in the cellar bar. This Grace was ancient and bright-eyed. Her hair was as white as dandelion clocks. Her head was framed by a foot-high collar made from gold wire and lace, the kind of thing you'd see in portraits of Elizabeth I. Ruby wondered which year Grace had travelled here from – some future period, where they'd revived renaissance fashions? Or maybe Grace had dispensed with fashion's whims altogether, and worn what she liked. She paused under the archway to survey everyone in the room. For an instant Ruby forgot she was there to discuss Bee's death. So impressive was Grace, it seemed everyone should drop to their knees in allegiance. Grace's eyes fixed on Ruby's – and then Grace gave the most luminous smile – only seconds before her body folded to the floor.

'Oh, hell,' Ruby muttered.

One of the barmen rushed to Grace's side, claiming his knowledge of first aid, and informed the room she was out cold. The other barman called emergency services.

'Her name's Grace Taylor,' Ruby said. 'She was here to meet me.'

Then she stood scratching her head, unable to give even the most rudimentary information about Grace's next of kin.

'We should probably ring the Conclave of time travel,' Ruby told barman number two.

'Wouldn't they know already?' said a patron, predictably. He had a point, though. How thoughtless of Grace to invite Ruby, merely to collapse in front of her. She seemed determined to play on Ruby's last nerve. Yet again, Ruby would have to wait to hear Bee's fate.

She didn't think that Grace was seriously ill. The installation at Tate Modern – not to mention several dozen scarves in the gallery shop – said her death date was still a decade away. By her own account, she was not in mortal danger. Barman number one was beginning to look sweaty, and Ruby wanted to reassure him: don't panic; she isn't actually going to die until 2027, but it didn't seem very appropriate.

The ambulance came to relieve him. There was terrible difficulty getting Grace out of the cellar. The nineteenth-century lift hadn't been built to accommodate stretchers; nor had the narrow, spiralling stairway. Ruby followed the paramedics, maintaining a short distance so she didn't get in their way. They reached the lobby, and Ruby was able to draw level with them as they carried her through the main entrance.

Grace remained unconscious, yet Ruby felt compelled to offer some soothing words. Bee would have wanted Ruby to be kind; she loved Grace.

Ruby took Grace's hand.

'I hope you feel better soon,' Ruby said, 'and that we can rearrange our conversation when you're back on your feet.'

These were polite parting words, for a woman she didn't know. Later, when she knew more, Ruby would wish she'd been warmer.

27

Odette

Once Odette's medical was completed, she was sent back to the waiting room with the others. After a short interval, Jim returned with a clipboard.

'Ms Sophola, Ms Morris and Mr Jensen – you are all cleared to time travel. Mr Roberts, might I have a word?'

Mr Roberts stood, rubbing the back of his head nervously, and stepped into the corridor with Jim.

They closed the door but their voices remained audible.

'I'm afraid, Mr Roberts, that your blood test showed levels of amitriptyline. Your medical notes didn't mention a prescription for this drug.'

'Is it a problem? I take it for back pain.'

'It's a tricyclic antidepressant, Mr Roberts. We have to exclude anyone on psychiatric medication. Our recruitment information is quite clear on this point.'

'But I don't take it for psychiatric reasons. I take it for back pain. The dosage is tiny.'

'Candidates sometimes lie about their reasons for taking a particular medication, because they don't want us to know their mental health diagnosis. We're therefore vigilant about excluding anyone on antidepressants, whatever they claim to take it for. It's really for your safety, you know.'

'So that's *it*? I'm out before I begin?'

'Thank you for coming today. We wish you the very best in your job search.'

Odette snorted with laughter – not from amusement, but disbelief. She thought again of Robert's threat. If the Conclave found out she'd been traumatised, it was clear they wouldn't give her a job.

'Might not be very nice, but it's all to our benefit,' said the woman in tartan. 'Now there's one less competition.'

*

At eleven thirty an administrator led the applicants down several corridors, into a windowless gallery. Oil portraits hung from green baize walls. One of them was concealed with a dustsheet. Fifteen minutes passed in uneasy silence. Odette noticed a security camera above the door. They were on tape. Maybe the test had already begun.

The doors swung open to reveal a pale, green-eyed woman in her late thirties. Odette recognised her with a jolt. This was the woman who had come to Mahé for her wedding. Odette wondered if she should mention having met before, and decided against. It would be awkward if the woman didn't remember. After all, Odette had only been a little girl.

'My name is Professor Elspeth Niven,' the time traveller announced. 'I'm the head of Criminal Investigation for the Conclave. You must be eager to start, so I won't beat about the bush. Your task today is to answer the question: how can time travel help us to prevent a crime?'

She walked past them, and pulled the dustsheet away from the hidden painting. It was a portrait, Odette observed, of a bullish man in an academic gown. The other paintings had small plaques with the sitters' names, but this man's identity seemed to have been removed, leaving a small pale oblong on the wall.

A gold knife had been plunged into the canvas, and jutted from the man's heart.

'The Conclave have owned this painting for decades. It *was* worth about sixteen thousand achrons,' Professor Niven said. 'But no longer. Between eleven and eleven thirty this morning, somebody stabbed the painting. If you were investigators, how could you use time travel to prevent this terrible vandalism?'

The square-jawed man spoke. 'We could travel back to eleven this morning, and alter the course of events.'

'I don't know about that,' demurred the woman in tartan. 'Wouldn't we cause a paradox?'

'Or end up with whole new lives,' Square Jaw mused. 'Like Marty McFly.'

'Let's find out, shall we?' Professor Niven said. 'In the next room are many dozens of time machines. One of them is at your disposal this morning. You may take one trip, into the past, to precisely eleven this morning. I will give you a set of tools, which you may use as you see fit.'

From a leather bag, Elspeth took three screwdrivers, and three catapults. Screwdrivers and catapults had very specific functions. Why those tools, and no other? Were they specially chosen because Professor Niven knew in advance what the hopefuls would need? The questions were making Odette's head spin.

Professor Niven hadn't finished. 'There's the knife too, of course. Does anyone want that?'

The candidates exchanged glances; they'd have to be fools to turn down any aid.

'Which of you should have the knife?' Professor Niven asked. 'Let's leave it to fate.'

Elspeth gripped the knife and pulled it from the canvas. She flipped the knife into the air with the ease of a circus performer. It landed, point down, at Odette's feet. Odette picked it up. The handle was engraved: I HAVE A SHORT LIFE AND A SINGLE PURPOSE. She slipped the knife into her jacket pocket.

'Why should she get an advantage?' the tartan woman murmured. 'It's not fair.'

'Fate isn't fair,' Professor Niven said. 'When you return, you will sit a timed essay where you will write your reflections and conclusions. Remember: the question you need to answer is, how can we use time travel to prevent crime?'

*

In the neighbouring hall, a technician explained he would set the machine for them.

'I think we should talk about our plans,' Odette said to the other applicants. 'Elspeth Niven didn't say we had to work alone. Why don't we consult each other first?'

'On what?' asked Tartan.

'We need to be strategic. The aim is to protect the picture, right? There's no point us undermining each other's efforts.'

'I was thinking I'd unscrew the picture from the wall before the vandal arrives,' said Square Jaw. 'If we arrive at eleven, we'll have enough time to remove the painting, and bring it back to the present, undamaged.'

'Good idea,' Odette said. 'Before we come back we could

use the catapults to smash the chandelier bulbs. Can't destroy any of the other pictures if it's too dark to see.'

'*I'll* be good at that,' said Tartan. 'My aim's straight as a die. I took the county cup for archery three years running.'

Odette hesitated. What was left? 'I suppose I could intercept the vandal – or distract them – do something to stop them getting to the gallery at all.'

Tartan rubbed her forehead. 'I *still* don't understand how we won't cause a paradox. If we succeed in stopping the vandal, our old selves will never hear that they're *supposed* to stop them.'

'I don't understand either,' Odette said. 'But Elspeth told us to try preventing the crime. So let's... try.'

With their plan agreed, they entered the time machine. Anxiety about the test curbed Odette's wonder at time travel, and something was bothering her about the task. The most interesting questions, to Odette's mind, were the vandal's motives. Why was this painting singled out for vandalism, rather than any other in the gallery? Surely the answer should shape how Odette used her time in the past? How could they prevent a crime before knowing the reasons for it?

In the darkness the engines shrilled, and Odette breathed a strange, pungent mix of scents that reminded her of photocopiers, and burning rubber. The time machine stopped. They waited until the decontamination phase was complete, then the trio walked into a room near-identical to the one they had left behind. Only the great clock on the wall confirmed they had moved back in time.

They returned to the gallery, where the painting was intact again. The top corners were screwed to the wall.

'I'm tall enough to reach,' Square Jaw said. 'You two support the base of the frame.'

Tartan and Odette did as he asked. The screws were impacted with rust, and Square Jaw grunted as his screwdriver repeatedly scraped the surface. A few red flakes fell to the floor.

'I can't get any purchase,' he said. 'I'll try the other side.'

As he stepped away, Odette noticed there was a plaque on the wall. The plaque that had been missing when Dr Niven unveiled the portrait. It read:

HEADMASTER
CHARLES THURROCK.

A man who caned his charge for
her vulgar accent.

Artist: Grace Taylor.

Grace Taylor must be the charge he caned. Why else would she paint him, and add that particular detail, if it weren't from personal experience? Odette understood about accents; the loss of one, the gaining of another, and what the switch signified.

Odette let go of the frame.

'What are you doing?' asked Tartan.

'Collecting a clue.' Odette took the other screwdriver from her pocket, and applied it to the plaque.

'A clue to what?' Square Jaw asked, pausing in his own efforts.

'Dr Taylor's life, I think.' The last screw wriggled out of its fitting, and she slipped the plaque into her bag.

'I don't think we can get this picture off the wall,' Square Jaw said. 'I can't get either corner to budge and we've only got fifteen minutes left before our old selves arrive.'

'Leave it,' said Tartan. 'We can start catapulting the chandeliers, before we run out of time.'

They took one chandelier each, a slingshot and ball at their right shoulder, and none of the trio – not even Tartan, archer for her county – made a direct hit. Their missiles arced too soon and too low every time. Odette's sailed past the security camera, and she noticed that its light wasn't flashing.

When Elspeth Niven had briefed them, the security camera was switched on; Odette was sure she had seen its light flashing, because she had believed they were on tape for the assessment.

Now the camera was off. Was the difference significant?

It might be. If the vandal did succeed in slashing the painting, the evidence should be captured on camera, and could help with prosecution.

The camera was too high for Odette to switch on manually. In the interests of experimentation, she raised her catapult again, and took aim at the camera.

With god-given precision, the ball struck the side of the camera, and the light flashed. Her success must be fluke. Yet Odette had *known* she was going to be successful, because she had seen the camera was switched on in the future.

And she knew, too, she wouldn't stop anyone vandalising the painting. She knew, because she had seen the portrait slashed in the future.

'It's eleven twenty,' Tartan said. 'We're going to arrive in ten minutes. Shall we get back in the time machine?'

'That's not what we agreed. The vandal must be on their way.' Square Jaw nodded at Odette. '*She's* going to intercept them.'

'Is there any point?' Tartan asked.

Square Jaw's lips parted in surprise. 'Yes! We need to do everything we can to change the course of history.'

'We *can't*. I've thought this all along. If we did, it would be paradoxical.' Tartan turned to Odette. 'What do you think?'

'We were asked how time travel can prevent crime,' Odette mused. 'I think we can provide an interesting answer even if we fail to stop the vandal.'

'So let's get back in the time machine!' Tartan said.

'I'm not going to fail at this task just because you two give up early,' Square Jaw said. '*I'll* intercept.'

Odette raised a hand. 'You're being rash. I didn't say I wouldn't try. As it happens, I want to ask the vandal a question.'

So Tartan and Square Jaw went one way – back to the hall of time machines – and Odette found a shady alcove in the corridor from which to spy. She saw a woman approach: Grace Taylor. Odette recognised her from the television. She wore a gold breastplate. A roundel of reflected light shone at her shoulder.

'Dr Taylor,' Odette called softly.

The time traveller stopped, and peered into the alcove. Odette moved out of the shadows.

'I'm one of the candidates,' she said. 'From the... near future. Very near.'

'I see,' Dr Taylor said. 'Can I help?'

'I wanted to know something. The picture you're about to vandalise – you chose that one for a reason, didn't you? I took the plaque as evidence. You took pleasure in painting someone you hated, just to destroy it.'

'How dramatic.' Dr Taylor checked her watch. 'I prefer to say I was making an artistic statement. Was there anything else?'

'Is that a standard exercise for Conclave applicants?'

'Yes – when they want to be investigators.'

'How many people have done this exercise before?'

'This exercise exactly? None. But around seventy applicants have endured a variation of it. Sometimes the crime's a theft, once it was arson.'

'Has anyone ever changed the outcome?'

'Not *yet*.' Dr Taylor paused. 'Now if you don't mind, I must be—'

A round, rubber ball struck Dr Taylor in the eye. Her hands leapt to her face.

'Fucking Nora!' she exclaimed.

At the end of the corridor stood Square Jaw, catapult in hand.

'She's about to *leave*,' he called to Odette. 'Pull the *knife*!'

Odette glanced down at her pocket. But Dr Taylor saw the direction of her gaze; she ripped Odette's pocket from the jacket, and the knife fell to the floor.

Dr Taylor picked it up, and shook her head. '*I'll* take that. You two have delayed me quite enough.'

Odette couldn't bring herself to speak to Square Jaw. By assaulting a senior time traveller, he had surely ruined his own chances of a job offer, and had possibly jeopardised Odette's opportunity too. She hoped Dr Taylor would distinguish between their actions. They walked back to the time machine in silence; Tartan had already departed without them.

28

FEBRUARY 1983

Margaret and Veronica

Since 1969, Margaret had followed Angharad's recommendations for recruitment. Only people with a clean bill of mental health, as demonstrated by their medical notes, were recruited as time travellers; and among new recruits, hazing rituals were commonplace. But Angharad's final recommendation – to issue ultimatums to employees with death anxiety – didn't have to be implemented until 1983. That year one particular employee was struggling, and failing, to manage her poor mental health. Her name was Veronica Collins; she was an interpreter, who was aged twenty-eight when her symptoms came to the attention of the Conclave's clinical psychologist, Dr Siobhan Joyce. Margaret's reaction would give Veronica a clear motive for subsequently placing Margaret's life at risk.

Dr Joyce picked up on Veronica's problems during a routine mental health check. She immediately telephoned Margaret to say she was bringing Veronica to see her. On arrival, Veronica's first comment surprised Margaret.

'I'm so grateful you're finding out in 1982,' Veronica said. 'It would have been dreadful, later in the century.'

'In what way?' Margaret asked.

'The silver Margarets are utter bitches. You're easier to talk to.'

'I see,' Margaret said. There was a tendency, among time travellers, to treat green and silver selves as separate people, but it was still a faux pas to criticise one to the other. Veronica's comment did not place her on a good footing.

To Siobhan, Margaret said, 'Would you care to outline the problem?'

'Veronica's using time travel in some troubling ways,' Siobhan said. 'Mainly to assuage anxiety. According to her psychometric results today, she meets the criteria for Obsessive Compulsive Disorder.'

In 1983, OCD was not a term in layman's usage, but Margaret had heard it used by travellers from the near future.

'Hand-washing?' she said. 'Checking the door is locked, that kind of thing?'

'Yes,' said Siobhan cautiously. 'But there's more to it than that. A person with OCD usually feels an excess of responsibility. All of us experience passing worries about whether we turned the oven off, but the person with OCD might imagine a disastrous gas explosion, involving fatalities, injuries, or loss of home, for which she is solely culpable. Checking provides relief from anxiety, but the relief wears off, so the person checks again, then again, eventually developing a ritual even if she's aware her behaviour is illogical.'

Extraordinary, Margaret thought. How glad she was not to have that weakness of mind. 'And this is true for Veronica?'

'In her case, she repeatedly worries that she's killed a person during one of her time travel trips and somehow forgotten her involvement.'

'I'm frightened that I've killed my grandchild,' Veronica added. 'I'm twenty-eight, for Pete's sake.'

'She keeps returning to his gravestone for reassurance,' Siobhan said. 'The epigram says he died peacefully of old age.'

'How many times have you returned?' Margaret asked.

'Hundreds. Thousands.'

The scale of Veronica's problem, then, was significant. Her mental weakness could jeopardise the Conclave, as Barbara's had done, if Margaret didn't strictly manage Veronica's decisions from here. That would be achieved more easily if they spoke to each other alone.

'Thank you, Dr Joyce, for diagnosing Veronica,' Margaret said. 'But I'll take things from here. Please don't let us keep you from your duties.'

Siobhan straightened in surprise. 'If that's what you think best.'

She left. Veronica searched for a tissue.

Margaret adopted what she hoped was a benevolent tone. 'My dear, have you told any family members about your difficulties? Any friends?'

'No, I... I didn't think they'd understand.'

'Good. Your instincts, I think, are correct. People don't understand. They propagate unfortunate stereotypes of time travellers and sadly this... disorder... would give them further ammunition.' *Against the Conclave, as much as Veronica*, Margaret silently added. 'But you still have options, and I will support whichever you decide upon.'

Veronica nodded uncertainly.

'Two paths are available to you,' Margaret said. 'First, you may remove the source of your anxiety by leaving your position at the Conclave. I will ensure you receive a good reference and severance package, provided you sign a non-disclosure agreement. It is essential that you remain silent on the reasons for your departure.'

'And the other path?'

'You stay. You tell no one of your distress. You undertake desk work, without access to the time machines, until your disorder improves. And you commit to a programme of reconditioning, which I'll oversee.'

'Re-what?' Veronica asked.

'Conditioning. The focus of your distress, Veronica, is the death of a loved one. I propose we neutralise your responses to the certainty we all must die.' Veronica should be familiar with hazing. Whenever wenches joined the Conclave, there was a degree of rough and tumble. But clearly the hazing had been insufficient in Veronica's case; it would have to be escalated, till she adjusted to Conclave life as the other time travellers had done.

'Neutralise my responses...' Veronica whispered. 'How will you do that?'

'Through a series of games. That doesn't sound so bad, now, does it?'

'I suppose not. Can I please have some time to decide?'

'You have until the end of the day. The sooner we know your next steps, the sooner you can start the next stage of your life.'

*

Veronica struggled to accept that the options Margaret presented were the only ones available. Could it be true that her only options were to leave – against her own desire for a career at the Conclave – or have her feelings *neutralised*? The word was so sinister. Why could she not retain her position and seek an independent medical opinion? Surely the law offered some protection? To understand this point better, Veronica visited the Conclave's legal department.

A woman named Fay, who had a drooping pompadour of ginger and grey hair, was at the duty desk. Family photographs were crowded round her telephone. Her matronly air appeased Veronica.

'I'd like to speak to an expert in employment law,' Veronica said.

'We don't have any employment law,' Fay said.

'I don't follow. England has lots of employment law.'

'Take a seat. I can see I need to explain a few things.'

Veronica obeyed.

'Policing people who can move between periods with different laws is complex,' Fay said. 'So the Conclave has its own governing body, and legislation, to regulate the conduct of time travellers. This constant, stable legislation takes precedence over the relatively changeable English and Welsh law.'

'But I'm English,' Veronica said. 'And we are *in England*.'

'No, love. You're in the Conclave. Think of us as an embassy – a little part of another country, right in the middle of London. And here, workers have no legal protections.'

If Veronica wanted to stay, she really did have to play by the Conclave's rules.

Fay was looking at her with open curiosity.

'If it makes you feel better, England's employment law isn't great in 1982. Margaret's trying to fire you, I take it?' she said.

'Not exactly, no.'

Fay rolled her eyes, apparently unconvinced. 'Can I give you some advice?'

'Sure.'

'Margaret's a risky woman to tangle with. Leave willingly. You're still really young. Take it from me – if you *could* stay, you'd only get callous.'

'I know you mean well,' Veronica said, 'but I'd never leave the Conclave if I didn't have to.'

She didn't wait till the end of the day to let Margaret know. The decision was plain, once she realised there really was no third option. If the only way to stay was to play Margaret's games, then that was what she would do.

29

Ruby and Barbara

After the ambulance had gone, Ruby was at a loose end because her train ticket wouldn't be valid until six in the evening. She idled her way through the civic quarter, and sat among the statues for a while, but decided to move on after the sixth charity rep approached for a donation.

Down one of the side streets she came upon an old cinema with bevelled windows. The cinema was called The Futurist, which made Ruby smile wryly. They had only one screen, which was showing Barry Lyndon. The woman in the ticket booth explained that the matinee had begun, and if Ruby bought a ticket now she'd be joining midway through the story. She'd seen the film before so it didn't bother her too much to miss the start. The chief appeal was being able to kill time undisturbed for a couple of hours.

She paid up and entered the auditorium. No one else was there. She settled into a cracked leather seat and promptly fell asleep. The previous night's restlessness, and the events of the morning, were to blame. She slept through the film's first act and woke, in some confusion, to a door banging shut. A second audience member had entered. Although the auditorium was dim, Ruby made out a woman's silhouette.

The woman walked with purpose up the steps and into Ruby's row, and sat right next to her.

Grace. Young Grace in a purple paisley dress. Her eyes were winged with black eyeshadow, Cleopatra style.

'Hello again,' Ruby said. 'I thought I'd seen the last of you today.'

'I knew you'd be here,' Grace said.

'Are you saying time travellers track my whereabouts?'

'Not all the time. But your location today is important.'

'Why?'

'Because it relates to my death. You were there, in the cellar, when I had a brain haemorrhage.' Grace spoke smoothly, as though relaying information she'd read many times. 'I'll survive hospital admission but I'll never regain consciousness. The Conclave will return me to my home timeline and I'll die there. In 2027.'

Ruby exhaled. Her first feeling was shame, for being flippant about Grace's condition – in her thoughts, if not comments. Had Ruby been flippant in her comments, back at the hotel? Maybe she'd betrayed her attitude.

'I'm so sorry,' she said, unsure how to express condolences to someone on their own death.

'Don't worry about it.' Grace gave a little shrug and shake of the head.

The coolness of her reaction was perplexing. Ruby was about to ask her if she was really all right, but Grace spoke first.

'You don't look how I imagined you,' she said. Presumably she hadn't met Ruby before – which would make her younger than the shoplifting Grace at Tate Modern.

'I hope you're not disappointed,' Ruby said.

'Oh, you.' Grace's cheek dimpled. 'No, I wouldn't say that.'

They were silent for a moment.

'You were expecting a conversation,' Grace said. 'If you like you can ask me your questions. That seems fair.'

'Thank you.' Ruby's expectations remained low. Grace had been too mysterious, too often.

'What do you want to ask?' Grace said.

Might as well go for the big guns. Ruby had nothing to lose.

'The inquest, next February. Is it for Barbara?'

'Good God, no. It's for Margaret.'

'Margaret? Margaret Norton?' Ruby had been so sure Grace would skirt the issue, it startled her to get a clear answer.

'That's right. Listen, is this going to be a long chat?'

'Are you in a rush?'

'No.' Grace smiled. 'But there's a bar around the corner with forty-four varieties of gin.'

*

Barbara had never visited the Conclave headquarters before. High arches of glass and granite spanned the foyer. With Breno at her feet, Barbara asked the uniformed man at the information desk if she could see Margaret Norton.

'Do you have an appointment?' the receptionist asked.

'No. But she'll want to hear what I have to say.'

'I'm afraid you need to have an appointment. Her diary is booked up so far in advance—'

'Let me talk to Margaret's secretary.'

'Madam—'

'Just her secretary! I'm sure she'll do an excellent job of sending me packing. What harm can it do?'

'All right, but if I allow that, you must accept it when Dr Norton declines to see you. I'd rather our guards didn't escort you from the building against your consent.'

'If she won't see me, I'll go as meekly as a lamb.'

Barbara was directed to the fourth floor. From the lift Barbara ventured down a long corridor, her feet sinking into a thick honey-coloured carpet. The secretary was standing at a filing cabinet.

Predictably, he said Barbara couldn't speak to Margaret without an appointment.

'Her next availability is in six weeks,' the secretary added.

'That's too long,' Barbara said. 'Please give her my name – Barbara Hereford. I wish to discuss strategies for recycling fuel.'

The secretary raised his eyebrows in recognition of the name, but replied, 'She can't be disturbed.'

'Very well,' Barbara said. 'In that case I'll be leaving. I spoke to a journalist only this afternoon; I'm sure I can ring him back and explain that Margaret is happy to waste taxpayers' money.'

The secretary breathed a heavy sigh, pushed the drawer back into the filing cabinet, and slipped through an oak door. Low voices travelled through the wood. A moment later the secretary returned.

'You've got five minutes,' he said.

Barbara let Breno run ahead of her, into Margaret's circular office. He waited by the captain's chair, wagging his tail, until she caught up with him and sat down.

Margaret watched from behind her desk, one eyebrow raised. It was many decades since they'd seen each other in person, and Bee observed that Margaret's style was unchanged. She still had the same smooth immovable hair and a discreetly expensive blazer. But her face, always haughty, had settled with age into a sneer.

'Hello, Bee,' she said. 'What's all this about journalists?'

'That was to get me through the door. I knew if I rang or wrote you'd ignore me.'

'Bee, of course I've ignored you. I couldn't tell you anything you wanted to hear. You would never accept that I had to cut you off.'

'I was perfectly aware that I'd been ousted, thank you. I'm not an idiot.'

'But you kept trying to get back *in*. That couldn't happen. You'd been a liability to the project. Stealing fuel was one thing, but you utterly shamed us on television. That was the worst of it. We looked terrible to the public. To the *public*, Bee.'

'Did you all feel that way – that you were ashamed of me?'

'When all's said and done, it doesn't matter how *we* feel about you – what matters is the Conclave's public image. Everyone outside these four walls thinks time travellers are liable to lose our minds, because of *your behaviour*. We've been fighting the image you left us with for fifty years.'

'What if we could change that?'

'How?'

'Give the public a new story. People love a reconciliation – let me come back, sane and ready to make my contribution.'

Margaret threw back her head and roared.

'Oh, Barbara. You are the *limit*. I've *just* said you wouldn't accept your time-travelling days were done! Stirring up people's memories of the whole affair would be foolishness. Why would I give you a job?'

'Because I have something to exchange – the findings of some independent research I've conducted. It could save you millions each year.'

Bee outlined her idea for recycling fuel. When she'd finished, Margaret looked thoughtful.

'It's an interesting proposal,' she said. 'But we'll never adopt it.'

'What? Why not?'

'Vested interests, my dear. There wouldn't be the political will for this kind of change, because too many of the individuals who say yay or nay to funding our missions also have a stake in the atroposium industry. We'd cause immense damage to their bottom line if we reduced our atroposium consumption on the scale you're suggesting.'

Bee sagged. Her bargaining chip had been refused. What else could she say to convince the Conclave to let her in? All that remained was to beg. She stood and placed her hands on the desk.

'Please, Margaret,' she implored. 'Let me time travel again. I'll do *anything* – the most menial, out of the way job you have. '

She was inches from Margaret's eyes, and Barbara thought she saw a glimmer of interest.

'You'll do anything?' Margaret queried. 'Are you sure?'

'Absolutely.'

Margaret massaged her temples.

'Very well,' she said. 'You can't publicly rejoin us. That *is* out of the question. But we do occasionally want covert employees. First, you'd need to take a few preparatory tests. There are other people in your position, ones we had to let go but who have skills that are still of use.'

'What do they do, these covert employees?'

'One step at a time. Do you want to take the prep tests?'

'Yes, definitely.'

'You can meet me tonight. Not here. I'll be at the toy museum in Rotherhithe. Come at eight o'clock on the dot. Don't mention where you're going to anyone.'

Barbara's smile froze. The demands for secrecy made her uneasy.

Go home, Bee heard Ruby say. *This is a trap.*

But time travelling again was what Barbara wanted to do most, and Margaret said time travelling was on offer.

'I won't be late,' Barbara said.

30

Odette

Odette took her seat in the small exam room. The candidates sat one behind the other, with Odette at the back. A draught from the door played on her bare ankles. The walls were marble, and when Elspeth spoke her voice echoed.

'You have an hour to write your reflections and conclusions on this morning's activity. I will notify you at half an hour, and five minutes, before your time is up.'

Behind Odette, the door whined open. Jim Plantagenet hastened past her.

'When I give you the instruction,' Elspeth continued, 'you begin.'

Jim reached Elspeth. Their heads drew close in whispered conference. Then both of them turned to look at the candidates.

Or to look at *Odette*. Their eyes were trained squarely on her – she was sure of it.

Elspeth straightened.

'I'm afraid,' she announced, 'there will be a short delay to the start of the exam while one of you is removed.'

Odette's legs shook. Robert had called the Conclave. She was sure of it.

She smoothed her tweed skirt as Jim walked back down the aisle. He was headed straight for her.

The man halted at the desk in front.

'Ms Morris. The technician has brought to my attention that you didn't wait for the time machine to decontaminate before you exited. You're now a threat to public health. You must leave with me *at once*.'

His face was scarlet. Tartan burst into tears.

Odette felt nothing but relief that her secret was still intact. If Tartan had been foolish enough to forget the rules, that was her failing.

Jim marched Tartan from the hall as she sobbed.

'You may now start,' Elspeth announced.

Odette opened her exam paper. There was the question in black and white: *How can we use time travel to prevent crime?*

Odette chewed her lip, considering how to respond. She jotted down an opening paragraph: *Detectives can interact with the past. But the outcome of their actions will always be consistent with events in their original timeline. The primary purpose of time travel must be to collect evidence, rather than prevent the offence. Justice can then be appropriately administered with all the information to hand.*

She detailed her own evidence, including the plaque and Grace Taylor's response to her questions. Lastly she noted that she had switched on the security camera, which would have captured the vandalism, should the video footage be required at trial.

Odette *had* failed to stop the crime, and that made

her fear for her prospects. But she had done her best and answered honestly. She had to hope this was enough to get her the job.

31

Julie

Veronica Collins might have been the first person Margaret threatened with expulsion, but she wasn't the last. Angharad's daughter, Julie Parris, joined the Conclave in 1993 as an environmental conservationist. When plants became extinct, it was her role to retrieve samples from the past in the interests of preservation. She had been born to time travellers, and might have taken to Conclave life as her dynastic birthright. But she didn't. From her first field trip she had felt frightened.

Seasoned time travellers can spend more of their lives in the past or future than their purported 'home' timeline. Julie had grown up observing this rootlessness in her parents. Before joining the Conclave herself, she had thought that she was familiar with all of the job's joys and challenges, and was ready to take them on. She had underestimated how upsetting she would find her own detachment from time. As soon as she stepped from a time machine, at the age of twenty-one, she felt like a ghost – what other name could be applied to a woman who walked among people born centuries after herself? To them, she should be dead. The feeling of dislocation outlasted her return to 1993.

The way that Julie expressed her fear was through food. She wouldn't try delicacies that were new to her, and she rejected her hosts' attempts to make her welcome with meals. Soon she rejected familiar meals, too, associating them with an old life that she was permanently severed from. Her body acquired hollows and sharp points. It was gratifying to watch her belly turn concave. The more weight she lost, the closer her physical form matched her inner self: she would be as thin and pared down as the air. Ghosts had no flesh.

Eventually, the circumstances in which she would eat anything at all narrowed to one very specific point in time. If she wished to eat, she would travel to the day of her birth in 1973, and make her way to the local park for 11.52 in the morning. She would only eat at this moment of her birth; and each time she travelled there, her other 'selves' were simultaneously in place. To have this moment marked out for meals reassured her, and gave her the sense of control that she otherwise felt was lacking in her life. All her silver selves in the park were close to her in age, so she knew that something would eventually interrupt the ritual she had developed, and take that control away. Whenever she returned to the park, she also saw a future version of her mother, with a stooped back and loose grey hair, watching from a nearby slope. This must have been an attempt on Angharad's part – still yet to happen – to gain insight into her daughter's distress.

*

For months, Julie concealed her shrinking body from those who loved her with artful clothing. But her face grew gaunt and furred with lanugo. Dr Joyce recognised the significance of this, and sent Julie to Margaret's office.

Margaret was now fifty-six. She had been secure in her power for a long time, and paid decreasing attention to social niceties. As testimony to her growing eccentricity, a rabbit – one of Patrick's descendants – watched them from the side of the room. He sat in the middle of the bookshelf, his nose twitching.

'Julie had the highest aptitude scores of her cohort,' Siobhan was saying. 'Nothing has happened to change that. At no point has her illness stopped her carrying out her duties.'

'But what might she cost the Conclave?' Margaret's voice was icy. 'That must be weighed against her contribution. Do you deny that every trashy paperback, every second-rate film, every cheap tabloid that dares to mention my work must reference Barbara Hereford's lunacy in the same breath? I will not pander to their view of us by indulging mental deficiency.'

Thus far Julie had been silent. Margaret's rabbit leapt from the bookcase and ran to Julie's feet. She picked him up. He settled in her lap.

The sight enraged Margaret.

'Parris! Have you nothing to say for yourself? Your weakness *disgusts* me. Are you so incapable of defending yourself that you must hide behind this doctor's skirts?' Margaret walked to where Julie sat with surprising speed and lightness. She lifted the rabbit from Julie's lap. 'Give me one reason why I should treat you with anything but contempt. Fussing over a lab rabbit as if it were a pet – you have the attitudes of a *child*.'

'Sometimes I think I am a child.' Julie spoke mildly, almost to herself. 'Or an animal – like a rabbit. Don't you ever wonder what it's like for the lab animals?'

Margaret stared, her expression incredulous.

'Julie,' said Siobhan, 'I don't think that question helps.'

'The lab animals in the time machines. The first ones.' Julie turned her head towards her psychologist. 'Rabbits have body clocks, you know. They must be sent askew by time travelling. Out of joint, like me. I just want routine and to forage and dig and sleep. Normal life, you know.'

'So take your normal life and go.' Margaret exuded contempt. 'But do not breathe a word of the reasons for your failure.'

'I can't go,' Julie said, matter-of-factly. 'My entire family are time travellers. It would break my mother's heart if I left.'

'Your mother would understand,' Siobhan said. 'Please, Julie. You'll die without intervention.'

'Get out!' Margaret barked at Dr Joyce. 'The girl's made her decision. If she's going to stay, she'll be following the rules I set. Your contribution is no longer needed.'

32

Ruby and Barbara

The bar Grace took Ruby to favoured Victoriana: the wallpaper was flocked, and a piano with candleholders and covered legs stood in the corner. A small bay window let in very little light. Grace bought two tulip glasses of genever, which Ruby hadn't tried before. They sat in a booth and Ruby sipped her drink.

'Good?' Grace asked.

'Very,' Ruby said. 'But I'm not here to discuss gin. How can the body be Margaret's? If the body isn't Bee's, what made you send her the inquest announcement?'

'I didn't send it. An older-me will.'

'That's just semantics.'

'It isn't. I don't know much more than you.'

'Oh, come on. You've seen the future!'

'I've seen *some* of the future. But my older-selves have always seen *more*. And they haven't deigned to explain why they left an origami rabbit on Barbara's doorstep.'

'Brilliant. So you don't know why we've been on a wild goose chase.'

'I have some guesses! Did you ever receive a save-the-date card before a wedding? Maybe they're like those. But for an upcoming death. The next few months are a bad run for the pioneers. You've already seen what happens to me, Margaret goes in the New Year, and then it's Lucille's turn in the spring. Hey!' Grace exclaimed suddenly. 'Did you work out what those engraved numbers meant on the ring? They're Lucille and her husband's birth and death dates. That's what time travellers engrave on their engagement rings.'

'Hang on, Grace.' Ruby spoke gently, because she wasn't sure this woman was right in the head. 'Why on earth would Bee want a save-the-date card for your deaths? She'd like a normal letter, or to meet you for coffee. If you're going to die, she'd like a chance to say goodbye. That doesn't mean she wants *riddles* about when it's going to happen. Do you think this is a game?'

'No?' Grace bit her lip in consternation.

Ruby waited for her to continue explaining.

'Gahhhh.' Grace raked her hair. '*I* don't think it's a game. My future selves do. They drive me loopy, quite loopy. Have you *met* any veteran time travellers?'

Ruby shook her head.

Grace clasped Ruby's hands across the table and looked at her intently. For a moment Ruby thought Grace was going to kiss her.

'Believe me,' Grace said. 'Old time travellers are an odd bunch. They're all so strange about *death*. It's like the longer you time travel, the more cavalier you get about people dying.'

'And that's true of you?'

'Evidently! I've spent a few Christmases with future Graces. They're a barrel of laughs, I can tell you. Would *you* want to spend Christmas with several versions of yourself?'

Ruby grimaced at the thought.

'Sad to say it, but I become very annoying.' She let go of Ruby's hands, and relaxed back into her seat. 'Though I'm not as bad as some. Margaret turns into the *worst person*. When I first met her she could be a bit of a control freak but she had a whip-smart brain – and she was always sensible. Everything she did was for a practical reason. It was a bad move for her to head the Conclave.'

'Oh?'

'Maybe being in charge of time and space would give anyone a god complex, but she's such a *mean* god. And it sets the whole tone there. She's cruel to the time travellers, and the old time travellers are cruel to the wenches, and they're all cruel to civilians. I can hardly stand to be around them, Margaret least of all.'

Grace's complaints reminded Ruby of her own feelings about university friends. People you'd once die for take appalling paths. It's not that they become unrecognisable. They become *more like themselves*. Personality quirks grow more pronounced, and so do values, until you wonder how you ever ignored the differences between you.

'How does Margaret die?' Ruby asked.

'She plays a dangerous game with a gun. One day it goes wrong.'

'No one else involved?'

'A rather lovely femme fatale – or so I've heard.'

'Fine. I'm relieved it's not my grandmother's body. That's all that matters to me.'

'If you want to know when Barbara *does* die, I can tell you,' Grace remarked.

'No!' Ruby almost shouted, thinking of how distressing the past few weeks had been. 'I don't want any advance warning. I'll enjoy the time I have with her, and when she dies it will be completely out of the blue. I won't have wasted a moment anticipating her death.'

'OK, OK.' Grace eyed her empty glass. 'Let's order another round.'

She went back to the bar, and Ruby took the opportunity to call Bee. There was no answer on the flat phone or her mobile.

'It's me,' Ruby told Bee's voicemail. 'The body's not yours. Ring me as soon as you can.'

Laughter travelled from the bar. Ruby watched Grace flirt with the barman. A shaft of evening light fell on Grace's face, and the illumination flattered her. She might be in a Terence Malik film.

Don't fall for her, Ruby warned herself. *She's* very *odd*.

But also beautiful, and a genius. Why wasn't Ruby angrier with Grace, for making her fear Bee would die horribly? Was it because Grace shifted blame onto her future selves, as if she were a different person completely? She'd acted as though they'd embarrassed her – as if she and Ruby were on the same wronged side. That was cunning.

Grace came back with the genever bottle, which she uncorked efficiently.

'By the way,' she said, 'don't tell anyone the body belongs to Margaret. That information's embargoed. If you pass it on, you'll be committing treason. Breaking a Conclave embargo is a capital offence and you won't want to lose your head.'

She sat down and topped up their glasses. Ruby stared at her.

'*You* passed the information on,' Ruby said. '*You've* committed treason. Aren't you worried about being executed?'

'Me?' Her eyes were wide. 'I died of a brain haemorrhage this morning, remember? Nobody's going to execute me.'

*

A hundred and thirty miles south, another time traveller – Ruby's grandmother – was browsing the Conclave store, which was the only section of the building open to the public. They specialised in the exclusive sale of food from other time periods. People could buy meals-in-pills, sonic-enhanced meat and fish, rum served in clouds. The candy accounted for most of the shop's wares. CitronGlows. Frozen Butter Pies on sticks. Sweet Algae. Cricketsnap and Honeyed Kernels. Everything looked good to Barbara. The colours on the packets zinged. All the songs from the speakers were exuberant. Soon, if Margaret's offer was genuine, Barbara would be travelling to new places – and experiencing the worlds her old work had promised. Barbara bought some biscuits for Breno, and a single tub of astronaut's ice cream for herself. She walked through the doors of the shop, back into the foyer.

The receptionist ran towards her.

'I wasn't sure if you'd gone,' he panted. 'Did you say you're Barbara Hereford?'

'That's right,' Barbara said, peeling back the tub lid.

'There's a call for you.'

'Are you sure?'

'I believe she said her name was Ruby.'

They headed back to the information desk, and the receptionist passed Barbara the receiver of a very peculiar phone. It had four different rotary dials, nested within each other. When Barbara pressed the receiver to her ear, the line wasn't crystal clear – there was a whining hum of radio static, and she thought she could hear crying.

'Ruby? Ruby, my love?' she asked.

'Yes.'

'How did you know where I was? Is something wrong?'

'No, Granny. I'm just so happy to speak to you. I have the most *amazing* news.'

33

Odette

After the exam, Odette reported to her interview with Elspeth Niven. Elspeth's office was at the north end of the building. The walls were ox-blood and the floors were polished concrete. A burnished copper desk and chairs were nailed to the floor. Everything was dark and shining. The cold edge of Odette's seat cut into her thighs.

Elspeth had Odette's exam paper in front of her.

'I liked your response,' Elspeth said. 'But how did the experiment make you feel?'

The question surprised Odette. 'I suppose a little anxious – as with any assessment. My teammates were sure we'd failed, and I wanted to pass very badly.'

'I should be more specific. How did you feel when you realised you wouldn't prevent the crime?'

'Oh.' Odette reflected. She supposed she should have been depressed on learning that she wouldn't swerve the course of events. Yet she hadn't been. She had switched her focus to evidence collection – and the possible motives of Dr Taylor. That process had been satisfying, in its way, rather than depressing. 'I think I liked feeling part of something bigger than me. My actions fitted in to a bigger pattern that I wasn't driving. I just wanted to see how everything fitted together.'

'Hm.' Elspeth's tone was impossible to interpret. She looked down again at the paper. 'The stakes were low, compared to our usual cases. You may feel more… despondent… if you couldn't prevent a murder, for example.'

Odette said nothing. The comment touched on her experience at the toy museum too closely. Her skin prickled. Had Papi already alerted Elspeth? Was she talking about Odette's trauma, and waiting for a confession?

Elspeth sat back again in her chair. 'Why do you want to work for us, Odette? Why not the police?'

Because a woman died, and the Conclave has something to do with it, and I want to know what.

'I've always wanted to be a detective.' This should have the ring of authenticity, at least, though it didn't answer Elspeth's question. Why wouldn't she join the police? Because they were racist. Maybe the Conclave was too, but they'd had Lucille Waters at the top from the start, giving an impression of greater opportunity. 'I think the Conclave is a better cultural fit for me than the police force.'

'Oh. *Culture.* The Conclave has its own culture, indeed. And it makes you fit by hook or by crook.'

'Is the training intensive?'

'We have a formal induction period. The Conclave has its own laws, and you have to be fully versed in them before you work as a detective, obviously. For the first few weeks you'd be carrying out administrative duties, but it's not quite as dire as it sounds. You'd get to shadow a detective before taking on your own caseload.'

'Could I shadow you?' No harm in creating a connection.

Elspeth laughed. 'Maybe. That would throw you in at the deep end.'

'Good. I like that. And can I request particular cases?' There was every chance the museum case was already under investigation. Odette wanted to be in the midst of it if it was.

'That would be unusual. Allocating caseloads takes a degree of managerial oversight.' Elspeth checked the clock. 'I think we have all the information we need. Is there anything else you'd like to know?'

'How many positions are you filling in this round?'

'One. And we don't have to fill it this round if there isn't a suitable candidate. Our timescales are flexible, obviously. Tell me, do you think you were the best applicant?'

This was not a fair question; Odette had to tread carefully. The Conclave might value team playing. 'I believe two have been excluded already. The third was clearly serious in his intent to work here. But we differed in our approaches to the experiment.'

'Grace's black eye?'

'Yes.'

'You wouldn't ever use violence in apprehending a criminal?'

'That would depend on the danger presented. Grace Taylor wasn't posing any physical threat.'

'Useful to know.' Elspeth's expression gave nothing away. 'We'll have an answer for you by the end of the day. Please wait in the reception area till then.'

'Thank you; I'll do that.'

They shook hands, bringing Odette's Conclave application to a close.

34

Siobhan

Siobhan Joyce was from the twenty-second century, where the field of psychology was a relic. It had largely been replaced by theological determinism: a belief that all human action was dictated by a higher power. New religions even used the experience of time travellers to bolster their worldview: if there was no divine plan, the theologians argued, it would surely be possible to use time travel to change the course of events. But it was not. Psychology was concerned with internal states and environmental influences, neither of which was deemed meaningful any more. Instead, theologians aggregated maps of people's life events, and searched for patterns computationally. They reasoned that any patterns in the data would be a source of divine insight.

Reading psychological texts had become at best a niche historical interest. The world had moved on. Job opportunities for psychological autodidacts, like Siobhan, were thus hard to find in her home timeline. As an independent scholar she had pored diligently over psychometric scales, finding a beauty in their enumeration of emotion. Fortunately for Siobhan, Margaret Norton was a woman of the twentieth century, not the twenty-second; and she saw a role for psychology in the Conclave. All vacant positions were advertised in all years the Conclave was active, giving Siobhan the opportunity she craved.

Her favourite psychometrics were the questionnaires for people with sleep disorders, and her knowledge had earned her the Conclave post. The Conclave took an interest in time travellers' dreams for practical reasons. Disordered sleep and unpleasant dreams can be part of a wider pattern of poor psychological health. As a basic safety precaution, time travellers were schooled in paying attention to their dreams, and reporting any issues to Dr Joyce. Siobhan drew on a variety of methods to record dreams, such as inviting the time traveller to tell their dreams as a story, ticking items on a prepared list of symbols, and drawing their dreams.

The job was one she felt immense gratitude for. She had faith in her tools, and was glad that the Conclave treated them with proper reverence. But a conflict arose for her. Siobhan had hoped to help people with her questionnaires and tests. The Conclave, however, had a different agenda. They used her expertise to marginalise vulnerable time travellers, rather than help them. Margaret's aggression towards Julie had troubled Siobhan deeply. At least, in Veronica's case, one might believe Margaret had spoken reasonably and for the general good – although Siobhan had no idea what bargain had been struck to keep Veronica in her job and she doubted it was to Veronica's benefit. Yet Siobhan did not publicise her objections: her own job security rested on an apparent willingness to follow Margaret's rules and there was no other venue available where Siobhan could work as a psychologist. She was sure there must be a compromise available – a way of retaining her position without being complicit in further mistreatment of sick staff.

On a commonplace day in 1992, Jim Plantagenet, from the biomedical department, saw Siobhan for a routine psychological check. This check included the monitoring of his recent dreams. Siobhan explained she would read from a list of symbols, and Jim should stop her if any of them were familiar. He agreed; she began to read.

'A future city burning with all of its inhabitants,' Siobhan said. 'Boiling oceans on a future coast. The earth cracking open from one future border to another. A future sky glowing in neon greens and yellow and pink.'

And Jim began to cry.

He was, at this time, only a recent recruit. Siobhan checked his notes and saw he had taken just three trips in the time machine so far. She wondered if he was having difficulty adjusting.

'Would you like to tell me what you're feeling?' she asked.

'My sleep's disturbed,' he said. 'I wake up screaming.'

'You're having nightmares?'

He nodded.

'With the symbols I described?'

He shuddered. 'I see my family dying from radiation sickness. Their skin is… ulcerated. Necrotic.'

'Is this an imagined scenario? Or something you've seen in the future?'

'A combination. There are moments where reality slips through.'

Siobhan leafed through the other psychometric tests. She checked Jim for depression, and found him sub-threshold, but his anxiety levels were very high indeed. Really she should report his situation directly to Margaret. Distress at death was something that Margaret took particular interest in – for the purposes of elimination.

Siobhan closed the psychometric file.

'What's your home timeline?' she asked Jim.

'Twenty twenty-seven.'

'Good. There's a great deal of private counselling available then. Take some leave, go home, and pay for anxiety treatment.'

'But that's forbidden.' Jim blanched. 'Am I going to be fired?'

'No. Not unless you've discussed your problems with anyone else at the Conclave?'

'I haven't.'

'Good. Keep it that way. As far as I'm concerned, this conversation didn't happen.'

'Very well.' He stood, and loosened his wristwatch absent-mindedly. 'Thank you, Dr Joyce. I'm glad it was you I spoke to.'

Siobhan nodded, and hoped – for his sake – he would maintain his discretion.

35

Ruby

Grace accompanied Ruby through New Street Station. They stared at the departures board.

'That's my train,' Ruby said. 'Platform two. What are you doing now?'

Grace bounced on the toes of her pilgrim shoes.

'I'm fancy-free. No ties, nowhere to be.'

'Do you have any family? In this year, I mean.'

'I probably have some cousins who are still alive. Who knows what age they'd be.'

'How old are *you* now?'

'Haven't a clue.' Grace tapped her tracker watch. 'This little chap counts my heartbeats. I'm up to... one point one billion. The Conclave uses that information to calculate what year I'd be in if I'd lived my life in the same chronology as everyone else. When I die, the number of my heartbeats will indicate I should be in 2027. That's why the Conclave will send my body there. Say, do you want to go there with me?'

'To *2027*?' Ruby found the prospect horrifying.

'No. To the *Conclave*. I'd give you a special guided tour.'

'Oh.' Ruby smiled with relief. 'How could I resist?'

'That's settled then. I'll catch the train to London with you now.'

She bought a ticket and they boarded the waiting train. It was packed with commuters, but Ruby and Grace managed to find two seats next to each other.

'Are you from London?' Ruby asked. 'Originally.'

'My home town's much less glamorous. Can't we pretend I sprang fully formed from the head of Zeus?'

'Your accent puts you somewhere between Hampstead and Philadelphia.'

'That's the middle of the ocean!'

'Yes. Maybe you're Venus, rather than Athena.'

'Ruby, you charmer! I'll tell you a secret.' Her voice dropped. 'This isn't the accent I grew up with.'

'You don't say.'

'Every Saturday I'd study how the film stars spoke in matinees. And – oh, this is a shameful genesis – one afternoon I saw a B-movie called *Hell or High Water*. A beautiful actress called Bella Darvi played a physics professor and I wanted to be just like her. Now tell me,' Grace said, 'I've been dying to ask. Weren't you the teensiest bit tempted to try on Lucille's ring? It's a darling little thing.'

A darling little thing hurtling through time. Ruby felt a twinge of guilt.

'It was too small,' she lied.

'What a shame! I was so sure it would fit you. It was a little loose on me. I worried it would slip off my hand without me noticing.'

'Why did you have Lucille's ring anyway?' Ruby asked.

'Before she died she gave it to one of my older selves. She didn't have any children to pass it on to.' She sighed. 'Maybe it's just as well you can't wear it. It would deter potential suitors.'

Ruby laughed.

'But if you'd worn it tonight,' Grace said, 'we could have played at being an engaged couple.'

'Have you played that game before?'

'Before I started time travelling all engagements between women were play engagements. There are some advantages to working in other time periods.'

'Do things keep getting better?'

'Progress isn't irreversible.' She smiled overbrightly. 'I can avoid the worst years. Right then, future wife. I'm going to have some beauty sleep. We have a long night ahead of us.'

'What do time travellers dream of?'

'Punch and Judy, and conspiratorial vicars, and schoolgirls with guns.'

'Get you with your John Masefield references!' Ruby said. 'Bee used to read me *The Box of Delights*. I can remember every single line, complete with page references. Did you know it's my favourite novel?'

'I did. Mine's *The Chrysalids*. Now hush.' Grace closed her eyes, and let her head rest against Ruby's shoulder.

36

Odette and Siobhan

In accordance with Elspeth's instructions, Odette waited in reception for the results of her application. She took one of the seats and contemplated the magazines fanned across the table. There was no point even trying to read one. Until she knew whether she had the job, she wouldn't be able to concentrate.

She closed her eyes and her head fell back as she allowed exhaustion to catch up with her. The day had been a prolonged test of endurance and her ability to dissemble. So far nobody appeared to realise her motives for working there were suspicious. Papi must have decided to hold his piece.

'Odette,' she heard someone say. Their voice was hushed. 'Are you sleeping?'

'No,' Odette replied, blinking. There was a woman kneeling down by her chair – a little older than Odette, with short strawberry-blonde hair.

'My name's Fay Hayes.' She held up a manila envelope. 'You got the job.'

Thank God. Odette beamed. 'Where do I sign?'

Fay removed Odette's contract from the envelope, and offered a pen.

Odette read the terms and conditions cursorily, and signed her name where indicated. 'Is that everything?'

'No. Come with me,' Fay said. 'I'll be overseeing your initiation.'

'I'm sorry?'

'We're going offsite – not far; just to a café down the road.'

'But why didn't Elspeth mention it?' Odette was thrown by the unexpected prolonging of her day. And *initiation* sounded worrying.

'Because it's not organised by Elspeth. You could call it… peer training.'

'Is it mandatory?'

'It's part of every employee's introduction to the Conclave.'

'OK,' Odette relented. 'What do I need to do?'

'Follow me. I'll brief you on the way.'

*

Siobhan Joyce was looking up holiday flights in her office. The telephone rang; it was reception.

'I'm really sorry to land this on you,' said the receptionist. 'We've had a call from a member of the public. He says he has important information about one of our job applicants.'

'What kind of information?'

'He says it's highly confidential. Won't give his name. I don't even know who he's talking about. But he's insisting on talking to whoever deals with mental health. Will you talk to him? Sorry if he's a nutter.'

'Put him through.' Siobhan picked a brown leaf from the pot plant on her desk and dropped it in the wastepaper basket.

'Hello?' a male voice asked. 'Who am I speaking to?'

'This is Dr Joyce,' Siobhan said. 'Can I help?'

'Are you a medical doctor?'

'A psychologist.'

'Oh. Oh, OK. I have information about a prospective detective. Her name is Odette Sophola.'

'I see,' Siobhan said.

'She won't disclose it herself. But she has a recent history of trauma. She was witness to a very violent crime and it affected her enough to require therapy.'

'You're quite sure she didn't put this on her application?'

'Positive. She saw a private therapist so it wasn't in her notes. I've worried sick over it. I just want her to be safe.'

'Has she recovered?'

'Yes. Yes, unquestionably. But the website seemed so clear – *any* history of trauma might be a risk. If she doesn't get the job, will she know someone provided this information?'

Siobhan considered. 'No. I can assure you of that.'

'Thank God.' The relief in his voice was tangible. 'She would guess it was me. She doesn't understand the situation she's put me in. She thinks that I'm trying to stand in her way. I just want her to be safe.'

'Rest assured,' Siobhan said. 'You've come through to exactly the right person.'

'Thank you.' The man sighed before hanging up.

Siobhan replaced the receiver and looked at her laptop again. Bangkok was cheap at the moment. Maybe she'd go when the rainy season was over.

37

Ginger

Ginger Hayes was in Euston Station, buying coffee on the concourse. Her commuter train to Tring was due shortly, and her thoughts were half mired in the problems of her outpatients. Gurpreet, who no longer perceived words at their normal volume, and begged strangers in the street to 'please, please stop shouting'. Sally, who had been deaf since birth but forgot how to sign when her brain was injured. Chloe, who confidently used neologisms in the expectation they would be understood. 'Mulmul' for garden, 'shwister' for tea, 'copterbop' for pencil.

The working day had finished late, because a team meeting overran. Ginger had argued at length with the neuropsychiatrist's assessment of a client. While the barista frothed milk Ginger was still arguing in her head, subvocalising the new points that occurred to her. Mixed in amongst this was the list of household obligations to be completed that evening. She'd forgotten to defrost the chicken before work, so she'd need to go to the supermarket, and then to the pharmacy, to pick up a prescription for her daughter Fay's eczema, and by then it would be time to collect Fay herself from Brownies...

Ginger took her coffee, and had just lifted the lid when she saw Ruby weaving through the crowds. At Ruby's side was a woman dressed like Megan Draper. They were laughing. In fact Ruby looked entirely different from her usual frowning, over-serious self; as though she'd received the best kind of news.

Did Ruby laugh like that with Ginger?

No. Ginger and Ruby were always brought together through a mutual sense of fatigue. Sex with Ruby was an escape, and yet it was the same kind of escape as drinking a bottle of wine alone in a darkened room. They didn't bring each other joy – or share anything of themselves. And Ginger had thought this was how she wanted their relationship to be. An impersonal release, easily segmented from her real life. Only now did she realise that she would be jealous of someone making Ruby laugh.

Ginger didn't lack self-awareness. She realised it was gross hypocrisy to want Ruby to herself. And yet when the service to Tring was announced, Ginger sleepwalked in the opposite direction, after the laughing women. They took the escalators down into the Underground station. Ginger kept her eye all the time on Ruby's shining hair, anxious that she would lose them among the tourists and the tired office workers. She followed them through the barriers and down again; they were taking the Northern line. Southbound.

When the next train arrived Ginger entered the same carriage as them, a couple of doors down. Between passengers' shoulders and upraised arms, Ginger could still see Ruby at the centre of the carriage. She was standing next to that other woman. Their heads were close to each other.

How else could they stand? Ginger scolded herself. *It's a busy train. Friends would stand as close. My head is as close to a stranger's.*

But Ginger knew sometimes we want proximity and a crowd gives us the excuse.

At every station she was poised to disembark, because she didn't know her marks' destination. The train passed through Angel, and Bank, and Borough. Ruby and her companion got out at Eligius. Ginger pushed her way to the open door, with more recklessness than before. Ruby would have questions if she realised Ginger was following her, but Ginger feared that she'd escaped detection not because she was a good spy, but because Ruby's attention was fixed so completely on Ginger's rival.

People funnelled from the platform. Ginger lost Ruby at the lifts. She rose to street level and ran through the parting doors, trying to catch another sight of Ruby's red flannel dress, but she was nowhere to be seen by the barrier, nor at the exit. Ginger rushed outside and looked up and down the street with rising panic. There, there she was! Turning a corner up ahead.

Will you follow her all night? that scolding voice asked. *What will you do when she comes to a stop?*

I'll tell her I want her, Ginger said back. *All of her, not just snatched sex in the blue hour before I climb back to bed with Seamus. I'll tell him about her. Then I can know her.*

Her conviction grew while she tracked the pair down roads of white stone buildings. She could catch up with them. She started to run, and was gaining. They were at the gates of the Time Travel Conclave. Ruby's companion was speaking into an intercom. If they went inside, Ginger's opportunity would be gone, for she couldn't follow them in.

'Ruby!' she shouted. '*Ruby!*'

The traffic drowned out her calls. She watched Ruby disappear into the Conclave, and the gate swung shut.

Ginger slowed her pace, now her quarry had gone. She walked to the gate and peered through the bars, to see if Ruby was still in view, but saw only a young woman in shades, coming down the path.

'Excuse me,' Ginger called. 'Is any part of the Conclave open to the public?'

The woman stopped in her tracks and cocked her head.

'It's me,' the woman said, and came closer. She took off her glasses. Her eyes, incongruously, reminded Ginger of Seamus. Guilt was making her imagine things. She pushed the thought away. The woman smiled at Ginger, and this too was familiar.

'It's me,' she said again. 'Mum? It's Fay.'

Ginger moaned. The woman's face was right, but it was upsetting to see one's daughter the wrong age.

'How can you be Fay?' Ginger whispered.

The woman laughed. 'I became a time traveller.'

Ginger looked for differences from the Fay she knew. This woman's hair was strawberry-blonde, and cut into a pageboy.

'Your hair's the wrong colour. My daughter's hair is red. Like mine.'

'We do still have dye in the future.'

'I have to go.'

The woman named Fay reached through the bars. 'Please wait. This is new to me too. I've *just* started.'

'How old... how old are you?'

'Twenty-four.' Fay beamed, proud.

'You're at Brownies,' Ginger said faintly. 'You're doing your Gardening badge.'

'I was going to come and visit you. Can I?'

'What? Yes.' This was Fay, then. And Fay could always come home. 'Do you mean now?'

'Well, actually I was on my way to a meeting—'

'That's fine. That might be better.'

'I'm sorry. I shocked you.'

'Don't be sorry. It's a surprise, a surprise rather than a shock. I can tell your father, and he'll be ready for when you come.'

Fay's eyes were shining. 'I can't wait to talk to him.'

'But if you're not coming to ours tonight, where will you get dinner?'

'Mum, I get all my meals here.'

'Oh, I see. And are you... are you happy?'

'Very!'

'Good.'

'So you had no idea I was here?' Fay asked.

'No. How would I?'

Fay frowned. 'What are you doing here then?'

Shit, thought Ginger. She was still flushed with the jealousy that fuelled her sprint to here from Euston. But she had meant to voice that jealousy to Ruby, not Fay. Ginger's cheeks flamed, and she knew she must answer Fay's question before the silence seemed too long.

'I was passing – and I thought I saw a colleague, here, by the intercom. It doesn't matter.' She brought her hands to her mouth. How dreadful if she'd stopped Ruby and told her she'd break their secrecy, only for Fay to arrive seconds later. What a way to hear her parents' marriage was over.

Except – it dawned upon Ginger – Fay would know already.

'Mum, you're shaking. Do you want some water? I'll let you in.'

'No!' Ginger's voice rose. She didn't want to bump into Ruby with Fay at her side. 'I should let you get to your meeting. Before I go...'

'What?'

'What do you remember of your childhood? Was it a happy one?'

'The happiest!'

'Even *this* year?'

Fay's expression was blank, then her eyes widened.

'Oh!' she exclaimed. 'You're talking about *Paige*.'

'Who?'

'My sister. What are you, four months gone? No wonder you're faint.'

A baby. Had she been so in denial? She'd not missed a period, but then she'd kept bleeding on and off till twenty weeks with Fay. *Four months gone.* Too late to reverse.

Fay held Ginger's hands through the bars.

'Don't look so worried. Wasn't she planned?'

Fay's enjoying the novelty, Ginger thought. Grown-up talk, with a mother barely older than herself. What was the grown-up reply?

'Well-laid plans can go awry too,' Ginger said. 'I'm just anxious.'

'You mustn't worry. Everything works out wonderfully.'

'All right. That's all I wanted to know.' She pulled Fay closer to the gate and kissed her on the cheek. 'I love you. Go to your meeting, and come see us tomorrow.'

'I'm so glad I saw you.' Fay hesitated. 'I'd forgotten you were this young.'

Ginger retraced her steps and caught the train home. There was no time for the supermarket or the pharmacy now. Even cutting those errands out of her journey, she was fifteen minutes late to the community hall. Fay was there with Brown Owl, who waved unconcernedly at Ginger's apologies.

'Fay has a brand new badge to show you,' Brown Owl said.

'Look!' Fay proffered a square of yellow fabric, illustrated with a watering can.

'Well done, sweetheart,' Ginger said. 'I'll sew it on for you when we get home. Let's get a takeaway to celebrate.'

'Fish and chips?'

'If that's what you want.'

What you want, what you want. The words repeated in Ginger's head. They left, and Ginger thought about the older daughter that she'd met that evening, who would now be sharing food with the other time travellers. She thought about Ruby, sleeping with a woman who could make her laugh. Lastly she thought of Seamus, and all the news she had to tell him. All the news, none of which was: *listen, I'm sorry, I like women not men, I'm in love with someone else.* For that headlong journey, from Euston to King William Street, she had acknowledged she wanted Ruby. A greater happiness seemed in reach. But now she knew the future. If Fay thought her parents stayed married, that's what would happen. The other, imagined life was gone.

38

Ruby

Ruby didn't have Bee's problems accessing the Conclave, thanks to Grace's invitation.

'Where to first?' Grace asked. 'The bar? Or the botanical garden?'

'Do you have plants from the future?'

'Some. But the main goal is preservation of existing varieties, so you'd recognise most of what we grow. You can see tropical flowers in the greenhouse that you're probably less familiar with. There are a few tortoises in there too.'

'I think that seals it. Greenhouse it is.'

Grace led the way. She opened a door disguised as a wall panel, and Ruby followed her into a semi-lit corridor. The walls were painted with art nouveau mermaids. Ruby could hear the distant splash of water.

'That's the greenhouse fountain,' Grace said.

'I expected the Conclave to be busier,' Ruby said. 'Where is everyone?'

'Drinking! Evenings are frantic in the bar but we might meet a stray horticulturist or two.'

They arrived at the greenhouse. Heat enveloped them. The sun was low on the horizon, turning Grace's cream skin gold.

'Look at all the orchids,' she said. 'Aren't they divine?'

'Very,' said Ruby.

Grace picked one, and tucked it into Ruby's hair. They walked to the fountain, as it was cooler by the water, and sat at the edge. Bright fish nosed the surface. Ruby admired the surrounding spice trees and inhaled the smell of vanilla. She saw they weren't alone; a woman in green overalls stood under a coco de mer palm, taking notes on a clipboard.

'Is the palm new?' Grace called.

'Newish,' said the horticulturist. 'Gift from Mahé.'

'We have replication sites,' Grace explained to Ruby. 'We also have Mahé to thank for the tortoises.'

'Where are they?'

'There's one peeking from the foliage behind you.'

Ruby turned to see a tiny, wrinkled face amongst the greenery. He was chewing on a leaf with gusto.

'He's not the only one hiding,' Grace whispered. 'Be subtle, but look over my shoulder.'

With affected casualness, Ruby scanned the expanse of plants behind Grace.

'I can't see anything,' Ruby whispered.

'Keep looking.'

Then Ruby's eyes rested on a couple, half submerged by trailing vines, locked in a kiss.

'Come on,' Grace said. 'Let's leave them to it. Next stop is the hall of time machines.'

She took Ruby's hand when they left the garden, and didn't let go as they walked back down the corridor.

*

The hall resembled an aircraft hangar and contained row

upon row of great grey cubes, any one of which could comfortably contain fifty people. All sides of the cubes were smooth, with a single entrance at the front.

'They're made from steel,' Grace commented.

'What are they like inside?'

'Pitch black. And when they're switched on, they smell good.'

'Good how?'

'Very clean. Like the air after a storm. It's because the fuel creates ozone. You'd get the same scent during radiotherapy – or if you dropped a nuclear bomb.'

Like the Candybox.

'Are the time machines open?' Ruby asked. 'Could I walk in and have a look?'

'Shhhh!' Grace made a show of looking left and right. 'Visitors aren't allowed, but maybe if we're very quick. Follow me!'

The machine door slid open at their approach. It didn't close again behind them. They stood in the arrow of light, and peered into the emptiness. Ruby might have been in any dark warehouse, except she knew this was the path to every memory she possessed, and that made her heart race. At her side, she felt Grace shiver. The machines weren't yet mundane to Grace either.

'Are these machines ever dangerous?' Ruby asked.

'Not when properly used.'

'Have they ever been wrongly used?'

Grace popped open her top button, so Ruby could see her décolletage. A scar marked her flesh, like a tyre track in snow. Ruby winced.

'That's thanks to a *huge* accident,' Grace said. 'All the time travellers who were caught in it have similar scars.'

'What caused the accident?' Ruby asked.

'Cost cutting. The Conclave hadn't been running very long... The year was...' She paused, to count on her fingers. 'Nineteen seventy-three. It was seventy-three. That's when Margaret said we could make recruitment more efficient.'

Grace explained that instead of using tests and interviews and qualifications, Margaret proposed a shortcut: skipping straight to hiring people that were named on future payrolls. The Conclave issued a contract to the one woman whose name was listed for that year. And after a few weeks, she botched the controls of the time machines. All four hundred and fifty-seven machines simultaneously malfunctioned. The same part came loose in all of them – a great hunk of steel, shaped like a smile with jagged edges. It flew through the air and scooped a ridge from Grace's chest like she was made of ice cream. Then she stepped outside. The other women were staggering from their machines, and they each had injuries just like hers.

'But you guys know the future,' Ruby said. 'Why didn't you predict the accident?'

'We did. That morning, we'd been laughing and joking about it. We were quite hysterical, in fact. Most of us still joke about it now. Although actually getting carved frightened Angharad more than she thought it would – she threated to leave straight after.'

'But *none* of you resisted going in beforehand?'

'Have you never done something that you knew would go wrong from the start?' Grace asked.

'Yes,' Ruby said, thinking of Ginger.

'There you are then.'

'It's not the same. Normally there's some upside to ignoring the warning signs.'

'There was an upside,' Grace insisted. 'You can't know, because you don't time travel. But if you've heard about an incident for years, actually experiencing it feels like a release. We call it—'

'Completing,' Ruby said, remembering Sushila Pardesi's phrasebook.

Grace nodded, surprised.

Ruby looked again at the faint tip of the scar, curving out from Grace's dress, and touched it.

'Does it hurt?' she whispered.

Grace shook her head. Her blue eyes had deepened to indigo in the semi-dark. Ruby could hear faint piano-playing.

'Shostakovich,' Grace said.

'I thought I might be imagining it.'

'No. He's one of Angharad's favourites. She must be in the ballroom.'

'There's a ballroom?'

They left the time machine, and the hall, to find the source of the music. It grew louder as they turned down corridors, this way and that, until they entered a gallery overlooking a gilded chamber. There were only two dancers below: ballerinas, with hands linked.

'My God,' Ruby said. 'They're *twins*.'

'No,' Grace corrected. 'Both of them are Angharad.'

The women wore one pointe shoe each, and were dressed in identical unitards of sunset orange. They pirouetted from opposite sides of the room, twisting their way to the centre – so nearly touching – before jerking back like one south magnet from another. Grace and Ruby watched the dancers close their fists and splay their fingers, twitch their torsos to the left, extend their arms jitteringly into the air until

Ruby lost her breath in sympathy. The performers leant into an embrace. One turned and dipped into a low arabesque, with her hip supported by her twin's hand. Ruby looked at Grace, whose shoulder was a hair's breadth from her own. The small gold figures flickered across Grace's irises. She turned to face Ruby fully and touched Ruby's waist. For a second Ruby thought they, too, were going to dance. But instead Grace kissed her. Her mouth was warm and alcoholic. Her skin smelt of jasmine. Ruby never asked what scent she wore, but for the next month she would spend her lunch hours at perfume counters inhaling swatches of paper, before she finally stood transfixed by a spray of Givenchy. It evoked Grace in an instant. Ruby could have drunk the bottle.

39

Odette

The sun was setting, and the streets were thick with people finishing their working day. Odette kept pace with Fay, but without the certainty of knowing their destination. Fay talked continuously.

'Tell me about yourself,' she said.

A worrying question, for someone working under false pretences.

'I want to be a detective,' Odette began cautiously.

'Let me stop you there,' Fay mimed zipping her mouth. 'Tell me about *you*. Your actual life. Where are you from?'

Always that question.

'Seychelles,' Odette said hesitantly. 'We moved here when I was still a child.'

'I grew up in Tring.' Fay stopped at the kerb as a passing lorry filled the air with dust and exhaust fumes. 'In fact I'm growing up there at the moment. I was born in 2011.'

'Do you visit often?' Odette asked.

'Yes. Not so much in this particular year. My sister was born in 2018 and my parents are flipping knackered. Do you have brothers or sisters?'

'I have a sister,' said Odette. 'But she's a lot older. My parents gave me almost as much attention as an only child.'

'Did that get on your nerves?'

'Not exactly. I felt special, I suppose.' Still, it had come with pressures. Nothing distracted Odette's parents from her academic performance. Maman had been able to keep an even closer eye on her because she was a teacher at Odette's school.

'And are you single?' Fay asked.

'Relationships aren't a priority right now.' Odette had had the same boyfriend through most of school. They'd broken up on A-level results day because she couldn't abide his sulking when she got a better grade than him in Chemistry. His mother still tried to convince her to give him another chance whenever they crossed paths. She'd acquired her next boyfriend in Freshers' Week. They'd gone out for two years. Sometimes she'd had the uneasy sense she was a novelty for him, and she wasn't terribly surprised when he left her for a horsey girl called Timandra. After that Odette focused on revision. Revision, and the corpse.

'I've been married for ever,' Fay said.

'To someone at the Conclave?'

'No. We worked in the same chambers, before I started time travelling. I suppose I was lucky to meet him then rather than later. The Conclave has a big impact on people's love lives.'

'Work stress?'

Odette had to wait for an answer; a queue of French students divided her from Fay, before they fell back into step.

'The job is stressful of course,' Fay said. 'But it's more that time travellers' relationships feel prearranged. Most time travellers check in advance who their partners will be.

They know the outcome before they necessarily know the person.'

'They still choose who to be with, don't they?'

'Sure. It just doesn't *feel* that way. Like, you meet someone, and you think, I end up attracted to *this* person? What was my silver-me *thinking*?'

Odette wasn't sure whether Fay was making general observations, or drawing on personal experience of relationships outside her marriage. Nor was Odette familiar with the phrase *silver-me*, though she could guess its meaning from the context.

'Are you excited about seeing your future?' Fay asked.

'I don't know. I really haven't thought about it.' She'd been so focused on investigating the death in the museum, she'd barely considered that she'd see how her life unfolded.

'Probably best to have few expectations. That way there won't be many big shocks.' Fay stopped outside a café, with tables and folding chairs on the pavement. 'This is the place.'

They sat down, and Fay asked the waitress for two coffees. Odette was still perplexed at why they'd come. Surely they might have drunk coffee in the Conclave.

For the duration of their walk, Fay had been carrying the large brown envelope that contained Odette's contract. She opened the envelope again. This time, she took out a piece of paper with a photo attached, though Odette only glimpsed the image. Her stomach twisted as she recalled the threatening post the Conclave sent to Zach.

'What's that picture of?' she asked.

'You'll need it for the ritual.'

'What ritual?'

Fay passed her the paper and photo in lieu of explanation. Odette almost smiled with relief. The photo wasn't a mortuary photo; it wasn't anyone in her family. It showed a girl, alive and laughing, aged seven or eight with a tow-coloured ponytail. Her name was written along the bottom: *Olivia Montgomery*. Odette read the typed page of information. *Mother killed in a road traffic collision outside Café Roberta*. There was a time and today's date, as well as a small map plotting the exact spot of the woman's death. Odette looked at the laminated drinks menu, at the side of the table. *Café Roberta* was emblazoned across the top.

'Explain to me what this means,' Odette said.

Fay leant forward, her voice too low for anyone to overhear. 'You're going to tell Olivia her mother's about to die. It's the Angel of Death ritual. Do it, and you'll be one of us.'

'*Angel of Death?*'

'Speak quietly, for heaven's sake. It's an initiation rite.'

'But you said this was *training*.' Odette couldn't believe Fay had wasted her time on false pretences.

'Officially this isn't part of your training. But unofficially – it absolutely is.'

Odette wanted to pause, and think. This little girl was about to experience a terrible loss. What impact would hearing about it, a few minutes in advance, have upon her? To Olivia Montgomery, Odette was a stranger. An unknown woman bringing news of death would frighten a child. And in the years to come perhaps Olivia would feel she should have prevented her mother's death, in those brief moments after Odette's announcement. No matter how kindly Odette tried to break the news, the ritual could heighten this girl's trauma.

'What happens if I won't do it?' Odette asked.

'You will do it.'

'What happens if I *won't*?'

'You'll not be one of us,' Fay said. 'You need to fit in, Odette. How will you fulfil your duties if the others don't trust you're one of them? The pranks will get more extreme. Eventually you'll give in and either complete the ritual, or leave.'

I can pretend, Odette thought. *Not do the ritual, but say I have.*

'I'll be watching you,' Fay said, anticipating Odette's strategy.

Odette was revolted. She'd have to go along with the ritual if she was to make allies – even fake allies – in the Conclave. On the corner of the street, she could see the little girl approaching, hand in hand with a man Odette assumed was her father. They took a seat at one of the tables.

'Shall we order for Mummy too?' the man was saying.

'No,' Odette said, her resolve hardening. 'I won't do it.'

'You're a fool,' Fay said. 'You have to accept this job will make new demands of you. You can't play by the rules you've known till now.'

Odette stood up, took a handful of change from her handbag, and dropped it on the table.

'Where are you going?' Fay asked.

'Home.'

'Are you going to take the job?'

'I don't know any more.'

'You've signed the contract. Do you want me to destroy it?'

'Yes.' Odette shook her head. She couldn't do that, not when the chance of getting inside was so close. 'No. *I don't know.*'

Horns sounded in the street. A tyre screeched, and cries went up; a woman was propelled through the air and landed on the bonnet of another car, her neck twisted into a right angle. All the other café patrons stood to look – including Olivia, and her father. He lifted her in his arms and crushed her head to his shoulder. He swayed, like a toppled ninepin.

'Rituals,' Odette said in disbelief. 'What are they for?'

'It's for your benefit,' Fay said. 'It accustoms you more quickly to being one of us. You're not like *them* now. It's better if you accept that as soon as possible.'

'But what's in this ritual for *you*, personally?'

Fay looked at Mr Montgomery, sobbing into his daughter's tow hair.

'Sometimes,' Fay mused, 'I like watching people have emotions I don't feel any more.'

40

Ginger

Ginger still read to Fay at bedtime. They were three chapters into *Charlotte Sometimes*. The copy was Ginger's own, from childhood, and she had wondered if Fay might find the prose old-fashioned. But Fay seemed relaxed with its staidness. When her eyes began to droop Ginger replaced the bookmark, kissed Fay on the forehead, and turned out the lamp.

She rejoined Seamus in the living room. His dark hair was a little wild and his skin was tanned from working in the garden. He was sitting in the easy chair, whittling a toy – a fox, from the look of it. A sitcom played on the television and Ginger turned the volume down.

'There's something I need to talk to you about,' she said. 'I wanted to wait till Fay was in bed.'

His eyes were still steadfastly trained on the fox. After a moment's reflection, he said, 'That sounds worrying.'

'It isn't, exactly, but... it's a rather unusual situation.' She took a deep breath. 'Today, I was walking past the Time Travel Conclave, and a young woman stopped me. She said she worked there, and that she was from the future. She told me she was twenty-four years old. And she introduced herself as Fay. Our Fay.'

Seamus paused in his whittling. He took a long look at Ginger, as if determining if she was serious. 'Any chance it could be a hoax?'

'No, I don't think so.'

'You're *sure* it was her?'

'Yes. I'm not really in any doubt about that.'

'Why on earth didn't you bring her back?'

'She had other commitments,' Ginger said vaguely, and it struck her that she had very little sense of what time travellers actually did for a living. 'But she is going to come to dinner. Tomorrow, possibly.'

'Why wait till then?' he asked. 'Let's ring her.'

'We don't have her number,' she replied, but he had already picked up his smartphone.

'I'll just look up the Conclave.' He flashed a grin, and she saw he was excited. 'I expect they'll put us through.'

He was filtering the search results, and then dialling, with gleeful haste. Ginger realised that there could be something rather thrilling in the prospect of meeting an adult Fay – to know she had grown up safely, and appeared to be thriving. But the circumstances in which Ginger had encountered her were so fraught there had been no opportunity to feel that buzz. Besides, it was always Seamus who was the more playful parent. Ginger was the worrier.

'Hello?' Seamus was saying on the phone. 'My name's Seamus Hayes. I'm trying to contact my daughter, Fay. She works for you.'

Fay could hear someone replying but the response was tinny and indistinct, then the line fell silent.

'The receptionist's checking for us,' Seamus said to Ginger.
Another tinny voice echoed through the receiver.

'Fay?' Seamus asked, elated. 'Fay, is that you?'

And then his expression rapidly changed from pleasure to confusion.

'She's just started crying,' he whispered to Ginger. To his daughter, he said, 'What's wrong? Darling? Do you need us to come and get you?'

Ginger wrested the phone from him. 'Has something happened, Fay?'

'No,' her daughter replied. 'Nothing's happened. It was just... hearing Dad's voice. It's been so long.'

'What do you mean, so long?' Ginger said, trying to keep her tone light. She could feel dread in the pit of her stomach as she wondered whether Fay had been completely honest earlier. Perhaps she and Seamus were not going to stay together as Fay had insisted.

'Since he died,' Fay gasped. 'I'm sorry. I didn't mean to tell you. I won't tell him.'

Ginger's limbs felt weak. 'I see. Do you want to talk to him another time?'

'No. Put him back.'

Wordlessly, Ginger returned the phone to her husband, and stepped into the back garden until she could regain control of the shake in her hands.

A short time after – Ginger had no watch, and her own phone was indoors – Seamus joined her on the patio.

'She wouldn't tell me why she was crying,' he said.

'Nor me,' Ginger lied.

'Did she react that way when she spoke to you earlier?'

Ginger evaded the question. 'Maybe she's crying because of... the stress of time travelling. People say it's stressful.'

A neighbour's cat, brown with a scar over its eye, paused in stalking their lawn.

'Do you think it happens soon?' Seamus asked, his expression flat.

'"It"?' Ginger queried.

'Come on, there's a limited range of things that could make her cry when she hears my voice. It must have occurred to you. Sometime between now, and whenever the hell she's from, I die.'

'Well it can't be soon. Fay told me her childhood was happy. She wouldn't say that, if you were just about to…'

'Wait – you said she was twenty-four, didn't you? So I have fourteen years at the most.'

They were silent. Ginger did the arithmetic. From some perspectives fourteen years sounded a lot – far more notice than people ordinarily had – and yet it also meant they were more than halfway through their time together. Seamus wouldn't live past forty-nine. The new baby would still be at school when he died. His death might not be imminent, but the time limit still lent Ginger's thoughts clarity. She did love Seamus more than she could love any other man, and she felt newly certain it was the right decision to stay with him. How dreadful it would have been to reveal her affair tonight, like she'd intended. Discovering his premature death on the same day as his marriage disintegrating would have left Ginger more guilty than she could cope with. Her relief at guilt avoided was immense. She had a new motivation to be a model wife; to make these next few years, with their children, as sweet as possible while he was still there. They would earn Fay's happy memories.

She took Seamus's hand. She could feel the calluses on his palm, at the base of every finger.

'Anyone can go at anytime,' she said. 'Let's see this knowledge as a gift.'

'You would say that.' He withdrew his hand, and there was a chill in his voice.

'What do you mean?' Ginger asked, and she realised she didn't really want him to answer. His tone told her that the world had shifted. Learning of his premature death made him drop a pretence that protected them both.

'Knowing when I'll die is a gift for *you*,' he told her. 'It must be a relief to hear when you'll be rid of me.'

'That's a wicked thing to say,' Ginger replied, to hide her fear.

'Do you think I don't know why you work in London?'

This was left field. 'I have to work where the jobs are, Seamus.'

'Yes, people only ever get brain injuries in London.'

'We live in a commuter town! Who *doesn't* work in London?'

'Me. Which makes it much easier for you to blame sudden absences on bad trains. And I won't run into the men you're fucking. The current one; does he know he's not the first?'

So he had sensed her duplicity, and guessed at her infidelity – but he had no proof. If he did, he would have known the threat was Ruby, rather than a man. She could still persuade him he was mistaken.

'I'm not sleeping with other men,' Ginger hissed. 'I never have. Please let's go inside. We're right below Fay's window.'

'You're a coward,' he said tiredly. 'You want to leave and you won't. So tell me why I shouldn't walk out.'

Ginger turned over what answers she could give. There was the pregnancy, which she was yet to share; it had seemed unreal, and now he might believe paternity was in question.

For the moment, she kept that news to herself. She needed another way to persuade him.

'Fay will visit us tomorrow,' Ginger said, taking Seamus's hand again. 'She will tell us what's coming. And she'll tell you, like she told me – she has a happy childhood. Doesn't that mean we're happy too? She wouldn't be happy if I was cheating on you. How can that not reassure you?'

'Maybe good lying is hereditary,' he said, then they heard their daughter rap the glass on the window above them, her face appearing small and pale in the evening light. The conversation, for now, was over.

4

Barbara

Barbara took Breno back to the flat before leaving for the museum. She rather regretted his absence on the walk from the station; he would have been company, and she felt very alone. The distance to the museum was considerable. Her preference would have been to catch a taxi, but she thought Margaret might be angry if a third party – the driver – witnessed her arrival.

She didn't meet another soul in the last few streets. A police siren distantly rose and fell. The museum was locked up when she arrived. Had Margaret chosen this place because of its quiet emptiness, the low likelihood that they would be seen? The venue was a strange one.

The walk had given Barbara a queer pain in her chest. She placed a steadying hand on the wall. *Nerves*, she thought. That was why she was nauseous and a little sweaty. As she contemplated how to get into the museum, she heard the creak of a door, out of sight. She stumbled to the side of the building. A staff entrance was wide open, but there was no one to be seen.

Bee peered inside. She saw a narrow corridor, with a

door on the left – presumably to the public areas of the museum – and a stairwell, leading to the basement. First she tried the door handle, but it didn't budge. The only other way to go was down. Down, to where no passer-by would hear her cry out.

Don't be silly, Bee scolded herself. Whatever differences had arisen between her and Margaret, they had once been friends. She wouldn't place Bee in danger. Bee had to believe that, especially now she was so close to getting what she wanted.

She went downstairs and let herself into the boiler room.

Margaret stood opposite the door. She wore a reefer and leather gloves, despite the warmth of the evening. In one hand she held a pistol.

'It's just the two of us?' Barbara's eyes flickered between Margaret and the gun.

'As we arranged. Do we need anyone else?'

'No.' The room smelt as fresh as April weather. Surprisingly fresh, for an underground boiler room. It smelt like time machines. 'Why are we meeting here, Margaret?'

'It has a personal significance to me. A sentimental value, you might say.'

Supposedly – if you had access to state secrets – obtaining keys and alarm codes to buildings that didn't belong to you was a relatively simple matter.

'Now.' Margaret extended her arm, pointing with her gun to a tower of bricks – around four foot high – that Bee had failed to spot by the wall. A Candybox was perched on the top. 'We're going to play a game of chance.'

'A game...?'

'If you shoot into the Candybox, there's a twenty per cent chance the bullet will rebound straight back into you.

Alternatively, it will pass through time, to the possible harm of whoever operates the machine in the future.' She held the gun out to Barbara. 'Call it my variation on Russian roulette.'

'But why?'

'It's a practical test, of my own devising. Willingness to play predicts smooth adjustment to the Conclave's norms.'

Barbara still hadn't taken the gun.

'You want me to endanger myself – or someone else,' she said.

'Yes. Those are the rules of the game. You told me you would do anything, Bee.'

'I meant I would do simple work – menial work, if necessary.'

Margaret let her arm drop.

'Fine. You can go home.'

Barbara thought her heart would crack. The chance to time travel again had been within reach, and now Margaret was taking it away.

'Wait,' Barbara said. 'Just... wait.'

'Are you going to play or not?'

'Please, I just... All right!'

The touch of the gun on Barbara's palm was cool. Her hand was trembling. She hooked her finger through the trigger guard. *Margaret's insane*, she thought; it was insanity to sport with Barbara's life, and other people's. Before today, Barbara hadn't seen Margaret in half a century. What had happened to her since to make her so cruel?

'I can't,' Barbara said. 'I won't time travel again at this price.'

Margaret took back the gun, aimed it at the Candybox, and fired.

'You were never going to shoot,' she said matter of factly. 'But I enjoyed watching you consider it. Duck.'

'What?'

The Candybox spat out the bullet as Margaret dropped to the floor. The bullet grazed Barbara's arm, spinning her off balance, then blood wept through the cotton of her sleeve. Margaret, unharmed, kept her foetal position at Barbara's feet, and she laughed and laughed. The seconds elongated. Barbara felt she was watching the scene from far away.

'Thank you, Margaret,' she said.

'What for?'

'It wasn't right to cut me out. But I was better off living the life I had.'

'Oh, for God's sake,' Margaret sneered. 'You're so smug, with your idyllic cottage on the coast, and your dog and your home-spun wisdom. We both know you're weak.'

'Strong enough to walk away from *you* without a backward glance.'

Which is exactly what she did.

Barbara's perception of time travel had been formed before the Conclave was born or thought of. In those early days, Margaret had been one member of a team where everyone's input was essential, so her personal qualities didn't dominate. This meant that the eventual character the Conclave took on came as a shock to Barbara when she tried, at the age of eighty-two, to return. She had the strength to walk away, but she was also glad she'd had the chance to see behind the wizard's curtain. It meant that when – less than a day later – Barbara died, she could go to her grave without regrets for the life she'd led. She'd loved her family. She was at peace with her health. She'd had years to tend her garden and watch the sea. In another life she'd invented time travel – but that was no longer a glory she needed to revisit.

42

Odette

It was dark when Odette arrived home. Only Maman was in, reading A-level essays at the kitchen table under a crisp circle of lamplight. She took one look at Odette's face, and put the essay down.

'You didn't get it?' Maman said.

Odette took a seat and undid her shoe straps. 'The job's mine. I've already signed the contract.'

'But, Midge, that's wonderful!'

'I'm not going back there. The people are terrible.'

Maman tsked, dismissively. 'Nobody likes their colleagues. Not me, not your father. Do you hear us complaining?'

'Yes.'

'Well we still go to work anyway. It might be frightening to leave university but you need to start your career now.'

'I'm not frightened of leaving university.'

'What then?'

Odette watched her own reflection in the kitchen window. What was she frightened of? She was comfortable enough with lying, to find out if the time travellers were murderers. But Fay's ritual had made it clear that blending in might also mean doing unpleasant things to innocent people. This time Odette had resisted. Could she keep resisting, and yet evade detection? Could she keep resisting while earning the time travellers' trust? Odette feared they might contaminate her. She wasn't sure you could work in a rotten system and keep your own hands clean.

'I spoke to lots of time travellers today. And one of them warned me I'd struggle to fit in.' Odette's voice trembled. 'I'm frightened they'll catch me out as someone who doesn't belong. And I'm scared that I'll be compromised – that I'll end up hating myself – because I'm trying so hard to be accepted. After today I feel so *alone*.'

To her embarrassment, a tear ran down her cheek. But it made Maman soften. She pulled Odette to her.

'This was a white time traveller, was it?' she asked.

'Yes, but... that wasn't what she was getting at.'

'It's always there when a white woman tells a black woman she won't be accepted – whether or not that's what she meant,' Maman said. 'You've shown determination, Midge, going to Cambridge and the Conclave. You must keep being determined. Nobody's going to hand a black girl anything. But you are *not* alone. You have me.'

'I know but—'

'You're not alone,' Maman interrupted. '*Ou pas tousel.*'

The sound of the words in Kreol surprised Odette, and gave her a strange ache in her chest. Maman hadn't spoken Kreol in years. Odette closed her eyes, and remembered the forgotten language, until they heard Robert's key in the front door.

43

Ruby

Grace didn't have to sleep in the Conclave's dorms. As a founding member, she had the privilege of a private apartment to the rear of the complex, on the thirty-sixth floor. She took Ruby there after they left Angharad to her rehearsals. The rooms were open plan and designed according to 1960s' Italian principles, which meant the furniture was white and sinuous, and the walls were hung with optical illusions. Grace put the Velvet Underground on the record player. She poured some Steinhäger into a pair of shot glasses and led Ruby out to the balcony to admire the city view.

On the patio table Ruby saw an arrangement of tiny objects: a matryoshka; a pearlescent pill box; a Swiss army knife; a Japanese coin; a ticket to see the Zombies; a dried sheaf of lavender; a pair of sea-green hurricane glasses; a heart-shaped eraser; a pharmaceutical capsule; an escargot fork...

'What are these for?' Ruby asked.

'My next exhibition. They're all examples of acausal matter. Or what some physicists call "genies" – because they appear out of nowhere.'

'What d'you mean, nowhere?'

'One of my future selves gave these to me, wrapped in a plastic bag. Eventually I'll give them to a past me. The objects only exist in that loop. They aren't made by anyone. They just *exist*.'

'That's impossible.'

'No, it isn't. We don't fully understand genies, but the laws of quantum mechanics allow for them. A surge of energy can spontaneously create matter from a vacuum. One theory is that the process of time travel creates an excess of energy that generates these objects.'

'I find that difficult to get my head around.'

'So do a lot of time travellers, especially the ones who work in support, because they rarely have a physics background. They tend to believe genies have a divine origin.'

'They're made by God?'

'Or a higher power of some sort.'

'D'you have a lot of them, these genies?'

'Every time traveller does.' Grace sipped her Steinhäger and placed the glass on the table. 'Not all genies are tangible. A genie can be a cake recipe. A piece of music. A mathematical equation.'

'A list of names on next year's payroll?'

'Yes. Using genies to avoid labour can be dangerous. Doing your own groundwork – like going through a recruitment process – means you can reduce the number of possible outcomes. But there are situations where accepting a genie can be beautiful.' Grace stroked Ruby's arm. 'Let's say my future self tells me that the Conclave ballroom, on an August evening, is the best place to kiss you. And when I get older I'll say the same thing to my past self. The idea wasn't my own. It's a suggestion that circles between my silver-me, and my green-me.'

'What does your future self say about women on balconies?'

'Nothing. We'll have to experiment without her involvement.'

She kissed Ruby again.

Ruby lifted the paisley dress over Grace's head. She kissed Grace's scars, and the border where Grace's shoulders met her oyster corselette. They made short work of Ruby's checked pinafore – but the unlooping of every hook in Grace's satin underwear was a slow pleasure – and then their hands were on each other's breasts, their hips, their thighs. They fell onto the tiles. Through the speakers Nico crooned, halted in a groove. *Eeeese*, she breathed, over and over. *Eeeese. Eeeese.* The world was nothing but the rhythm of her voice, and Grace's mouth on Ruby's skin.

*

'Tell me a secret,' Grace said afterwards. 'Something no one else knows.'

'I didn't have sex till I was twenty-seven,' Ruby replied.

'Is that late?'

'Don't you think it is?'

'Not necessarily. These things can take longer to work out, if you're a woman who likes women. Is that why you waited?'

'No, I don't think so. I didn't wait deliberately. My favourite theory's that I had a limited communication repertoire. I grew up in a house where nobody got too emotional, so I kept everything hidden, including attraction. I certainly didn't flirt.'

'A "limited communication repertoire"! I think that's nonsense,' Grace said. 'You talk to people for a living.'

'No, I listen, and I ask questions from behind a very crisp boundary. I'm ideally suited to my job.' Ruby propped herself up on an elbow. 'Does your job never frighten you – with how dangerous it is?'

'When I was a little girl, I expected to do dangerous work.'

'Really? Why ever did you think that?'

'I'm from a mining family, in the Midlands,' Grace said. 'My mother pulled iron nuggets out of the banks of Tipton. That would have been my fate, too, only I was evacuated during the war, and the woman I stayed with offered to pay for my education. She said I was intelligent, which was true, but I think that really she liked the idea of rescuing me. Manual labour horrified her – so did manual labourers – and she enjoyed being horrified. I became a pet project that she could tell people about and they'd praise how generous she was.'

'That's horrible.'

'Hm? Yes. Still. I went to boarding school. When I'd finished, I felt out of place at home, but it didn't matter any more. I could go to university; I wouldn't be dead by forty, like my grandparents, or lose my livelihood through mine closures, like my cousins. The risks of time travel seem quite manageable in comparison. Particularly when you think of the benefits. I've always loved it. When we invented time travel, I stopped noticing how I didn't fit in any place. Because time travellers were a new thing, they didn't have a particular accent, and you didn't do it because that's what your mother and grandmother did. I know that changed. People have an idea by now of what time travellers are like—'

'Mad,' Ruby said. 'People think time travellers are mad.'

'They do,' Grace said. 'But I can live with that.'

'It's your turn to tell a secret.'

'I practically have. Everyone's forgotten I should have been a miner.'

'Tell me another.'

Grace sat up. She reached for her dress and pulled it back on.

'How about something from the future?' she said finally.

'Ugh. No.' Ruby shuddered.

Grace didn't reply. She was looking at the clock on the wall, which read half past eleven.

'I didn't mean to be rude,' Ruby added. 'It was a kind offer – to tell me about the future. The idea just makes me nervous, that's all.'

'No, it's fine. Ruby…' Grace tapped her fingers against her mouth, as if trying to raise her words to the surface. 'Ruby, I think you should go now.'

'Oh. Have I done something wrong?'

'No. I just hadn't realised it was this late. I think it would be best if you went home.'

'I'm sorry. I knew I'd put my foot in it.'

'Please, go back to your flat. I can arrange a Conclave car, it's no problem.'

Ruby put her clothes back on. She felt cold now, even when she was fully dressed. Neither she nor Grace spoke again before the chauffer pressed the buzzer, and then Grace only said goodbye, with no farewell kiss. She watched from the doorway until the lift took Ruby away.

*

Breno greeted Ruby at the door, but Bee was already in bed. The flat smelt strongly of time machines, meaning Bee must have been playing with the Candybox again. Ruby took a shower and brushed her teeth. She slumped over the sink with tiredness, yet she doubted she'd sleep. She was upset by Grace's sudden haste to be rid of her. Ruby must have misread the situation. She'd foolishly thought tonight was the start of something. Whereas Grace had clearly got what she wanted, and couldn't wait for Ruby to leave.

And was Grace being unreasonable? What could exist between them beyond a few hours? You couldn't get involved with someone who spent most of their life in a different time period from you. What would such a relationship look like? Just thinking about it made Ruby's head hurt. She put her toothbrush back in its mug and turned off the bathroom light.

On her way past Bee's open door, Ruby heard her grandmother stirring.

'Tony?' Bee mumbled, her voice slurred with sleep.

'No, Granny,' Ruby said. 'It's me.'

'Oh, Ruby... come in. Let me see you.'

Ruby did as she was told, and sat on the edge of the bed.

'I was so sure Tony was here. I must have been dreaming about him.'

'Does that make you sad?'

'No. No, not at all. It's like seeing him again. A chance to catch up. I never fancied remarrying, you know. He was the only man I wanted.'

'For all that time?'

'A little time with him was better than all my life with anyone else. I still had Dinah, and you.' Bee patted Ruby's cheek. 'Remember that. When you go, you want to have people you love to think about. You need enough money to feed yourself, and a sense of purpose is nice. But the rest is superfluous.'

Breno leapt onto the bed and curled round Bee's feet. Ruby kissed her grandmother on the forehead.

'I love you,' Ruby whispered – unheard, because Bee had already fallen back to sleep.

Those were the last words they'd exchange. Bee didn't wake up again. She died, asymptomatically, of a blood-borne infection. It was contracted from Margaret's bullet.

Ruby knew something was wrong as soon as she opened her eyes the next morning. Not because of a sixth sense, or anything as silly as that. She knew because Bee was usually an early riser. While she'd stayed in the flat, her chatter with Breno and quiet singing and clinking of breakfast cutlery and pots were the soundtrack that roused Ruby. So when Ruby's eyes focused on her bedside clock, which clearly read ten twenty, and the flat was silent, she knew Bee was gone. She pretended, for the last few minutes, that her grandmother had overslept. But when Ruby entered the other bedroom she picked up Bee's hand and it was quite cold. Ruby thought over their conversation, and wished she could know that Bee heard that Ruby loved her. She wanted to talk to her again – to make sure she'd received the message. The certainty that would never, ever happen made Ruby weep.

44

Robert and Odette

As soon as Robert entered the kitchen and placed his trilby on the table, Odette gave him a watery smile and announced she was going to bed. He assumed the tears were because the Conclave had rejected her application. They must have done; he had told them about her therapy.

'Bad news?' he asked Claire, once Odette had left.

'She says she got it, but she has cold feet.'

Robert glanced over his shoulder, to check if Odette was really out of earshot. He was sure she had lied to Claire. She wouldn't want to admit the Conclave had turned her down. Or perhaps they did offer her *something*. But it wasn't the prestigious job she imagined. A support role, safe for people with fragile mental health, that didn't involve use of the machines. That would make sense.

'Did she say what put her off?' Robert asked. He took a seat at the table.

'Some woman made her feel unwelcome. I tried to persuade her she should take the job anyway. She shouldn't give up on an opportunity like that.'

'Don't lean on her too hard,' Robert said. 'Maybe the place *is* a bad fit for her.'

His guilt had lessened. Odette had wanted this job so much, and it hurt him, of course, that she should be distressed. Yet he was convinced his action was the right one. No job was more important than Odette's health, and the Conclave clearly thought a history of trauma made you unfit for service.

'I thought she was more resilient,' Claire said in bewilderment. 'She applied herself so well at school and university.'

'She hasn't been herself since finding that body,' Robert said. 'Since then she's been... vulnerable. We need to watch over her for a while. And perhaps be a little gentler than we have been.'

Claire removed her glasses and rubbed her eyes. 'You think we're putting too much pressure on her?'

'From the best of intentions, my love.' He kissed her cheek. 'But now it might be time to pull back.'

*

The day had been long but Odette was too agitated to attempt sleep. Instead she slipped into the front room, where the bookshelves were kept. Following Claire's unexpected lapse into Kreol, Odette wanted to find the stories they had once brought to England. She finally located them on the bottom corner shelf, dropping to her knees on the rug. Picture books, mostly, which were simple enough for Odette to still understand. She ran her fingers over the illustrations in primary colours and peeled apart the pages that had curled together. Each book took only a few minutes to read. She reshelved the last of them, wishing there were more.

Then a green spine caught her eye. *La revanche de*

Peredur. It was the book she had bought outside the inquest – the old crime story, in parallel French and Kreol. She hadn't touched it since that day in February.

It fell open at the title page. No publishing house was listed there – and no date of publication. That was odd. But the glue in the spine had grown brittle, and perhaps a page had fallen out.

Her French was sufficiently fluent to read the opening paragraphs. An unnamed woman – referred to throughout as *la Mère* – challenged drinkers in a bar to a game of Russian roulette.

Odette's eyes drifted to the Kreol text. A prior reader had circled four words on the page. *Get. Disan. Rezilta. Ankar.* The words appeared in different sentences, but there must be some connection between them. Why else would they be circled?

Odette took the book to her bedroom. At her desk, she flipped open her laptop, and quickly located an online translator. *Get – look at. Disan – blood. Rezilta – results. Ankar – again.*

Why would someone circle those words?

On the smooth melamine of her desk, Odette pencilled:

> *look at*
> > *blood*
> > *results*
> > > *again*

She rubbed the words into a grey smear with her thumb. The book's previous owner had been playing at cryptography, sending hidden messages. She wondered who the intended recipient was.

As ever, her thoughts drifted back to the body in the museum. There had been blood tests at the inquest. She sighed, a little exasperated with herself. No matter what distractions she sought, there was always some detail in the film or book or song that reminded her of the case. And now she'd been reminded, she wouldn't sleep till she'd looked again through her notes on the mystery, for any clue that she'd missed.

Her ring binder was in reach, on her desk, as it had been for months. She flipped to the pathologist's testimony and tapped her nail on the blood results. The pathologist said the dead woman had bacteraemia. The same bacteria was on the bullets. The bacteria was macromonas.

Odette read the name once more and let out a small cry. *The bacteria was macromonas.*

Before meeting Jim, Odette hadn't known that macromonas was associated with time machines. Was it possible the bullets had passed through a time machine? Might they, then, belong to a time traveller? Either the dead woman – or her killer?

Odette closed her laptop and watched her reflection in the dark square of her bedroom window. Zach believed the body was Margaret Norton's; wasn't that consistent with a macromonas-ridden bullet? His theory now had extra heft. Odette's choice, to join the Conclave or preserve her own integrity, grew less tractable. She might be compromised if she was in their ranks. But to ignore this real, physical evidence was immoral too. Claire had told her not to be afraid, which felt like futile advice, because Odette was very frightened of the path that lay ahead. Still, she would have to endure it. She was going to accept the Conclave job.

45

Grace

There was one genie in Grace's possession that Ruby hadn't seen, because she kept it beneath the bedroom floorboards. This genie was a book. According to Conclave lore, every time traveller has an acausal book – a volume with no writer, which is passed from silver selves to green selves, and is superstitiously said to reflect something of its owner. The contents are always in the owner's native tongue and are always bound in a single, unique, unduplicated copy.

Sometimes the contents are little more than word salad with recognisable prosody but no meaning. Angharad, for instance, had a book called *Quantum Wombs* which she couldn't make head or tail of. Lucille's book was a collection of verse titled *The Philharmonic Dining Rooms* and Margaret owned *Daisy*, a hefty pseudobiography – which was somewhat opaque but in a literary fashion that could be deciphered with effort.

Grace had received her book soon after the Conclave's formation, from one of her eldest selves. It was called *A Ring of a Very Strange Shape* and contained handsomely illustrated allegories, one of which was struck through with fluorescent highlighter. The fables' relevance to Grace's life was unclear. She looked for connections to her favourite tales – to the Wyndhams, and Butlers, and Tiptrees already on her shelves – but found none. She resigned herself to not knowing the book's significance and concealed it beneath the floor of her flat.

But the book had come back to her thoughts the day she met Ruby. Their conversation about favourite stories on the train had brought it to mind. That night, after Ruby had left, Grace rolled back the carpet and prised up the wooden panel to examine the book again. It was in pristine condition. Although some acausal books spring into existence with dog-eared corners and the scent of aging lignin, they are oddly resistant to further damage and decay. Grace leafed through the pages. It was as she thought; there were references to mice, and gangs pretending to be clerics, and Punch and Judy men. This book was the words from *The Box of Delights* in another order.

Grace reread the paragraph scored in yellow. Now she knew her connection to the book was Ruby, she could interpret the words more easily.

A whole village went fishing in a sea of burning garnets. The oldest gave instructions: take this, hold that, stop daydreaming, and don't take part with the past. Their haul hit the base of the boat with a slap. In the middle of the net was a woman of rubies, red as the heart, who scorched the wood. The oldest said, By law I must dance with you. The woman of rubies replied: What else must I do by law? The oldest replied: You must keep vigil at my death. But, the woman of rubies said, you must do the same for me, and how can that be possible? Because, said the oldest, my life is a ring of a very strange shape.

The allegory was telling her what her silver selves told her: she was going to end up with Ruby. Sleeping with Ruby had, indeed, felt like completion. But amidst the usual symptoms of infatuation – the short attention span, the dwelling on Ruby's appreciable charms, the desire to be desired by her – Grace was panicking. Fate was closing in, and she wanted, for just a little while longer, to be only *her*, without Ruby in the picture.

For it seemed to Grace there were only two ways a couple could survive stretches where one partner was either dead, or yet to be born. The first was to rework one's understanding of binding commitments, and accept a degree of openness in long-term relationships. The second was to maintain a single partnership which admits no others even after one partner dies – because that partner continues to exist in the past, and is thus still reachable. Grace leant towards the strictly monogamous, fundamentalist approach. She believed this solution was both elegant and romantic – while it was theoretical. Now that reality approached, Grace was frightened. The days before time travelling, when Grace was free to fall in love with any woman or man she met, were officially over. Ruby was *it*. After her, there was no one else.

*

The following evening Grace was due to leave 2018 for 2075. On arrival in the future she reported for her psychological debriefing with Dr Siobhan Joyce. Grace completed her psychometric tests speedily and was content to chat while Siobhan recorded her scores.

'What brings you to 2075?' Siobhan asked.

'The new replication sites, in Cuba. I'm going there to help.'

'Oh! Lovely. Any other plans?'

'Ruby's due to die this week. I should be with her when it happens.'

Siobhan paused in her scoring.

'How do you feel about that?'

Grace worried that her ardour wouldn't survive Ruby's death. The fever of Grace's thoughts, which made Ruby relevant to any disparate subject, was new; it might be destroyed by seeing Ruby old and frail. And because Grace felt promised to Ruby, she wanted to hold on to their attraction. If it dissipated Grace didn't feel free to extract herself. The future was set.

But Grace had no wish to explore such issues with Siobhan. The Conclave's psychological services were oversensitive to these kinds of doubts and anxieties, reading into them the signs of burnout, or incipient breakdown. Grace gave a more nonchalant reply.

'I'll have to go to her deathbed at some stage. Might as well get it out of the way.'

'Like a dental appointment,' Siobhan mused.

'Or a smear,' Grace suggested.

Siobhan returned to the psychometric scoring.

'Doesn't that ever worry you?' Grace asked.

'What?'

'When we start to see people's deaths that way. An unpleasant inconvenience, to tick off the chores list? A date we write in the calendar so it doesn't slip our minds?'

'Mm. I'd call it an adaptive strategy.' Siobhan came to the end of her score sheet. 'All your psychometrics are fine. You're good to go.'

Grace went to her apartment, to pick up the wings she'd need for her flight. They were in her dressing room among her pilgrim heels and go-go boots, which had been dulled by a layer of dust. She strapped the box of wings to her back.

I could fly straight to Cuba, she thought. *Be as nonchalant as Siobhan thinks I am. Pretend I forgot to look at the calendar, and Ruby's death escaped my notice. Leave it for my silver selves to do. There's no rush. There's the rest of my life to turn up at Ruby's death bed. I could spend a little longer without Ruby in the picture.*

On the balcony the yellow sky awaited her. The doors could be left open when she departed. In her absence the apartment had grown stale and needed airing. She flung herself from the balcony and spun three times through the air before she pulled the cord. A wing's breadth of twenty-four feet shot out from her shoulder blades. The current caught her and she began to glide. Buildings below her righted themselves. One of them contained Ruby.

Ruby, who had been there when Grace died, sixty years before.

It was fair to repay the favour. If Grace's feelings changed so be it. Seeing Ruby die, and being changed by it, would remind her she was still human, and not yet Siobhan, or Margaret, or even her own silver selves with their casual disregard for death. Seeing Ruby die, Grace would feel something. With this thought Grace looped in the sky, the streets disappearing and reappearing through layers of cloud.

46

Ruby

September came, and with it autumn. Around the crematorium the trees were bronze and burgundy. Inside, Ruby sat in the front pew. She was dressed in black silk, held together with pearl buttons. Dinah was also at the front – with Henry, who Ruby had never met before, at her side. The mourners, row upon row of them, awaited the eulogy. To Ruby's sadness and disappointment Grace was not among them. It had been a month since they saw each other.

Mrs Cusack, Bee's friend, stood among the lilies at the lectern. Both Dinah and Ruby had declined to speak. Neither believed they could provide a reading without breaking down. Dinah's grief was fluid and seeping. The hair that framed her face was stiff with salt water. Her breath juddered. *I'm an orphan*, Dinah had said that morning. *I've been orphaned.* Inwardly Ruby protested that she had been orphaned too. It was Bee who'd mothered her. Ruby could never voice in Dinah's hearing that Bee was the true parent to both of them. That would be cruel, she knew. But she still felt her loss was as great as Dinah's, and resented the expectation that she would be less affected.

They'd agreed that Mrs Cusack would be the best person to speak at the funeral. She'd known Bee for decades – longer than Dinah had been alive – and her advanced age made her practised at funerals. She was a monochrome column in her mourning dress and veil. Her voice was steady as she addressed Bee's neighbours, the village shopkeepers, the dog walkers Bee knew from her morning constitutionals, and the worshippers from Bee's church. The only people missing were the pioneers.

'Bee rarely mentioned her scientific career,' Mrs Cusack said, from the lectern. 'But her silence was not from shame at her departure.'

Next to Ruby, Dinah stiffened. During their preparations for the funeral, Dinah had insisted the eulogy should focus exclusively on Bee's later years. But Ruby was gratified that Mrs Cusack swept aside this restriction.

'Her family wanted to live outside that particular shadow, and she deferred to their wishes. My friend lived alone after raising her family – excepting her long-time companion, Breno, who was third of his line and will be making his new home with Bee's daughter Dinah. Those of us who were lucky enough to be Bee's neighbours will all remember her ability to spin a good yarn. I will be forever thankful for the kindness she showed during my mother's final months, because she relayed all the news of the village when my mother could no longer leave the house, and read novels to her when the print finally grew too dim. Bee showed me compassion when my mother departed, because she understood grief. The loss of her beloved husband early in their marriage was always present in her mind. Both Barbara and Antonio believed in the life to come, and it is a great consolation to me – as I'm sure it will be to you – that they are now reunited.'

They were reunited before, Ruby thought, remembering how Bee had tricked herself into thinking Tony was at her bedside. A delusion, but a happy one, that Ruby hoped took fresh hold at the moment of Bee's death. Mrs Cusack returned to her seat. The coffin rolled through the velvet curtains to the sound of Scott Walker. Ruby accepted then – not a second before – that she would never see Bee again.

*

It was on the walk to Bee's house that Ruby saw the stranger. An elderly woman stood among the sand dunes, the tide going out behind her, while the mourners progressed along the road. She wore a pastel pussy-bow blouse with a large patent handbag. Her short hair was ash-blonde and carmen-rollered.

She was Margaret Norton.

Ruby broke away from the mourners. She removed her funeral heels so that she could walk across the sand, and felt the grains rise between her toes. Margaret did not come to meet her halfway.

'Why are you here?' Ruby asked her.

'To express my condolences.' Margaret smiled and blinked slowly.

'Is that all?'

'No. I came to speak to the executor of Barbara's will.'

That was Dinah. If she were confronted by Margaret, there would be a scene.

'Surely you don't think you'll inherit anything?' Ruby asked.

'No, I don't expect to be a named beneficiary. My aim is to ensure any stolen property in Barbara's estate is returned to us.'

'Stolen property?'

'By which I mean atroposium.'

'You investigated Bee for that. The police reclaimed your fuel.'

'Yes. However, a more recent development awakened my suspicions that she still had some. In the week of her death she badgered us at the Conclave to consider a new strategy for maximising energy extraction. She provided many notes detailing her experiments with atroposium. I find it hard to believe she was buying it at the cornershop. Presumably she was drawing on old stockpiles, originally purloined from our research team.'

This was close enough to the truth to make Ruby uneasy. Bee's Candybox still appeared to be running several weeks after her death. Every day Ruby had woken to the smell of ozone. She didn't understand how the Candybox could still be running on just the one stolen briquette. Bee must have had more fuel hidden away.

'I don't know where Bee would get atroposium,' Ruby said. 'If we find any, we'll let you know.'

She turned to go.

'How are you holding up?' Margaret asked.

The question surprised Ruby, given the mercenary slant of their preceding conversation.

'It's a difficult day to get through,' Ruby said. 'As you'd expect.'

'I suppose it's easier, when someone's so old.'

Ruby gasped at the lack of tact. She saw Margaret's eyes gleam and thought, *No, not lack of tact; she's deliberately getting a rise out of me.* Margaret smiled her slow smile and blinked her slow blink again.

'Is *that* why you're really here?' Ruby asked coolly.

'Whatever do you mean?'

'To witness my grief. To poke it with a stick.' Ruby recalled what Grace had said of time travellers. They were all so *weird* about death. 'You want to feed on my feelings. You're a vampire.'

'Really, Ruby,' Margaret said. 'You do have an imagination. Just remember, return anything to the Conclave that's rightfully ours, won't you?'

Margaret walked away then, following the coast southward. Ruby watched until Margaret's path curved round the rocks, and Ruby could see her no longer.

*

Ruby failed to catch up with the mourners on the street. They were already in Bee's house when she entered the kitchen by the back door. The table was covered with trays of egg and cress sandwiches. Dinah and Mrs Cusack were mid row.

'Your eulogy,' Dinah hissed. 'I told you not to mention *them*.'

'Who?' Mrs Cusack said, baffled.

'Time travellers.'

'But, Dinah, you can't pretend that part of her never existed.'

'It's true, Mum,' Ruby added quietly. She pushed the door shut behind her.

'How dare you refuse my request?' Dinah said.

'All right,' Mrs Cusack said hastily. 'I apologise. We're all upset.'

'The Conclave were *bad people*,' Dinah said. Ruby noticed her reversion to a child's lexicon. 'They weren't her friends. Do you see any of them here?'

'One of them sent flowers – with a handwritten card!' Mrs Cusack said.

'What?' Ruby worried that this was another example of Margaret's intimidation. 'Who sent a card?'

'I don't want anything of theirs in the house,' Dinah said. 'Where is it?'

'The flowers are still at the crematorium,' Mrs Cusack said. 'The card's with the others – on the hall table.'

'Who was the card from?' Ruby asked.

'Oh – her name's on the tip of my tongue. The one who sold the broken pencil for a lot of money.'

'Grace,' Ruby said, and she enjoyed saying her name, out loud, when it had been in her head all month long. If Grace had sent flowers, she wasn't cutting Ruby off.

'I don't want anything of hers in the house,' Dinah repeated. She left the kitchen. Ruby followed her.

The unmarked envelope was on the shelf beneath the mirror. Dinah seized it and tore it in two. She cast the pieces on the floor and covered her eyes, her words a jumble of English and the Konkani she'd learnt from her father, spitting invective about a woman called Fay who was an Angel of Death. Ruby wrapped her arms round her.

'Shhh,' Ruby said, over and over. 'I'm here. Shhh.'

The guests were taking their leave at the noise. Mrs Cusack emerged from the kitchen, and ushered Dinah back with her, to give her sweet tea.

Ruby picked up the triangles of card and flattened them on the hall table. She pushed each piece into place until she could read the clear, sloping script. Grace had written: *I will be grateful all my life for knowing Barbara, and for everything she made. G.*

The clock in the hall read half past one. If Ruby left

now she could make it to London by evening. Whether or not Dinah expected her to stay, Ruby could think only of escaping. The house was too full of sadness. She needed to feel something – anything – but grief. So Ruby donned her cycling jacket and boots. She rode her motorbike to London, then walked through the Conclave parks where they were burning leaves, and arrived at Grace's flat with the smell of bonfires in her hair. 'Make me forget,' she implored Grace.

'Forget what?' Grace asked.

Ruby undid the pearls of her blouse and let it fall. 'Death,' she said.

47

Odette

Odette's first day at the Conclave was dedicated to training. Until she'd been appropriately briefed by her superiors, she wouldn't have full privileges. Her movement round the building was restricted. She told herself to be patient. If she couldn't confirm the identity of the corpse just yet, she could still observe and listen to her new colleagues. She might pick up important details on Margaret's whereabouts.

Although Odette was polite to other employees, she was also wary. During the introductory tour she was startled to see that the Conclave bar was open and busy, despite the early hour. The atmosphere there was coarse. Too much swearing, and too many sick jokes about death and sex. The drinkers didn't make any concessions for a wench's nervousness. She felt badly situated, for a spy. Not only did she know nothing about her colleagues, they might know things about her future she didn't. The imbalance troubled her.

And yet there were glimpses of a life that she could love. She took another trip in a time machine, to report for a training session with Lucille Waters. It was attended by all investigators at least once, before commencing duty. The topic was handling sensitive information, which Lucille addressed from her position as Head of Knowledge. Odette tingled at the prospect of the secrets she might access.

They assembled in the marble hall where Odette had taken her recruitment exams. Lucille stood on the platform above them. She wore an olive linen suit and smoked a cheroot which she periodically tapped in the ashtray on her lectern. The cigar's sweet, dirty scent filled the room.

'Your job as investigators,' Lucille said, 'is to gather evidence. Time travel gives us many valuable opportunities to collect, and revisit, evidence in the past. But knowing the future can impede proper investigative processes. You must not, therefore, check the outcome of an investigation in advance. Who knows how the Conclave enforces this?'

Hands waved, reed-like, across the hall. Lucille gestured with her cigar at a wench on the front row.

The wench stood up. 'All investigations are conducted in secret. They may only be discussed with Conclave employees who are directly involved in the case. It's forbidden to discuss a case with your green selves. Breaking these rules constitutes treason.'

'Exactly,' Lucille said. 'Note that this secrecy extends to the trial. The verdict, and sentence, are embargoed in perpetuity. And an embargo breach is punishable by death.'

There was a pause in the *scratch scratch* of the recruits' notetaking. Odette recollected the anonymous source who sent privileged information to Zach Callaghan. Was that person in this hall? Had they endangered their life by contacting the press? Who were they? Odette needed to know – the leak could be a valuable witness.

Lucille extinguished her cigar.

'Enough threats. You are welcome to the Conclave, where you will find not only death, but the million quotidian experiences that make us love humanity. I hope you will cherish our work – in all its rich mystery – just as much as I do.'

She beamed. Hesitantly, the recruits commenced their applause.

Lucille left the stage. The recruits rose, their chairs squealing on the marble, and they exited with a subdued air; no doubt wondering what kind of information needed protecting with the threat of execution. Odette was bolder. She wanted to question Lucille directly about the intricacies of embargoes.

Lucille had her own suite of rooms. The door to her study was open when Odette got there. Lucille was already at her desk, turning the pages of an atlas. A large bay window let in light behind her, filtered through the water of a substantial fish tank.

'Take a seat, Odette,' Lucille said. 'What can I do for you?'

Odette noted, once more, that there was no need to introduce herself here. Yet she didn't feel uncomfortable, as she had with the drinkers in the bar. Lucille had a warmth that the drinkers lacked. Her welcome reassured Odette. It told her: *you have a place among us.*

'Can I ask some questions about embargoed information?' she said.

'Feel free.' Lucille closed the atlas. She smiled over steepled hands. A solitaire glinted on her ring finger.

'How many people have been on trial for breaking an embargo?'

'Impossible to say, because of the secrecy of the trials. But time travellers have sometimes gone missing without public explanation, and one of the possible reasons for that is execution. I know of twenty-seven such disappearances.'

Twenty-seven missing time travellers, at minimum. That was a frightening thought.

'When there's a leak, how can we identify the source?' she asked.

'We can't, unless someone comes forward with information.'

'OK... Let's say a piece of embargoed information is reported in the press—'

'I take it this question's hypothetical?'

Was that a twinkle in Lucille's eye? Odette had no idea what Lucille might be party to. Better, for now, not to reveal too much; Odette didn't know, yet, whether Lucille was to be trusted.

'The question's entirely hypothetical,' Odette lied. 'If information is leaked in the press, but we don't know how it got there, could we narrow down the potential sources? Could I check the time machine logs – to see who'd travelled to the right year?'

'Yes,' Lucille said. 'But a canny employee could leak information remotely, to someone in a completely different period, without time travelling at all. They could use Beeline.'

'But surely they could only reach another time traveller? I thought Beeline was just for use within the Conclave.'

'It is. However, the system could – theoretically – be hacked to send messages to people other than colleagues.'

'What kind of messages?'

'Radio transmissions, obviously. With a little tweaking you could also use the bandwidth to send internet data.'

'Could you send an email?'

'Certainly.'

'Wouldn't there be a record of that? We must be able to trace any transmissions to a particular year.'

'I'd be the only person able to check.'

'So, I could ask you what data was sent when? And that would give me a list of possible leaks?'

'Odette,' Lucille said softly. 'How would you rule *me* out as a leak?'

'I couldn't.' Monitoring the Conclave effectively relied upon the cooperation of all its members. 'We'd be back to the problem of needing voluntary reports.'

Lucille chuckled. She rose from her chair and stood by the fish tank. As she upended a shaker of fish-food over the water, she commented:

'There's another question you didn't ask.'

'What's that?' Odette said.

'Is a leak ever defensible in the Conclave's court of law?'

'Is it?'

'It should be. Sometimes, we have a moral duty to break the rules. Particularly where the rulemakers are corrupt. Do you see how that argument would apply to Zach Callaghan's informant?'

Aha. Lucille *did* know that the case wasn't hypothetical.

'I agree Zach's leak had a strong moral defence,' Odette said. 'I'm not looking for the leak to prosecute them. I think they may have information I can use.'

'I doubt they can share anything openly.'

Odette tried to conceal her disappointment. 'In that case I'll have to be creative. Thank you for answering my questions.'

'A pleasure.'

Odette walked to the door, and stopped. 'Actually, Lucille... there is a last thing I'd like to know. Have you ever been tried for an embargo breach?'

'No.' Lucille winked. 'To prosecute me, they'd have to catch me.'

*

On her return to her own time, Odette had a meeting with Elspeth to attend, to discuss her initial caseload.

'Have you considered which criminal department you'd like to be placed in first?' Elspeth asked. 'Please don't say homicide; everyone always does, and we can't accommodate you all.'

'Actually, I was thinking of Environmental Health,' Odette said.

'Good grief. You're virtuous.'

'I'd like to look into breaches of hygiene protocols after using the time machines. Surely it counts as public endangerment?'

'Yes, it would. What strategy would you take?'

'Tracking health records to see where there are any outbreaks of macromonas. Mapping them to see if we can isolate the source.' And in the process, pin down the identity of the toy museum corpse, and that of her killer.

'Very well,' Elspeth said. 'I'll draft you into Environmental Health, effective from tomorrow morning.'

48

Grace

Ruby was in Grace's bed; her lipstick, like peach halves, adorned the pillowslip, and her scent lingered on Grace's skin. Grace watched Ruby sleep until she heard the click of the apartment door. The sound of reedy singing followed. Grace wrapped herself in a silk housecoat and tiptoed to the kitchen.

A very silver Grace, stooped but glamorous in a teal turban, was unpacking groceries on the counter top.

'What are you doing here?' Green Grace whispered.

'I'm *terribly* sorry,' Silver Grace replied. 'Was I disturbing you?'

'Yes.'

'I suppose I'm only the help.' She moved from cupboard to cupboard, packing away the dry goods. Pausing, she ripped open a large bar of cooking chocolate and bit into it. 'Without me fetching things for you, you'd be in a pickle.'

'Please, keep your voice down.'

'Whatever for? She needs to get used to there being more than one of us. She needs to get used to a lot of things.'

'Not yet. Not today – she's only just come from the funeral!'

'Pffft. The sooner the better.' She raised her voice still more: 'Ruby! Ruby!'

When, thought Grace desperately, was she going to get so brash? Or was this how she came across even now, and she failed to see it in herself?

'*Ruby!*' Silver Grace called again.

They heard Ruby's approaching footfall, and then she was there, yawning, with her hair tangled like the wool shepherds save from hedgerows.

'Would you like some coffee and chocolate?' Silver Grace asked.

'Darling,' Green Grace cut in. 'Go back to bed if you wish. My older self is just about to leave.'

Ruby's eyes were wide. She looked from one Grace, to the other, and back again.

'I'd like a coffee,' she said. 'But no chocolate, thank you.'

'Now,' said Silver Grace. 'I've come to do what she won't.'

'What's that?'

'Tell you straight. If you want to keep doing *this*, there have to be a few rules. It's very simple.' Silver Grace poured hot water into the cafetière. 'Whenever I, or she, learns something about your future, she has to be able to tell you.'

'I don't want to know my future,' Ruby said.

'And that's fine, darling – that's absolutely fine!' said Green Grace.

'No,' said Silver Grace. 'It isn't.'

'Why can't things carry on as they are?' asked Ruby.

Green Grace felt uncomfortable, because Ruby's discomfort with the future had already caused problems. She hadn't wished to know when Barbara died. So when Grace had encouraged her to go home, to spend her last night with her grandmother, Ruby had assumed Grace was giving her the brush-off.

'A relationship between equals isn't possible if one person has all the knowledge,' Silver Grace announced.

'I just can't cope with more bad news right now,' Ruby said.

'What if it were good news?' Green Grace asked suddenly.

Ruby smiled sadly, and pulled up one of the breakfast stools.

'Good news would be very welcome.'

Green Grace crouched before her. 'You live a long time. Like Bee did. For another fifty years.'

'All right.'

'We have two children. A girl and a boy, named Emily and Icarus.'

'Am I happy?'

'I think so. You make other people happy. You make me happy.'

'There's something else you should know,' Silver Grace interrupted.

'Please don't,' Green Grace said.

'About Bee,' Silver Grace said to Ruby. 'About why she died. And what *you* do next.'

'Get out,' Green Grace roared, fearful of what her older self was going to reveal.

Silver Grace held up her hands in defeat. She slung her bag back over her arm, and left.

'What are you going to tell me?' Ruby whispered. 'Is it really terrible?'

Grace didn't need to give her the whole story. Not the worst part; not what Ruby was going to do. She could leave Ruby out all together.

'Bee's death,' Grace said. 'It was Margaret's fault.'

49

Ruby

Though she spent two months trying, once Ruby knew how Bee died she couldn't get it out of her mind. Margaret's actions were a final insult to Bee after many years of contempt. Since Bee's death, nothing had changed for Margaret, she was still at the Conclave, treating people as cruelly as she'd treated Bee. The Toy Museum was where it happened and Ruby believed if she saw the scene she might understand how to make Margaret pay.

Ruby was relieved, when she visited, to be the only patron. It was better to be there in silence. Vacationers with cameras, or busloads of schoolchildren, might have overwhelmed her. She stared at the Roman dolls and wheeled horses without really seeing them. There was only one museum assistant in the hall. The minute he strayed from his post, Ruby would make for the basement stairs. Until then she pretended to browse. Just when she was beginning to worry no opportunity would arise, a phone rang in the distance. The assistant smiled apologetically and rose from his seat, leaving the way clear.

Quickly Ruby made for the door. She took the little dark flight of stairs, glancing over her shoulder as she went, and the boiler room door was ajar when she arrived.

She flicked the light switch. The boiler room must contain some clue of how Margaret's mind worked. Grace had told Ruby that Margaret would die of bullets from the Candybox game. That must be significant. With every player that Margaret invited here, was she rehearsing the scene of her eventual death? Did coercing other people into violent acts lessen her sense of impotence?

I should pretend I'm Margaret, Ruby thought. *I can get into her head.*

She stood with her feet apart, and pretended to raise a gun. She shut one eye. The shelf of stock was in front of her. There, in the middle, was a Candybox. *The* Candybox.

At closer range Ruby could see the Candybox had aged badly. She lifted it off the shelf. The plastic had bubbled and cracked, and was rough to the touch. Tears dropped onto the toy and Ruby swiped the back of her hand across her eyes. This was the instrument of Bee's death.

Her own invention.

Ruby put the Candybox back on the shelf. An idea was beginning to form.

*

'This is going to be such a wonderful Christmas,' Grace said.

They were in Liberty's, looking at brown diamonds in the jewellery section. Most years Ruby was not an early Christmas shopper – they were barely into November – but Grace's enthusiasm was infectious. She would be the only Grace to spend Christmas with Ruby. The other Graces could spend Christmases with other Rubys, and *this* Grace was glad none of her silver selves would be around.

'I've made a decision,' Ruby said.

'Ooooh! And I don't have the first idea what it is. I *love* it when that happens!'

'I'm going to apply for a job at the Conclave. I'd be a good candidate for their Psychological Services department.'

Grace gaped.

'Honey, no,' she said.

'Won't my application be successful?' Ruby asked.

'I haven't the first idea. I don't understand why you'd *want* to work for the Conclave. After everything you know about them!'

Ruby didn't want to work for the Conclave; she wanted to retrace Bee's steps. She would ask Margaret for a job and, presumably, be put through the same ordeal as Bee. Except this time, Margaret would get her comeuppance. Ruby resisted telling Grace this. Grace's reaction suggested she would dissuade Ruby, or try to.

'*You* know how bad the Conclave is, and you still work there,' Ruby pointed out.

'That's different. I was embroiled before I knew how bad it was going to get, and then it was too late to extricate myself.'

'Wouldn't life be easier if we could both move through time?'

'Oh, sweetheart. I understand why you'd think so but I don't want that for you. Being at Margaret's beck and call, my God. Spare yourself. Now, look at that beauty of a necklace – it would look perfect on you.'

'How could you not know this conversation was coming?' Ruby asked.

'Maybe none of the silver Graces thought it was very significant.'

'Or you're lying.'

'*That's* quite an accusation.'

'You might want me to think there's no point applying.'

'This is ridiculous. First I'm the villain for giving you information from the future. Then I'm the villain for lying about it. I can't win. You're impossible.'

'Jesus fucking Christ!' Several heads turned. Ruby lowered her voice. '*I'm* not impossible. *We* are. Us. You have all the power. I can't check you're telling the truth, I don't get to pick which parts you tell me, and I'm never going to be the one telling *you* about *your* future. We can't be on a level footing. I'm fucking done.'

'No such luck,' Grace scoffed. 'I'm stuck with you.'

Ruby wailed. Grace had proved Ruby's point, using foreknowledge as the opportunity for a barb.

'I can't see you right now,' Ruby said. 'I just – need to be by myself.'

*

But she didn't want to be by herself. She wanted to be with someone who knew nothing about her future; who knew hardly anything about her at all. So she went to the brain injury unit, for the first time since the summer, and sat on the front wall for an hour, and caught Ginger on her way out. Ginger's mac was uncharacteristically shapeless. The folds of her dress hung oddly. She placed a self-conscious hand on her middle.

'I can see why you've not been in touch,' Ruby said, taking stock of the bump.

'Weren't you busy too?' Ginger's tone was sardonic, which surprised Ruby. They didn't normally criticise each other for unexplained absences.

'It's all been happening with me.' Ruby slid her hands into her pockets. 'Love, death. Not birth, though.'

'Love? So what was the attraction of this person you're in love with? Fewer vices than me? Prettier?'

Of all the ways Ruby thought Ginger would react to her arrival, she hadn't anticipated jealousy.

'She's not prettier than you,' Ruby said. 'And she probably drinks as much – though she's more interested in mother's ruin than the grape.'

'So that's your type. Decorative alcoholics.'

'Don't forget intelligent. I outdid myself this time. She's a genius.'

'It was *brains* you were interested in? I really played things the wrong way.'

Ruby hesitated. She thought of the barman, in Birmingham, that she'd seen Grace flirting with, and said: 'You're both bi.'

'I'm not bi.' Ginger's tone wasn't defensive; it was resigned.

'OK. Whatever.'

Ginger waited for some colleagues to walk past, then said, 'How can it be love with her, if you're here with me now? I missed you. I kept thinking of contacting you but… things seem a lot more complicated than they did.'

'Only as complicated as we make them. Come home with me.'

'Ruby… I don't know…'

'I'm not asking more than an hour or two. You can say a client overran.'

'You know how to make a girl feel special,' Ginger said in that sardonic tone again.

'Since when do you want romance?'

'Yes, you're right. That's not what this is.' Ginger sighed. 'Let's go.'

They weren't even halfway there before Ruby started having doubts. The train took her further and further from Grace, who might still be standing at the counter in Liberty's for all Ruby knew, and as her anger at Grace dissipated, she realised she had said, out loud, that she thought she was in love with Grace for the first time, and it was to the wrong person. She pushed the doubts aside and slept with Ginger anyway. That path, Ruby told herself, had already been set. There wasn't any turning back now.

50

Odette

In the Environmental Health department, Odette had access to a variety of public and ordinarily private records. The ones that were of most interest to her were inquest reports, and medical records, for the years 2017 to 2018. For that period she was able to identify several cases of macromonas. Several residents had died at an old people's home in Nottingham. A nurse had died at a hospital in Oldham. Barbara Hereford, the mad time traveller, had died of a deep infected scratch – which seemed likely evidence of a hygiene breach, as she might plausibly have had contact with a Conclave employee carrying the germ. But for now there was only one report among the documentation that Odette wished to follow up: the unnamed woman at the museum, with macromonas in her blood. The pretext of investigating hygiene breaches meant Odette could justifiably contact the police, and request the museum case evidence. It arrived on a wooden palette, in stacks of inauspicious boxes. She spent several days unpacking and examining their contents.

When she thought back, Odette could vividly recall hard, white fragments that had crunched under her feet on the day she found the body. She'd assumed they were shattered pieces of bone. In fact they were plastic, and had been bagged as evidence. The police had concluded they were probably ricochet debris, formed from the museum's toy stock – some of which was stored on the cellar shelves.

She took the pieces to the Conclave's digital archaeologist, Teddy Avedon, because he had software to reconstruct broken objects. Teddy was in his late twenties, and Odette quickly learned they had studied the same degree at Cambridge; for a few minutes they exchanged news of mutual acquaintances, before moving on to the matter of plastic ricochet debris.

'Reassembling the parts should be straightforward,' Teddy told her. 'For an object of this weight... with this many pieces... we can get a good reconstruction.'

The broken parts were placed on a concrete plate in the centre of an empty room. A thin line of green light moved back and forth over the pieces, as Teddy's equipment collected data about the shape of each section. Odette watched the pieces jostle round each other, as they were moved, remotely, by signals from the computer. Even the tiniest shards slotted into place, creating a three-dimensional jigsaw from the bottom up. When the reassembly was complete a cuboid, made from yellowing, cracked plastic, with a hole in the top, sat on the concrete plate.

'What do you know,' Teddy said. 'A Conjuror's Candybox. Did you have one when you were a kid?'

'We didn't play with those where I grew up. They're for party tricks, yes?'

'Yes. You pretend you're a wizard, you can make objects disappear and reappear. But really the object's travelling through time.'

'Send it to ballistics,' Odette said. 'I want to document what happens if you fire a bullet into a time machine.'

Teddy laughed. 'Are you talking about Candybox roulette?'

'What's that?'

Teddy grinned ingratiatingly. 'Let me explain.'

*

The ballistics specialist scheduled the tests for the following morning. In the meantime, Odette convinced Elspeth they could travel back to January 2018 and set up surveillance cameras at the museum, to check if the dead woman was a known time traveller. They took a small Technical Operations team, who parked a battered van opposite the museum, where they could capture images of anyone who came in or out the main gate or fire doors. This felt very low tech, compared to Teddy's wizardry, but it would satisfy Odette's requirements without drawing attention from the public.

Everyone got out in silence. Approaching the building again perturbed Odette, taking her back to the day she found the body.

Then is not now, she thought. Ruby had taught her anchoring techniques when she felt the first signs of panic. She looked for differences from the last time she had walked here, on that January morning. *It is now night, not morning. I am with colleagues. I am here to solve a mystery. I am here to solve a mystery. I am here to rebuild a world, not watch one crack open.*

Odette soothed herself with these refrains while they walked through the lobby and the exhibition hall and down the stairs. Did the others notice her disquiet? Maybe not the Tech Ops team, who went ahead into the boiler room, but Elspeth was watching Odette closely. Odette raised her chin, feigning composure.

The room was lit by a fluorescent light. That helped; the illumination showed her a plain room, just a room, not the dark cavern of blood and decay she'd dreamed of. Only the sound of the boiler threatened to drag her back in time. The rumble and click of its innards was the same.

She walked round the room while the team set up their cameras. What details would be important to the case? The shelves were lined with boxes of games and playthings – she couldn't have seen that before, in the dark, when the room was dim and her lungs were full of foul air.

Mid shelf, at eye level, one particular toy arrested her. It was made from yellowing plastic, and was cracked with age, though it didn't have the deep fractures Odette saw after its reconstruction.

As soon as the surveillance equipment was installed everyone returned to the van to await the victim's arrival. On a small monitor images of the empty basement strobed in the blacks and neon greens of night vision footage. They'd had to turn the lights back off.

The waiting was dull. They played word games, and because Odette was still a wench, the others teased her. They relayed future celebrity scandals, interspersed with lies, and invited her to guess which were true.

'I don't read celebrity scandals in my own time,' Odette complained, but the others enjoyed themselves, and they were laughing at her when the Surveillance Officer interrupted:

'Look! Look over there! For fuck's sake!'

The leader of the Conclave was walking down the street.

'It's *Margaret Norton*,' the Surveillance Officer said.

They all watched Margaret under the moonlight. Shining court shoes, a wide-lapelled coat and smoothly set hair. A sensible yet expensive-looking handbag.

Shouldn't we try to stop her? Odette thought. *She's walking to her death. We should intervene.*

When Margaret reached the door, she turned around on the step, and took a last look at the winter night. Her final night. Cold, bright, with the heavens curved over them like a glass bowl.

Odette reached for the handle of the door, but the Tech Ops manager gripped her coat.

'Remember your training. You can't stop Margaret dying,' he said.

'I have to try.' Odette couldn't stand by and watch someone die. She opened the door, just as Margaret disappeared into the museum. Odette broke into a run.

'Margaret!' she called. 'Stop! Margaret!'

A hand clamped Odette's mouth from behind and an arm encircled her waist.

'You could get us all executed,' the Tech Ops Manager whispered in her ear. 'If anyone saw you it would be an embargo breach.'

He carried her back to the van. After he released her she lay back, breathless, on the floor.

'You need to keep your fucking trap shut,' he said.

'Enough,' Elspeth told him. She looked at Odette then – not with disapproval, Odette noticed, but with interest – and said, 'We need to watch what happens next.'

The surveillance team watched their small monitor as Margaret entered the basement. Their night vision cameras captured four alternating views of the room. They would observe her death from every angle.

Margaret had slid the bolt across the basement door, and taken her gun from her bag. She stood motionless, with one side of her body pressed against the door.

'What's she doing?' Odette asked.

'Listening for anyone following her,' the Techs Op manager said. 'I wonder why, Odette.'

'Hush,' Elspeth said.

Suddenly, Margaret rattled at the bolt. The Candybox spat out half a dozen bullets. Her body jerked and crumpled with the impact. The Candybox smoked for a few seconds, then a final bullet flew from its mouth. The bullet caught the rim of the hole, shattering the box.

'That's weird. Why did she go there? Who turned the Candybox on?' Odette asked.

'Dunno,' the Tech Ops manager said. 'But we know one thing. She didn't switch on the machine, or fire her gun into it.'

'The bullets must have come from a previous player,' Odette surmised.

The team watched the body onscreen, in silence. They'd identified the victim. Now they had to find the murderer.

51

November 2017

Grace

Grace was in her forties – she wasn't quite sure where in her forties – when she sent Barbara the origami rabbit. She was prompted by a visit to one of the oldest Lucilles, who in late 2017 was dying of a brain tumour in a palliative unit.

Lucille had lost the use of her legs but her cognition was unimpaired by the tumour. She and Grace played gin rummy while they talked.

'Not one of my greens has visited,' Lucille commented.

Grace slid a five of hearts into the discard pile. She sympathised with Lucille's younger selves. Time travellers could avoid grief with ease – it's why they were so blasé with uncarved mourners – but they tended to be abnormally anxious about their own deaths. Every other dead person was reachable by time machine, which made one's own death uniquely final and lonely.

But to say this seemed less than tactful. Instead, Grace said:

'The other Lucilles probably think they're being kind.'

'Kind how?'

'You might get upset, if you saw yourself how you were. In good health, everything ahead of you.'

'Poppycock.' Lucille picked up a card. 'They're terrified. I know from the inside – I remember well enough. I'm sure they tell *you* it's kinder to leave me alone.'

'Hm. Maybe.'

'Do you know what that excuse reminds me of?'

'No.' Grace discarded again, and laid out her melds.

'Barbara. D'you remember how we said it was kinder to leave her alone?'

'I do.'

'Did you believe it at the time?'

'I believe it now.'

'I suppose it might have been true, but that wasn't why I stayed away from her. I felt *guilty*. Getting into that time machine fucked her head up, and we were all to blame.'

'Bee would have been manic depressive whatever her job was. Angharad says so. Time travelling was a trigger but an air hostess would have the same problems. Are you going to show your melds, or what?'

Lucille did, and laid off a king of diamonds. 'That's gin. Angharad doesn't know everything. We should have taken better safety precautions – we shouldn't have sent the other workers away, we should have spaced out our missions, and we shouldn't have rushed to the BBC. At least if we hadn't been live on television Barbara's breakdown would have stayed private. If I'd visited her afterwards I'd have to face my guilt. Much easier to say she was better off without us.'

Grace gathered the cards and shuffled them.

'How's Ruby?' Lucille asked.

'She's great,' Grace said. 'Unless – hang on – where in the year are we?'

Lucille squinted at the calendar clock hanging on the wall. 'November.'

'Ah, then she's not great, I don't think. She's busy plotting her revenge on Margaret.'

'Geez, somebody has to. I wish Margaret wasn't coming to my funeral.'

'Don't invite her if you don't want her,' said Grace.

'She comes regardless. Might attract public attention if she snubs her old colleague. But she gets nothing in the will. Speaking of which...' Lucille removed the ring from her wedding finger. 'This once cost me and George a month's salary. You might as well take it now. I know you won't get another chance to come over before I kick the bucket.'

'Lucille. You're such a sweetheart.' Grace kissed her friend on the cheek.

'Don't pretend you're sad. You'll keep seeing me anyway.' Lucille laughed, but her eyes were wet. 'Go see your silver selves, Grace. It's terribly lonely, dying.'

'I've already made arrangements for my death. I won't be on my own. Do you want to play another round?'

'Go on then. God, I'd kill for a cigar. With a nice single malt! I wish you'd smuggled some in.'

*

Grace went back to the Conclave, where she placed a call on Beeline to her secretary. She wanted inquest announcements from Southwark Coroner's Court, for the month of February 2018.

As she'd told Lucille, Grace didn't worry about her silver selves. Instead she was newly sorry for Bee. Lucille's confession had sparked some recognition in Grace. She, too, had professed to acting in Bee's interests by staying away from her old friend. There was nothing Grace could do to change that. But if Bee was anything like Lucille – if she was anything like Grace herself – she would be frightened of dying. Grace could do something about that. Now she knew why she sent the dates of their deaths – in August 2017, the last weeks of Bee's life. Grace wanted to tell Bee that she wasn't alone. Death wasn't uniquely final to her. It was coming for them all.

Grace collected the inquest announcements from the mailroom, and threw away the irrelevant ones. Neither Grace nor Lucille's deaths were embargoed, but Margaret's was. That meant the messages would have to be anonymous. There, between the mail sacks and pigeonholes, she creased and folded her sheet of paper until the rabbit was complete. All it needed was Barbara's name.

52

November 2017

Ruby

Ruby didn't apply for a job at the Conclave. Grace's reaction implied Ruby would fail, and that shook her confidence. But she didn't abandon her plan to confront Margaret. She considered her options for a week. What could she offer Margaret, in exchange for an audience? Ruby laughed when she realised. Margaret had already suggested the perfect bargaining chip. It placed Ruby at risk of arrest, but she no longer cared.

She made the phone call from her flat, with a glass of red in her hand. It was only half ten in the morning but she needed to steady her nerves.

'I'm afraid you can't speak to her now,' Margaret's secretary said. 'Her telephone calls are diarised some time in advance.'

'It's about Barbara Hereford's legacy. She specifically asked me to call if I had information.'

'One moment please.'

A few bars of muzak played.

'Dr Rebello,' Margaret said. 'Did you find something in Barbara's will after all?'

'Not exactly. But you were right about the stolen atroposium. She was using it for experiments.'

'I see. How much are we talking here?'

What had Bee said? A single brick was worth about five hundred thousand pounds. Which was a life-changing sum of money to Ruby, but probably peanuts to the Conclave. A little bit of embellishment would be required, if Ruby was to have any bartering power.

'We have a suitcase of it. About fifty bricks, I'd say.'

'Very well. Thank you for alerting us. You can make arrangements with my secretary for its safe return.'

'Not so fast. I want something in exchange.'

Margaret laughed. 'My dear, we're talking about stolen property. If you don't want to return it to its rightful owner, we can call the police.'

'I think we can make things more interesting than that.' Ruby sipped her wine. 'I want to play the Candybox game. If I lose you take the fuel.'

'What's the Candybox game?' Margaret asked.

She didn't want Ruby to play, that much was clear. Somehow Ruby must be different from the players Margaret usually picked. They must be more eager for Margaret's approval. Or maybe they were more susceptible to Margaret's intimidation. Perhaps Margaret preferred players who were too scared to shoot. She enjoyed their humiliation.

What could Ruby do – other than show vulnerability, which she refused to do – to make Margaret play?

She could attack Margaret's vanity.

'Are you too frightened to play with me?' Ruby asked.

'The very idea,' Margaret said. 'You're really not like Barbara, are you? You're not like her at all.'

'Are you going to play or not?'

A long pause followed. 'All right. Do you know the venue?'

'Yes. I'll see you there at eight.'

'Seven. I won't spend my whole evening waiting for you.'

'Nor I for you.'

Ruby hung up. She didn't have fifty bricks of atroposium, of course. But she wasn't intending to lose the game.

53

Odette

The firearms examiner had been shooting into the Candybox, as Odette requested.

'We've fired a hundred bullets, over the course of an hour,' said the examiner. 'The Candybox used an atroposium briquette, size B12. Eighty bullets rebounded immediately. The other twenty successfully dematerialised. None of them have rematerialised yet – we're keeping the Candybox in an isolation room to manage the bullet discharge safely. The bullets will rematerialise after forty-eight days, eight hours and ten minutes. We know because we've already received a call on Beeline to tell us.'

'That's fantastic,' Odette replied. By counting back from Margaret's death, they could work out when the fatal bullet was fired into the Candybox, and set up surveillance for that date. Forty-eight days before Margaret's death would be the nineteenth of November. 'I had an additional query, if that's OK. Does firing a gun sterilise the bullets?'

'Not necessarily, no. Obviously some germs may die off due to heat and deceleration but it's quite easy to transfer bacteria by firing a bullet. In fact, there's an entire field dedicated to bacteria ballistics.'

'And – I hope you don't mind a follow-up question – if there were bacteria on a bullet, just ordinary everyday bacteria, and the bullet was fired into a Candybox – would the radiation encourage an overgrowth of macromonas?'

'That's certainly a possibility.'

It stood to reason that playing Candybox roulette would be associated with macromonas outbreaks. If you liked playing high risk games fuelled with atroposium, you probably didn't implement hygiene protocols. Odette returned to the other macromonas cases she'd unearthed in case they included Margaret's fellow roulette players. Of the people who died, Barbara Hereford seemed the most likely participant, because she knew Margaret. But she couldn't be Margaret's murderer; she died in August, well before 19 November.

None of the other macromonas deaths matched names on the Conclave's staff lists – but perhaps they'd had contact with a time traveller who was carrying the bug. In an attempt to identify vectors for the infection, Odette requested a list of residents and staff from the old people's home. She also requested patient and staff lists from the hospital, in the week of the nurse's death. Finally she cross-referenced the lists with the Conclave's own staff lists, and yielded two historical hits. The first was Veronica Collins, a resident at the old people's home who had joined the Conclave as an interpreter in 1982. The second was Julie Parris, a hospital patient who had commenced work as an environmental conservationist in 1993. Both women had resigned in the past twelve months. Odette telephoned each of them. She said she had some questions about hygiene breaches, and would like to interview them as soon as possible.

*

Veronica Collins came to the Conclave that very morning. She was a bright-eyed woman with a dowager's hump, her face lightly liver-spotted. No one would imagine her as a gun fiend. Odette eschewed the interview rooms for their conversation. They went instead to the gardens, as Odette believed Veronica might open up more in relaxed surroundings. They scattered seed for the birds.

'It's a while since I took a trip without the other residents. The activities there run like clockwork. Normally we play golf on a Thursday. The nurses hire a coach to the course.'

Odette apologised for keeping Veronica away from her game.

'I don't mind. Glad to break up the routine, actually. It's always good to have new ears for my old tales.' Veronica replaced the cap on the tube of millet. For a while she talked about the kind of assignments they'd given her at the Conclave, before Odette steered her towards the topic of Margaret. Had they got on? Odette asked.

'Up to a point.' Veronica gave a short, sardonic laugh. 'The thing about Margaret was – if you were in her group, she was clannish. She never let you forget that time travellers were different from everyone else. We were special. But we also were terrified of not being special any more. The prospect of readjusting to normal life, if you have to quit time travel, is really daunting. It made us put up with extraordinary things.'

'What kind of things?'

'You know. Encouraging people to carve themselves up in those time machines? Did you go along with that? No? I wish I hadn't. The weird pranks and assaults. And that thing where she shows you a little cache of your relatives in the morgue? Seeing those pictures really did a number on me. Is it any wonder I got totally neurotic about bad things happening to my family? But I was so desperate to be a time traveller I took the initiation stuff as the price of admission. And what's really unpleasant is that those rituals do bond you together, once you've been through them. The suffering becomes something you've all shared, and that makes it harder to leave. For years I didn't have the strength to quit.'

'Was there a particular incident that prompted you to resign?'

'Hmm? No... I wouldn't say that, not at all. When I was young I said I'd never leave. But I realised gradually I had to go.'

'The thing is, Veronica,' Odette said slowly, 'we've been tracing hygiene breaches back to games of Candybox roulette.'

Veronica dropped the tube of millet.

'That wasn't me!' She put her hand on her chest. 'I never fired – I never...'

'Fired what, Veronica?'

'The gun – during Candybox roulette.'

'Tell me about Candybox roulette.'

'It was one of Margaret's sick games. Games – oh, for years she made me play games – she said I couldn't stay at the Conclave if I didn't let her recondition me to stop fearing death. It wasn't shooting to begin with – that was at the very end. And it was the final straw for me. I'd endured it for years but that Candybox roulette game was the worst.'

'Did you fire the gun into the Candybox, Veronica?'

'No! No, you must believe me. Margaret fired, and the bullet rebounded. She made me pick it up and swallow it. But I never fired the gun myself.'

Odette sensed she was lying – from fear, or perhaps

shame. She needed to check whether Veronica was alibied for the day in question.

'When did you play this game?'

'I didn't fire, you must believe that. We played the game last year. August, it must have been.'

'You're sure about the date? It wasn't November?'

'November?' Veronica looked blank. 'No. I was in Canada that month, with my niece.'

'Send me the details of your ticket payments and your niece's contact details.'

'All right. All right. May I go now?'

'In a moment. Can you think of anyone with a motive to harm Margaret?'

'Deliberately, you mean? Of the colleagues I remember... no one would have been open about hating her that much. We presented a unified front. She was one of us. And to set out purposely to kill her... well... what would be the point? The satisfaction would be so fleeting. After all, you'd need to take a trip into the past at some point, and there she'd be, issuing her edicts.' Veronica picked up the fallen vial of millet. 'I suppose you'd take solace in knowing what was coming for her. I suppose that could buoy you through the difficult days.'

'Thank you, Veronica,' Odette said. 'You've been very helpful. I'll see you out.'

*

Julie Parris arrived a couple of hours later. They went to the Conclave canteen. Odette was immediately aware of Julie's thinness. The loose silk blouse concealed Julie's size, but her wrists and neck were fragile, and her skin looked tissue-thin

– as though she were made from origami. Her hair was folded into a pleat and her nails were beautifully manicured. She wore a delicate gold crucifix at her neck.

Odette began by asking why Julie resigned.

'I'd wanted to leave for years. I've had mental health problems for a long time, and you know what the Conclave's like about that.'

Odette nodded.

'The first thing I did when I left was check into a clinic for eating disorders.' Julie sipped from a glass of water. 'Do you know what I learnt? I found this very interesting. Lots of the girls there were self-harmers as well as anorexics – scratching themselves, razoring their arms, you know the kind of thing – and the psychiatrists told us that one of the reasons why people cut for stress relief is that blood-letting lowers your blood pressure. It's a simple physiological response. You quickly feel a sense of tranquillity. It made me think of the Conclave, on the day the time machines malfunctioned – we queued up to hurt ourselves and came out dripping with blood but I felt so calm the second my skin broke.'

'Was Margaret aware of your mental health problems?' Odette asked.

'Oh yes. And she was vicious the day she found out.' Julie tapped the side of her glass. 'As if I'd personally affronted her.'

'Why would she take your illness personally?'

'I've thought about it a lot. And I've wondered if she saw something of herself in me. Because she had problems, too, you know. Don't you think it's weird how she quit using time machines? I think it's because she's a control freak, and time travelling makes you realise how little control you have. Nothing ever changes the past, or the future. I bet she was going crazy inside, just like I was.'

'When did you last see her?'

Julie shifted in her chair.

'When I resigned, last year.'

'She didn't contact you afterwards?'

'No.' Her fingers interlocked round the water glass, whitening her knuckles. 'What does this have to do with hygiene?'

'There was a breach on November the nineteenth, 2017, and we need to know your whereabouts for that date.'

'I was in *hospital*,' Julie said rapidly. 'The Royal Oldham. I'd hurt myself again. That's all you're going to get.'

'At no point did you leave the hospital? No stepping outside for a breath of fresh air, perhaps?'

'No.'

'Very well. I'll verify with the Royal Oldham that you remained onsite for the full day.'

Julie stood up and slipped her jacket back on. Her elbows were set square sharp as she fastened the buttons.

'Do you miss it?' Odette asked. 'Time travelling?'

'The Conclave made me ill.' Julie looked into the middle distance, letting her arms fall to the sides. 'To miss it I'd have to really hate myself.'

When she'd gone Odette contacted the hospital again, to verify Julie's whereabouts. She also asked why Julie had been hospitalised. The reason supplied was a gunshot wound.

54

Angharad

Angharad sat next to Julie's bed, swilling coffee from the vending machine. A television in the corner showed rolling news. The sound was high enough to be distracting but too low to make out the words. Julie was yet to come round. She'd had surgery to repair a gunshot wound in her shoulder. The doctor said Julie had been shot during a mugging. Around the fifth time that Angharad had watched refugees climbing under a razor wire fence, Julie stirred.

'Mum?' she said.

'I'm here.'

'Here?'

'The hospital. You've been all patched up.'

'Oh... oh. I remember. The gun.'

'You don't need to think about that now, sweetheart.'

'Where's Margaret?'

'You're not at work, sweetie. This is the hospital.'

'You don't understand. Margaret brought me here. She saw me get hurt.'

Angharad stroked her daughter's head. 'Don't try to talk. You need rest.'

'We were playing a game.' Julie closed her eyes. 'A secret game.'

Why would they be doing such a thing? Playing shooting games with Margaret had to be an anaesthesia dream, didn't it? Angharad watched Julie sleep for a while. She gave up on the cold coffee dregs and went in search of the nurse who'd checked Julie's vital signs. She was in the corridor, a sombre woman with a Spanish accent.

'She's disorientated,' Angharad said.

'That's to be expected,' said the nurse. 'We've treated her for infection but she still has a fever. Give her some time to come round properly.'

'Were you on duty when she was admitted?'

'No. Why?'

'I just wondered if she was alone when she was arrived.'

'I don't know. I'm sorry.' The nurse opened the door to another patient's room, and Angharad returned to Julie's side.

*

By the next morning, Julie was lucid.

'How did you get to the hospital?' Angharad asked. 'Whoever helped you, I'd love to thank them.'

'I don't know.' Julie smoothed the creases out of her bedsheet.

'Yesterday you said Margaret brought you here.'

'That's not true,' Julie said, quickly. 'Why would Margaret be with me?'

'That's what I wondered. You said you were playing... secret... games.'

'How silly.' Julie laughed, then her shoulders began to shake, and Angharad realised the laughter had turned to weeping. Angharad leapt up. She put her arms around Julie and felt, with dismay, how slight her daughter was beneath the gown.

'You can't tell anyone this,' Julie whispered. 'But Margaret did bring me to the hospital. She said we were going to tell everyone I'd been attacked – by a mugger. No one could know what we were really doing.'

'Which was?'

'Playing Candybox roulette. Do you know what that is?'

Angharad did. She'd taken it for an urban myth; an artefact of Conclave gossip, rather than a real game. 'Why would Margaret play that with you?'

Julie gave a juddering sigh. 'This was the first time we'd played roulette, but there have been other games. So many – for years. It was because I told her I couldn't cope with time travelling. With seeing what comes *after* me. I told her... that time travelling made me feel like a ghost. And she said the games would blunt my feelings about death. But this time, the game went too far.'

Angharad's stomach lurched. A memory returned to her, from decades before: *not brutalising, but hazing*. Margaret hadn't stopped at the initiation rites to toughen wenches – rites that Angharad had encouraged. But Angharad never anticipated her daughter would be among the worst affected. 'Why would you keep this secret?'

'Margaret said that was the only way to stay at the Conclave. I can't leave.'

'You can leave, Julie. You *must*.'

The crying intensified. 'I didn't before... because...'

'Yes?'

'I didn't want to disappoint you.'

'You could never do that,' Angharad whispered. She kept

her guilt to herself – that it was her fault Julie had been subjected to years of damage, and lay in this bed now.

Over Julie's shoulder, through the internal window, Angharad could see one of her silver selves in the corridor. Not much more silver. At Angharad's age, there weren't many silver selves left.

'I'm going to fetch you some water.' Angharad pulled back from Julie, and stroked her cheek.

'Don't leave me for too long,' Julie said.

'You won't even miss me.'

The silver Angharad had disappeared, but only into the waiting room.

'What are you doing here?' Angharad asked. 'It's not bad news, is it?'

'No,' her silver self said. 'Not for us, anyway.'

'Then for *who*?'

'Keep your voice down. Do you want Julie to hear you get overexcited? I've brought you a genie.'

'What kind of genie?'

'Information. I'm going to tell you what you need to pay Margaret back.'

'Pay back?' Angharad swallowed. 'Are you saying I should *hurt* her?'

'Yes. Because of how she's treated Julie,' her silver self said calmly. 'You've let Julie down dreadfully. Revenge is the only way to atone.'

55

Ruby

Ruby was hyperalert when she arrived in the museum's boiler room. She was wearing her motorbike leathers. The visor of her helmet functioned as a mask. It made her anonymous, and that freed her of her conscience.

Margaret was already waiting for her.

'You take a turn first,' Ruby said.

Without saying a word, Margaret pointed her pistol at the Candybox, fired with precision, and stepped neatly to the side before the bullet ricocheted from the machine.

She handed the pistol to Ruby. The trigger guard was a tight fit, due to Ruby's gloves.

'Have all your bullets ricocheted?' Ruby asked.

'Yes,' Margaret replied.

'What about the other players? Did their bullets bounce back too?'

'Only Julie Parris attempted it. Barbara was like the others – she refused to even try. Whose footsteps will you follow in?'

'I'll shoot. Don't you worry.'

'What are you waiting for?'

'I'd like to give my professional opinion of you.'

'Really? I think that might be the most flattering stalling tactic I've ever heard. Do go on.'

'You're narcissistic. You empathise with people only to further your own ends, you charm people as long as you receive admiration in exchange, and you feel shame, but not guilt. You think you're entitled to people's compliance. You try to enliven your loveless world by inflicting pain on others and sensation-seeking with games like Candybox roulette. The Conclave is dysfunctional because anyone who doesn't fulfil your narcissistic needs is eliminated, or self-selects out. You've made the whole organisation narcissistic. Convinced of its specialness and distinction from everyday people, obsessed with novel and high risk activities, and blunting its members' empathy from the first day of their employment.'

'You're boring me. Shoot, or give me the atroposium.'

Without taking her eyes from Margaret, Ruby shot all the remaining bullets at the Candybox. Fate would dictate if she hit her target. She didn't see if she'd succeeded. She saw Margaret's reaction and knew the bullets had dematerialised.

The director of the Conclave tottered, taken aback by Ruby's success. For the first time Ruby saw Margaret's frailty. Ruby knew something that Margaret did not: Margaret had just edged closer to death.

That was when Ruby felt ashamed. She'd repaid Margaret for past cruelties. But the victory didn't assuage her grief for Bee. It just lost Ruby her moral ground.

She threw the gun at Margaret's feet and ran from the basement, out of the museum and into the night. The bike was waiting for her on the road. The emptiness of the streets was a blessing, because she wove at too high a speed. Perspiration condensed on her visor. By the time she hit traffic she thought she'd regained self-control, then she had to stop to vomit in the gutter. Her stomach heaved long after she was hollow. She wanted someone to tell her everything would be all right. Only one person could do that. Grace, with her secrets from the future; Grace, who Ruby had discarded.

56

Odette

Odette was working at her desk when Tech Ops rang.
    'Good news,' said the Tech Ops manager.

'Go on,' Odette said.

'We have the images from November the nineteenth. Margaret was definitely playing Candybox roulette that night, and she wasn't alone.'

'Who was she with?'

'Looks like a woman, but she's in full motorbike leathers, and she never takes off her helmet.'

'If she came by motorbike, get the number plate.'

'We did. The bike belongs to a Ruby Rebello.'

Odette stood up. Her stomach lurched. The name was a shock. Why would Dr Rebello be playing Candybox roulette? She wasn't a time traveller, like Barbara Hereford, or Veronica, or Julie.

'I'll bring her in,' Odette said, and hung up.

She contemplated walking out of the Conclave. She'd come to solve a mystery, and she had: she knew who the dead woman was, and who killed her. But if Odette waited, just a little longer, she might hear Dr Rebello's own explanation; and Odette realised she wanted this very much.

Her thoughts went back to the day she'd found the body: how Dr Rebello had been waiting to give Odette the therapy card. At the time Odette assumed the police must have alerted Dr Rebello she was in need of victim support. But now she guessed Dr Rebello had come of her own accord, trying to keep tabs on the case.

Yes; Odette wanted to wait for Dr Rebello's explanation.

It was Elspeth who lent greater urgency to proceedings. Odette had just finished a telephone call, arranging for Ruby to be picked up, when the Beeline receiver on her desk started ringing. She hadn't known it ring before, and stared at it momentarily before lifting the handset.

'Hello?' she asked hesitantly.

'Odette? It's Elspeth.'

Through the office door, Odette could see her boss was talking to a colleague.

'Which Elspeth?' Odette asked.

'A day ahead of you. I wanted to say you have four hours until Dr Rebello's trial.'

'Why so fast?'

'The trial is usually scheduled this quickly, we don't have the administrative burden that the English courts do. But, Odette – this is important, you must listen – Dr Rebello will let slip you were her patient. Do you know what that means?'

The Conclave would demand Odette's resignation. Her lies at the time of her application would cost her the job. Odette would join all the other men and women the Conclave had discriminated against.

'Should I leave now?' Odette asked.

'Wait until Dr Rebello reveals you were her patient. You won't be escorted off the premises until the end of the trial

– once you've entered the courtroom no one can leave till the ordeal's over – but as soon as it's done you'll be out the door. So tie up any loose ends *now*.' Elspeth was breaking an embargo to help Odette leak information. Odette wondered whether she'd been an ally all along, or whether the investigation had persuaded Elspeth that the Conclave was rotten.

'Thank you,' Odette said. Her eyes fell on the case notes, splayed over her desk. Four hours was enough time to find a better home for them. First she needed to know whether the threats against Zach Callaghan and his family were ever acted upon in the future. She asked Elspeth if she could obtain any connected medical and police records in the coming decades, via Beeline.

'I'd do it myself, but I don't have the clearance to make outgoing transmissions. I'm not senior enough.'

'Well, I am,' Elspeth said. 'I can get that to you in seconds.'

*

Odette ran to the station. She caught the train, and then she ran to the college where Zach Callaghan worked. She checked the lecture theatre where they'd first met, but he wasn't there. Nor was he in any of the other theatres. There was a wall map on the second floor, which she deliberated over for some minutes. It was no help because it didn't mark any of the staff rooms or offices where he might be hiding – only the halls that she'd already searched.

It was important to see him in person. She didn't trust the receptionist to pass on the message he needed to hear. But she was running out of time.

She was heading back downstairs, contemplating the best way to get his home address, when she caught sight of him through the centre of the stairwell. He was on the ground floor, talking to a student.

'Mr Callaghan!' she called. He didn't hear her. He was turning to go.

She ran the rest of the way, just in time to see him leave by the main entrance. She followed him outside. He was opening his car door.

'Zach!'

He looked up, and waved in acknowledgement. She ran across the car park to meet him. All she wanted to do was lie down. She had to make do with leaning against the bonnet.

'Are you all right?' He touched her shoulder in concern.

'Sorry. Let me catch my breath.' She pulled at the collar of her shirt. She must look sweaty from her trek through London grime. That didn't matter, she thought, what mattered was what Elspeth had found in the records.

'Here...' He took a bottle of water from his car. She drank it gratefully.

'I have something to tell you,' she said. 'I know you said you'd given up on Conclave stories. This might tempt you back. I infiltrated the Conclave. And I got this.'

The transcripts and fingerprint report were in her bag. She handed them to him.

'What's this?' he asked.

'Enough material for several reports. I'll help in any way I can.'

He read the first few paragraphs of transcript, then skipped ahead, skimming the later pages. 'This is incredible, Odette.'

'I know!'

'But I can't write this story.' He held out the transcript. 'I told you why before.'

'You did,' she said. 'I haven't forgotten. When I was in the Conclave I could check your future – and your family's futures. You will cover this story. You need to, to call the Conclave to account. There won't be any retaliation. I can say that for certain.'

'I don't know what to say.' He looked at the transcript again. 'You've been brave, Odette.'

It felt so good to give away the case notes. Odette felt physically lighter. For nearly a year she'd thought of nothing but the body in the museum. Now, she might finally be ready to leave it behind.

'Have you thought of becoming a journalist?' Zach asked her.

'It's not the most stable career path,' she said. 'I don't think I have a future in it.'

He laughed. She saw he was lighter too, and she saw, as well, what her silver selves might like about him. Elspeth had unearthed some surprises in his documentation. The most notable was his marriage certificate, dated six years hence. Odette didn't really know Zach. She didn't know yet why anyone would want to marry him. But she was curious. He was, she realised, a new mystery to solve.

'If I were you I'd take a holiday,' he said. 'Better to be away from everything when the story breaks. You've earned it, anyway.'

'That's a good idea.'

They smiled at each other, neither speaking nor moving away. Until Odette remembered Ruby's trial and swore.

She darted from the car towards the road. If she hurried she could still make it back in time.

'Where are you going?' Zach called.

She ran backwards as she shouted her reply.

'My therapist's being tried for murder, and I have to be fired by the Conclave!'

'What?'

'I have to be somewhere! I'll call you!'

She waved, and he waved back.

57

Margaret

Margaret didn't expect Julie's gunshot wound to cause trouble. November ended, and so did December, without anyone challenging Margaret's version of events. So she rested easy. She didn't realise those two months were being used to plot against her. Not until the New Year.

She was reviewing the year ahead with her senior staff. When the meeting came to a close, all of her subordinates stood to leave – except for Angharad. And Margaret felt a flicker of premonition. Angharad wouldn't meet her eye. Margaret waited until the last departing time traveller had closed her office door, and she was alone with Angharad, before saying, 'Is there something you'd like to discuss with me? Only I'd rather you make a separate appointment—'

'Julie's wound's healing well.' Angharad sat with her hands clasped at the knee, her fingers white. Normally her movements were fluid – the muscle memory of a ballerina, even at her advanced age – but her pose today was rigid. 'Now that Julie's stronger, she intends to take you to court. To the Conclave court. She wants to tell them about Candybox roulette.'

So Julie had squealed, and intended to squeal some more. What a little fool. 'I see.'

'We've been friends a long time, you and I.' Angharad's fingers unlocked. She reached for Margaret's hand. 'With each other's help we can dissuade her.'

'Why would you do that?'

'If there were a trial, it would come out that you acted on my advice. Julie can never know I was involved. I couldn't bear it.'

'What do you suggest?'

'If you eliminate all the evidence, perhaps I can persuade Julie that she won't be believed.'

That would be for the best. And then Margaret would take her much delayed retirement. Disappear, in case Julie changed her mind, into some halcyon year of Margaret's choosing. She thought about the blank death certificate in her drawer: was it blank because she was missing, believed dead? To vanish, Margaret must liquidate her assets. At the first opportunity she would sell her property for achrons. She could covertly exchange them, for local currency, in her destination decade. But not before doing the necessary clean-up.

'The bullets in the wall,' Margaret mused. 'Blood in the basement.'

'And the Candybox,' Angharad said. 'You must go back for the Candybox, too.'

Margaret laughed. 'You don't have to worry about that my dear. I destroyed it.'

'Destroyed?'

'Smashed it into little pieces.' As soon as Bee's granddaughter scored a direct hit. Margaret didn't want anything flying out of the Candybox at a time she could no longer choose. She'd envisioned buying a new machine, before the next game.

'What did you do with the parts?' Angharad asked.

Margaret unlocked the bottom drawer in her desk – the drawer where she kept everything she didn't want to think about. She took out a jewellery box and placed it in Angharad's hands. Angharad looked Margaret in the eye, as though asking permission. Margaret nodded. The lid flipped up, revealing the mosaic pieces that had once been the Candybox.

'Let me take these,' Angharad said. 'I can destroy them properly. Obliterate them – in the Conclave lab. Then no one can say they ever existed.'

'Very well,' Margaret agreed. 'And I'll return to the scene of the crime.'

There was nothing to worry about, Margaret reasoned. Julie was no match for her. Even Julie's own mother wouldn't take her side.

58

Ruby

So Ruby rang the Conclave in the hope of speaking to Grace. She was told no Graces were there at present. In the weeks that followed Ruby continued to see clients and pretend nothing was wrong while quietly being eaten by guilt for firing the bullets that would kill Margaret. When the guilt got too much Ruby went to the nearest police station and confessed. She told them she'd played a shooting game with Margaret Norton and in a matter of weeks Margaret would die because of it. The duty officer brought her tea and arranged a psych consult. They contacted Dinah, as Ruby's next of kin. After that, Dinah telephoned daily to make sure Ruby was looking after herself. They argued about Ruby's laundry pile and the mouse infestation behind the skirting boards. On Christmas Eve they also argued about Ruby's refusal to go to Great-Aunt Jane's for Christmas dinner, because Ruby was determined to spend the day alone, drinking herself into a stupor while slumped in front of *Top of the Pops* and *Doctor Who*. Ruby had just hung up when the doorbell rang.

It was Grace, on the step with a round leather suitcase.

'What are you doing here?' Ruby asked.

Grace looked at her as if she were mad. 'I've come for Christmas. Like we arranged. You didn't forget?'

'I assumed it was off. Because of what happened in Liberty's.'

'Oh. That? Really? I suppose that's recent to you. Do you want me to leave?'

'No, actually.'

Inside, Grace was nearly as aghast at Ruby's Christmas preparations as Dinah.

'Not even a tree, Ruby! We must go out and buy one at once.'

'There won't be any left by now. I suppose everything does look drab,' said Ruby, and she promptly burst into tears.

'Dear heart!' Grace said. 'You needn't take on. I misspoke. It will be fun for the two of us to dress up the flat – much more fun than you doing it alone. And apart from the decorations everything's dandy. It smells divine in here – like time machines!'

'That's Bee's Candybox. It's still going. God knows how she got so much juice from one briquette.' Ruby sniffed. 'I'm not really upset about Christmas decorations.'

'Then why are you crying, lovely?'

'I killed Margaret Norton.'

'Is that all? I thought you might be sad from missing me.'

'It's not funny, Grace.'

'I know.'

'What do I do?'

'Do? There's nothing to do. Margaret invented a game that she knew could be fatal. What difference does it make? Every time I travel back in time she'll be still at work and on my back. I won't mourn her.'

'But I should repent—'

'There is no repenting. You just have live with yourself. And to live with me, too, when I'm in town.'

Ruby cried harder.

'What now?' Grace exclaimed.

'I thought I'd scared you away. I was so stupid. There's this woman I know. Her name's Ginger. And straight after we fought I—'

'Don't.' Grace put her finger to Ruby's lips. 'You need to keep some secrets. It will be better for us, if you know some things that I don't. Now. Do you have a saw?'

'In the toolkit, above the washing machine. Why?'

'There's a fir tree in the street that I could fit through the door. It'll look charming with some fairy lights.'

*

They woke, on Christmas morning, to a low beeping sound.

'Surely you didn't set an *alarm*?' Grace said.

'I think that's the Candybox,' Ruby mumbled. She pulled the pillow over her head.

'I'm going to investigate.' Grace tugged the pillow from Ruby's fingers. 'Who knows what's arrived from the past?'

'It could be dangerous,' Ruby said, suddenly alert. 'I'll come with you.'

'Oh-ho, now you're interested. Bags I if it's anything good.'

The Candybox was humming in the living room. Ruby and Grace approached hand in hand.

'I can't look,' Ruby said.

Grace craned her neck over the hole in the Candybox.

'It's a ring,' she said.

Lucille's ring. Ruby had dispatched it, months ago. And now it was here.

Grace retrieved it. The setting had contorted en route. Before it had been a conventional, if pretty, solitaire; now the stone sat in a curling, organic web of gold. The circumference had shrunk and the numbers engraved inside had gone. In their place were the words *A Ring of a Very Strange Shape*.

'I'm glad I staked first dibs.' Grace tried it on the middle finger of her right hand. 'Dash it. Too small.'

Ruby took it, and slid it onto Grace's left ring finger easily.

'It's an engagement ring,' Ruby said.

'Look at that. So it is.' Grace admired the diamond. 'It won't be an easy marriage. I might as well be on an oil rig, for all you'll see me.'

'That means we won't take each other for granted.'

'We'll have to spend so much time apart. For most of your life I'll be officially dead.'

'You're the most alive person I know. Oh! The ring should have our dates in it.'

'I like these words more.' Grace kissed Ruby. 'Not all time travel customs are good ones.'

59

OCTOBER 2018

Odette

As Ruby's crime involved time travel technology, she was to be tried by the Conclave rather than an English court. The accused was allowed legal representation – in this case, Fay Hayes. The Fay who turned up in Odette's office was relatively young, possibly because the case appeared to be straightforward and manageable for a less experienced lawyer. Odette assumed that their disagreement over the Angel of Death ritual was still fresh in Fay's memory, as her tone was slightly clipped.

'I'm heading up to the court now. Have you attended any other trials yet?' Fay asked.

Odette shook her head.

'Once you enter the courtroom you can't leave till the end of the trial. I want to take Ruby up there now so she has some time to adjust to the room and I can walk her through the process. At the moment it's empty and we will need privacy to discuss the case.'

'Good luck. We attempted to question her on arrival and she didn't respond. She wouldn't stop crying.'

'Yes – because you're not on her side. I am.'

But Odette's loyalties were not clear-cut. Ruby had

helped Odette cope with a trauma. A trauma that was ultimately the fault of Margaret Norton. While Odette thought Ruby should account for her actions, Margaret was almost certainly the bigger villain and everyone at the Conclave was complicit. Perhaps – if she could communicate that to Ruby – Odette might still get the answers she desperately needed.

'Take a message from me.' Odette thought back to their therapy sessions, and their careful reconstruction of her memories into a narrative she could live with. 'Tell her – the story almost makes sense to me now. But I haven't decided what the ending is.'

Fay departed. Ten minutes later, Odette received a telephone call from the courtroom.

'Dr Rebello says she'd like you to be here while we prepare,' Fay said. 'Just you, mind, not anybody else on the case. I counselled her that it was not in her interests for you to attend, but she was quite clear in her instructions.'

'I'll be there right away,' Odette said.

*

The Conclave courtroom was in the legal department. It resembled a theatre, with a proscenium arch dividing a raised platform from the gallery. On the platform was a great stone table, behind which was the room's sole window, a large pane of modernist stained glass. At the front of the platform was a stone bench, where Ruby and Fay were seated.

Odette took a seat in the dim gallery, so as not to disturb them unduly.

'As you're not a Conclave employee,' Fay was telling Ruby, 'I want to spend some time explaining the way we dispense justice. Fate will decide whether you're guilty or not in a *trial of ordeal*. Do you know what this phrase means?'

'Isn't that like ducking stools?' Ruby asked weakly.

'A similar kind of thing, yes.'

'What ordeal will they put me through?'

'The judge will receive a genie from her silver self, normally in the form of a scroll, which describes how you will be tested. Do you know what genies and silver selves are?'

'Yes. Won't anyone present any evidence?'

'No. If you fail the trial of ordeal, the judge will need to pass a sentence. That's when I come in. I need to present any mitigating factors you can give me. I know you pulled the trigger, but did you mean to murder Margaret Norton? Did you take part in the game freely?'

'N-no one forced me,' Ruby stuttered. 'I don't know whether I wanted to kill Margaret, not that exactly. I just wanted her to suffer.'

'Why?'

'She was responsible for the death of my grandmother, Barbara Hereford.'

Odette gasped. That was the link she had missed: Barbara Hereford had died before November, so Odette ruled her out as a suspect, but hadn't considered that Margaret's murderer might be motivated by Barbara's death.

'Blood revenge is a good mitigating factor,' Fay said. 'Just as long as we get a twenty-fourth century judge. Otherwise you're looking at a potential capital punishment.'

Ruby didn't react to this statement at all; maybe she believed she deserved what was coming to her. Odette tried to catch Ruby's eye, to get a sense of her feelings – and for the first time since Odette's entrance, Ruby seemed to register she was there.

'I let you down, Odette,' Ruby said, her face crumpling. 'I went back to the crime scene, the day you found the body, because I couldn't bear the guilt. Then I spoke to you because I was panicking. I wanted to find out exactly how much you knew, and what you'd relayed to the police. It was despicable to get that information by offering you therapy. I regret it every day.'

Fay's eyes widened in surprise at the mention of therapy. She looked from Odette, to Ruby, and back again. To change the subject, Odette said, 'It's nearly time for the trial to start. The judge is due any minute.'

Fay was still watching Odette, but said, 'Are you ready, Ruby?'

'Not quite. This trial by ordeal,' Ruby checked. 'Are the verdicts always accurate?'

'No,' Fay said bluntly. 'They are always *fated*. That might not seem very fair to you. But no system of justice is perfect.'

*

At the allotted hour, Elspeth arrived, then the court notary, then Judge Astrid Insch – who positioned herself at the stone table. The law permitted Ruby one additional moral supporter, who would be bound by the same secrecy as the rest of the court. Ruby had chosen Grace Taylor, who took a seat on the front row. Naturally the trial was otherwise closed to the public.

Odette watched the judge's silver self approach the table holding a scroll tied with magenta ribbon, then leave the court again.

Lifting a monocle to her eye, the judge read the unfurled scroll.

'Could the accused please stand,' she announced.

Ruby did as she was instructed.

'Your trial of ordeal is a test of memory. You will be asked three questions relating to *The Box of Delights* by John Masefield.'

'Yes!' Grace cried out. The judge stared at her with disapproval. Ruby hadn't moved. A hanky was balled in her right hand, and her hair was in disarray.

The judge continued.

'When I ask the three questions, you must respond to all of them correctly to survive the trial. Do you understand?'

Ruby half shrugged, half nodded.

'The trial by ordeal will now commence,' Judge Insch said.

'Ruby Rebello is ready,' Fay confirmed.

'The first question you must answer is this,' Judge Insch began. 'How does the law act?'

Ruby murmured under her breath.

'I must beg you to raise your voice,' Judge Insch said. 'I don't have the ears I once did.'

'By the shutting of eyes; by putting its foot down.'

'That is correct. Next. What does the lady of the castle advise Kay about travelling to the past?'

'That it is not wise to do so – that others have been lost to it.'

'Very good. This will be your final test.' Judge Insch cleared her throat. 'Kay is instructed to meet a woman in the cold. What is she wearing?'

'She's wearing a... wearing a...'

Two creases appeared above Ruby's nose.

'Wearing a…'

Odette wanted to help her. But she didn't know the book. The stories of her own childhood were folk tales; the escapades of Soungoula and other tricksters. In her teens she'd read English novels but she'd never heard of *The Box of Delights*, much less memorised its lines.

At that moment Grace Taylor stood up. She brought her hand down, sharp, on the steel barrier before her. The sound of a ring striking metal chimed through the gallery.

Judge Insch glared at Grace.

'Silence,' she intoned. To Ruby, she said, 'I must ask you to complete the line, Dr Rebello. The trial requires one hundred per cent accuracy for an innocent verdict.'

But Ruby was smiling; she was looking at Grace, and her cheeks were flushed.

'The line is: "You will see a woman plaided from the cold, wearing a ring of a very strange shape",' she said.

'That is correct,' Judge Insch said. 'I'm satisfied to rule that you are innocent of murder.'

Odette cried then. The case was done. She walked to the exit. Security guards from the future were waiting, on Fay's information. They marched Odette from the Conclave, for ever.

60

Margaret

When Margaret planned her last journey to the Toy Museum, she was prepared to be ruthless. The stakes were high. Any evidence that Julie could take to the Conclave court placed Margaret at risk of a blood tithe. To avoid that, Margaret would dispatch whatever threats stood in her way with a clear head. She only needed her gun and a few handtools. To make room for them, she emptied her handbag. Then she dismissed the chauffeur for the day. There was no need to create unnecessary witnesses.

She drove the car herself, late that night, from her Georgian house. Once she reached the outskirts of London the scenery grew dispiriting. The streets were still festooned with limp Christmas lights. Trees had been abandoned in pathways. Despite the hour, traffic was heavy and her progress was slow. But she would have all night, she reasoned, to clean up the basement on arrival. Eventually the cars cleared and the last half mile was quiet. As was her habit, she parked three streets away. It was half past midnight when she locked her car. The lighting was poor but so much the better for reaching the museum unnoticed. And if, as a woman in her eighties, she was taken for easy prey by some attacker in the shadows, her gun would give him a nasty shock.

The museum was deeply familiar to her. It had been built at the instruction of her grandfather, who was a philanthropist with an interest in toy theatres. As a small child, she had donated several theatres from her own nursery to the museum's displays. In the years since, their exhibits had diversified. Margaret remained a patron, which lent legitimacy to her sporadic presence.

At the museum door she was just turning the key when she heard a woman calling.

'Margaret! Stop! *Margaret!*'

Who was that? Might it be Parris? Or one of the other Candybox players, in cahoots with Parris to press charges?

She hastened inside, locking the door again behind her. When she reached the cellar she drew that lock, too, as quietly as she could. To be prepared she took the gun from her handbag. The seconds lengthened.

Her breathing began to slow: no one was coming. She would remove the bullets from the wall undisturbed.

Briefly, she allowed herself to be reassured by the cool air of the basement and the clean, strong smell of the Candybox. That smell was home.

The smell of the Candybox.

Her hand leapt to the bolt again. The Candybox shouldn't *be* there. She didn't know what had happened – she had broken the pieces herself – but some ghost or memory of the Candybox lurked in the dark.

Something punched her in the stomach. It couldn't be a bullet. She expected – more pain. Shock anaesthetised her.

She staggered into the room, but her eyes didn't adjust to the darkness. The Candybox had come back from the dead.

How? How? What had Angharad done when she took it to the lab?

Margaret dropped to her knees. The end unfolded so slowly. Strange how time shrank and expanded that way. There was time enough to realise: Angharad had remade the Candybox. Put the pieces in that machine, run by the silly boy with hair like a troll – Teddy something. Angharad had betrayed her. People said mothers always put their children first. It was Margaret's fatal error, to believe Angharad was any different.

Margaret's blouse was sodden. Oozy. She hated being a mess. More bullets tore her hand. Her nerves screamed. Imagine it! This was Margaret's dirty secret – the secret kept by the coroner, when he omitted her cause of death – she could be rent apart like any human. But she hadn't fallen yet. She hadn't—

The Candybox spat out its final missile, which broke the box's rim. Every hairline crack raced through the Candybox until it shattered. Pale stars and pyramids of plastic were propelled through the air. Some landed beneath Margaret's lock, and would grit Odette's path the next day. Others swam in Margaret's blood. The Candybox was destroyed when she was. That, at least, would have satisfied her. She wanted to believe she was the ruler of the Candybox, and not that it was the ruler of her.

61

Ruby

Two women, who'd already witnessed each other's deaths, married on the first day of spring. Ruby and Grace. Grace and Ruby. The ceremony was officiated by the Conclave chaplain. Several silver Graces attended. They were all cheerful and full of good wishes, which the other guests agreed was a good omen. Lucille acted as best woman. Angharad and Julie were there, as were many, many more time travellers from past and future.

After the ceremony, they ate in the ballroom where Grace and Ruby had first kissed. The wedding feast was salmon. Each bride had her own rich wedding cake, topped with a figure of her true love. The crumbs were scattered over their heads for good luck. Entertainments followed: fifty-five Angharads danced a ballet. She took principal roles *and* performed in the corps. Orange blossom fell from the ceiling during the climax. The rest of the guests took to the dance floor in Angharads' wake.

The day was almost, yet not quite, perfect. Dinah had refused to attend any wedding held at the Conclave, much less Ruby's to a time traveller; and Ruby's guest list was missing another person who she thought should be there.

With the plates cleared, and the speeches delivered, and the guests entertaining themselves, Ruby had an opportunity to reflect. She may have looked wistful.

'Come on.' Grace interrupted her reverie. 'I have a wedding gift for you.'

'What is it?'

'Wait and see! You always say you want to be surprised.'

Grace led Ruby into the corridor – past Fay, who was crying on a lover's shoulder; past Lucille, who was smoking with Elspeth; past Judge Insch, who had caught Ruby's bouquet and was now contemplating it with some puzzlement.

Ruby and Grace reached the lobby. Here the sound of the music had dwindled to the bassline. No one was at the front desk. Grace turned her attention to Beeline. She picked up the receiver and obtained a connection to August 2017.

'Is that the receptionist?' Grace asked. 'This is a call from Ruby Rebello, for Barbara Hereford.'

Ruby shook her head, incredulous. *'How...?'*

'Hush!' Grace said. To the receptionist, she added: 'I believe Barbara just attended a meeting with Margaret and she should still be on the premises. I'll hold.'

Ruby began to cry.

'You silly,' Grace whispered to her. 'Take the receiver. And make the most of this.'

So Ruby pressed the Beeline receiver to her ear.

'Ruby? Ruby, my love?' Granny Bee asked.

'Yes,' Ruby said.

'How did you know where I was? Is something wrong?'

'No, Granny. I'm just so happy to speak to you.' Ruby held Grace's hand. 'I have the most *amazing* news.'

62

Odette

'Odette! Odette!' Maman was calling. 'There's a letter for you.'

Odette lay on the decking of her parents' garden. The cherry blossom was falling. She heard Maman's footfall draw near.

'*Oli lét?*' Odette asked, opening one eye. She had been trying, with variable success, to remember her Kreol words, although Maman always answered in English.

'Here.' Maman passed Odette a typed envelope.

Odette turned it over. There was no return address.

'What's the letter about, Midge?' Maman asked. 'Is it a job offer?'

'I don't know yet. Wait till I open it.' Odette sat up, and the decking creaked. She slid her little finger under the seal and tore it open. Inside was a leaflet for Grace Taylor's work at Tate Modern. The leaflet said the collection had recently expanded, with the addition of several older installations from storage, and one exhibit that had never been displayed before. The reverse was blank except for a handwritten message – a date, time, and the instruction: *Meet me. E.*

'Well, is it a job?' Maman asked.

Odette laughed at her mother's nosiness. 'It's a mysterious invitation. From my old boss, I think.'

'Mysteries!' Maman. 'That's all you need.'

*

But Odette couldn't resist a mystery. It was a weakness she shared with Elspeth; and with Zach, come to that. She went to Tate Modern at the appointed time. There was plenty to interest her; she enjoyed looking at the sampler, and the oil portrait, and the broken pencil. The gallery assistant told her the most recent additions were in the neighbouring exhibition hall, so Odette moved along to the next room.

The wall was papered with newspaper clippings. Dozens of them, yellow with age and trembling as people walked back and forth. Amongst the fading print a name stood out to Odette – Zach's name; his piece on Margaret's disappearance. The date was July 2019. Last time he'd called Odette, he said he was struggling to find an editor who'd run the piece. But clearly persistence would soon pay off. She allowed herself to feel thrilled, for her own involvement in its publication.

Her pride was brief. She turned her attention to the other articles. They were all about Margaret, and her disappearance. But none of them told the same story twice. A political assassination here. A suicide gone wrong there. One journalist said that Margaret had absconded into the twenty-fifth century after faking her own death. Odette's dismay grew. Most of the journalists cited insider Conclave sources. There was nothing to mark out the truthfulness of Zach's report. It was just one account, among many others.

'Those stories are Angharad's doing.' A silver Elspeth had approached without Odette seeing.

'Angharad made up *all* these stories?'

'Not personally, no. She delegated that aspect. They were fabricated, and leaked, at her instruction.'

'But why?'

'Because she failed to keep Mr Callaghan's exposé from the public. Oh, she made a decent stab at it, a lot of moguls fell into line and refused to print the story, but she's never been quite as well connected as Margaret, you know. Or as frightening. The next best thing was to muddy the waters. Flood the media with so many ludicrous alternatives that any speculation about Margaret Norton's whereabouts had the whiff of the tin hat brigade.'

That wasn't a technique Margaret would have used, either. Margaret would have died before propagating a glut of salacious rumours about the Conclave. Angharad's motives had never been quite clear to Odette, though she suspected she may, again, have been trying to deflect attention from Julie.

Odette sat down on the nearest bench. The thought of her hard work – of Zach's hard work – being undermined this way made her heart heavy. Angharad had achieved the opposite of solving a mystery: she had obfuscated, and deceived, until the truth was no longer discernible.

'Does Angharad want me tried? For the embargo breach?' Odette asked.

'Careful!' Elspeth said. 'She doesn't know who breached the embargo. It could be Ruby, or Grace, or even Judge Insch for all she can tell. No need to let on.'

'How can you carry on working for her?' Odette cried. Even if Angharad weren't as brutal as Margaret, she was poisonous in her own way.

THE PSYCHOLOGY OF TIME TRAVEL

'I can't. That's what I wanted to talk to you about.' Elspeth took the next seat. 'A number of us at the Conclave have discussed how we might improve the Conclave's culture. The chief barrier is the impossibility of leaving the past behind. All our years intermingle and that makes change impossible.'

'So *leave*.'

Elspeth raised a hand. 'I have another proposal. We can establish replication sites – other time travel centres in cities across the world, where we can start afresh. With staff of integrity.'

'What's this got to do with me?'

'I hope you'll consider joining us. The reasons for your earlier dismissal would no longer count against you. And an outpost in the Indian Ocean would be strategically valuable.'

'No,' Odette said without hesitation.

'Understood. But, Odette, you and I – we swim in the same cut, do we not? When you were a little girl in Mahé – yes, I remember our meeting – you said you wanted to be a detective. Here's your opportunity.' Elspeth stood, and sank her hands into her coat pockets. She glanced at the wall of clippings. 'I'm not over-fond of Grace's art. Too post-modern for my taste.'

She walked away without farewell.

Odette was in no rush to leave. Maman would be at home, with questions Odette didn't know how to answer yet. She could linger a while. The last installation stood close to the exit. A black, cubic hut, reminiscent of a miniature time machine. She walked into it and a video screen was playing in the darkness. The woman on the screen was Fay. Fay before she was jaded. A luminous Fay. Was she being interviewed? She was sitting alone in a chair. Then she spoke.

Whenever I visit my father, the trees in his garden are young again, and so is he. I will *never* take that for granted.

The screen cut to black. Odette had missed the start of the story. She would wait for the story to begin again.

Glossary

Closed timelike curve (CTC): A path of spacetime that loops back to its starting point. CTCs are associated with a breakdown in causality, because causality demands that any event is preceded by its cause.

Completion: To live an incident you've already read or heard about.

Consistency principle: This principle states that the probability of any action or occurrence that would cause a paradox is zero.

Common chronology: The sequence of events experienced by non-time travellers.

Echoing: Returning to an incident you've already experienced.

Emus: People who don't time travel, and thus pass through time in a single direction. Emus are unable to walk backwards.

Exotic material: A technical term for the material used to build scaffolding in wormholes. Time-travelling adulterers also use the term lewdly, to refer to conquests in far-off decades.

Forecasting: Intercourse with one's future self.

Green-me: A time traveller's younger self.

Legacy fuck: Intercourse with one's past self.

Liebestod: A trip to see a lover for the last time before one's death. The term is Germanic in origin, with liebe translating to love and tod to death. In a non-time travelling context, it is more usually applied to the final music in Wagner's opera *Tristan and Isolde*, from 1859.

Me-timing: Ongoing infidelity committed with a past or future self. This is largely tolerated among time travellers but regarded as emotionally unhealthy.

One-way travellers: See Emus.

Palmist: A time traveller who uses her knowledge of a person's future to manipulate them into sex. Technically this is illegal under time travel law, as it violates consent. Over a three century period there have been eighty-seven prosecutions, fifty per cent of which reached guilty verdicts. However, anecdotal reports suggest that the incidence of the crime is higher than the prosecution number.

Personal chronology: The sequence of events experienced by an individual time traveller, which will differ from common chronology, and may differ from the personal chronologies of other time travellers.

Plodders: People who don't time travel, and who must therefore experience events at the pace of common chronology, rather than a pace of their own choosing.

Quantum tunnelling: Detection from the opposing side of a barrier, in the field of quantum mechanics. Also a slang term for intercourse.

Silver-me: A time traveller's older self.

Swim in the same cut: People whose personal chronologies match well, because they belong to the same team. A 'cut' is a term for a canal, typical of West Midlands dialects.

Tipler cylinder: Early plans for time travel machines proposed a long cylinder spinning around on its longitudinal axis. The rotation would twist spacetime, rendering CTCs traversable, and permitting time travel into the past. As the design could not accommodate travel into the future it was eventually abandoned. However, the term has persisted as anatomical slang, because early diagrams of tipler cylinders suggested they would be phallic in appearance.

Topology change: Manipulations of time and fields which allow time machines to function.

Wenches: Freshly recruited time travellers. Historically wench has been used in a number of British dialects to refer variously to a young girl, a servant, or a sex worker. These nuances of meaning may be revealing of how time travellers perceive their newest team members. The adoption of a feminine term may partially reflect the high representation of women among the Conclave's staff; however time travellers apply the name to male as well as female entrants to the profession.

Zeitigzorn: Feeling angry with someone for things they won't do wrong for years. The word is German in origin, with zeitig translatable as early and zorn as anger. Zeitigzorn is particularly common during the early stages of a time traveller's career. The converse is under-reacting to objectionable behaviour, because the time traveller has known it is coming for decades.

Time Travel Conclave's Battery of Psychometric Tests

Selected Questions

Death Anxiety Scale for Time Travellers (DASTT)

Indicate your agreement using the following scale:

1 = strongly disagree, 2 = disagree, 3 = neither agree nor disagree, 4 = agree, 5 = strongly agree

i	I worry about my physical health being poor before my death	1 2 3 4 5
ii	I worry about my mental health being poor before my death	1 2 3 4 5
iii	I worry about what happens after death	1 2 3 4 5
iv	I don't mind being forgotten after my last time travel trip	1 2 3 4 5
v	I don't mind being gone for ever after my last time travel trip	1 2 3 4 5
vi	The thought of dying makes me feel alone	1 2 3 4 5
vii	The thought of dying makes me feel out of control	1 2 3 4 5
viii	The thought of dying makes me sad	1 2 3 4 5
ix	Discussing aspects of my death with my older selves does not disturb me	1 2 3 4 5

x	Discussing aspects of my death with other time travellers does not disturb me	1 2 3 4 5
xi	Discussing aspects of my death with ordinary people does not disturb me	1 2 3 4 5
xii	I'm not afraid of dying of cancer	1 2 3 4 5
xiii	I'm not afraid of dying from heart disease	1 2 3 4 5
xiv	I'm not afraid of dying from stroke	1 2 3 4 5
xv	I avoid reminders of the known way I am going to die	1 2 3 4 5
xvi	I hate not knowing what will happen after death	1 2 3 4 5
xvii	I hate not knowing what death will feel like	1 2 3 4 5
xviii	I hate not knowing what the world is like after the curtain call	1 2 3 4 5
xix	I think of death as something that affects my older selves, not me	1 2 3 4 5
xx	I think of death as something that affects me, not other people	1 2 3 4 5
xxi	I think of death as something that is very remote	1 2 3 4 5
xxii	Other people's deaths are abstract to me	1 2 3 4 5
xxiii	Other people's deaths are funny to me	1 2 3 4 5
xxiv	Other people's deaths feel temporary to me	1 2 3 4 5
xxv	Death will be a reunion with loved ones after my last time travel trip	1 2 3 4 5
xxvi	Death will be oblivion	1 2 3 4 5
xxvii	Death will be a reckoning for the life I've lived	1 2 3 4 5
xxviii	Looking at another person's corpse has no impact on me	1 2 3 4 5
xxix	Attending another person's funeral has no impact on me	1 2 3 4 5

xxx	I am not anxious about death whenever I get ill	1 2 3 4 5
xxxi	I am not anxious about death when I take risks with my health or safety	1 2 3 4 5
xxxii	I am not anxious about death	1 2 3 4 5
xxxiii	Compared to before I was a time traveller, I fear death more	1 2 3 4 5
xxxiv	Compared to before I was a time traveller, I fear death less	1 2 3 4 5
xxxv	Compared to before I was a time traveller, my feelings about death are unchanged	1 2 3 4 5
xxxvi	Ordinary people have commented that my attitudes towards death are strange	1 2 3 4 5
xxxvii	My worries about death are in line with other time travellers of similar experience	1 2 3 4 5
xxxviii	Death is the doorway to a new existence	1 2 3 4 5
xxxix	Death is an unavoidable, normal event that comes to all life on earth	1 2 3 4 5
xl	Death is an escape from the cruelties of this life	1 2 3 4 5
xli	Reading of my death in the archive upsets me	1 2 3 4 5
xlii	The idea of attending my own death upsets me	1 2 3 4 5
xliii	The idea of attending my own funeral upsets me	1 2 3 4 5
xliv	I worry about dying	1 2 3 4 5

Reference: Joyce, S. (June 2020). 'The course of death anxiety in time travellers: A longitudinal study.' *British Death Journal*. 13 (2). 110–119.

Bereavement Scale for Time Travellers (BerSTT)

Using the following scale, indicate how frequently each item is true for you:

1 = never, 2 = rarely, 3 = sometimes, 4 = often, 5 = always

For use where the bereavement pre-dates the first field trip:		
i	I avoid reminders of the person who's gone	1 2 3 4 5
ii	I am shocked that the person is gone	1 2 3 4 5
iii	I have accepted that the person is gone	1 2 3 4 5
iv	Life has no meaning now the person has gone	1 2 3 4 5
v	Losing this person made me angry	1 2 3 4 5
vi	Losing this person made me bitter	1 2 3 4 5
vii	I can move on from this loss	1 2 3 4 5
viii	I feel numb because of this loss	1 2 3 4 5
ix	It's hard to complete necessary life tasks because I think about this loss so much	1 2 3 4 5
x	I'm upset by places and objects that remind me of the person who's gone	1 2 3 4 5
xi	Sometimes I worry I have the same symptoms as the person I've lost	1 2 3 4 5
xii	Sometimes when I'm out I think I've seen the person I've lost, and feel sad	1 2 3 4 5
xiii	Sometimes when the phone rings I think it's the person I've lost, and feel sad	1 2 3 4 5
xiv	I feel guilty for living when this person has gone	1 2 3 4 5

xv	I'm envious of people who haven't experienced grief	1 2 3 4 5
xvi	Other people have remarked on how unaffected I am by this person's death	1 2 3 4 5
xvii	My feelings of grief are intense compared to other people in the same position	1 2 3 4 5
xviii	My feelings of grief are typical compared to other people in the same position	1 2 3 4 5
xix	My feelings of grief are not intense compared to other people in the same position	1 2 3 4 5
xx	When I am in the field I expect my feelings of grief to lessen	1 2 3 4 5
xxi	When I am in the field I expect my feelings of grief to feel the same	1 2 3 4 5
xxii	When I am in the field I expect my feelings of grief to worsen	1 2 3 4 5
For use where the bereavement post-dates the first field trip:		
xxiii	I avoid reminders of the person who's died, including seeing them in other timelines	1 2 3 4 5
xxiv	I am shocked that the person has died	1 2 3 4 5
xxv	I have accepted that the person has died	1 2 3 4 5
xxvi	Life has no meaning in timelines where this person is dead	1 2 3 4 5
xxvii	This person's death made me angry	1 2 3 4 5
xxviii	This person's death made me bitter	1 2 3 4 5
xxix	I can move on from this death	1 2 3 4 5
xxx	I feel numb because of this death	1 2 3 4 5
xxxi	It's hard to complete necessary life tasks because I think about this death so much	1 2 3 4 5

xxxii	I'm upset by places and objects that remind me of the person who's died	1 2 3 4 5
xxxiii	Sometimes I worry I have the same symptoms as the person who's died	1 2 3 4 5
xxxiv	Sometimes when I'm out I think I see someone who's currently dead, and feel sad	1 2 3 4 5
xxxv	Sometimes when the phone rings I think it's a person who's currently dead, and feel sad	1 2 3 4 5
xxxvi	I feel guilty for living when this person has died	1 2 3 4 5
xxxvii	I'm envious of people who haven't experienced grief	1 2 3 4 5
xxxviii	Other people have remarked on how unaffected I am by this person's death	1 2 3 4 5
xxxix	My feelings of grief are intense compared to non-time travellers in the same position	1 2 3 4 5
xl	My feelings of grief are typical compared to non-time travellers in the same position	1 2 3 4 5
xli	My feelings of grief are not intense compared to non-time travellers in the same position	1 2 3 4 5
xlii	My feelings of grief are intense compared to time travellers in the same position	1 2 3 4 5
xliii	My feelings of grief are typical compared to time travellers in the same position	1 2 3 4 5
xliv	My feelings of grief are not intense compared to time travellers in the same position	1 2 3 4 5

Reference: Joyce, S. (September 2020). 'Do time travellers grieve? The Bereavement Scale for Time Travellers (BSTT).' *English Journal of Adjustment Disorders*. 20 (3). 34–40.

Religious Belief Scale for Time Travellers (RBeSTT)

Indicate your agreement using the following scale:

1 = strongly disagree, 2 = disagree, 3 = neither agree nor disagree, 4 = agree, 5 = strongly agree

i	It's important to me to think about religious issues	1 2 3 4 5
ii	Spiritual topics are interesting to me	1 2 3 4 5
iii	Staying informed about religious questions has value for me	1 2 3 4 5
iv	I believe in a higher power	1 2 3 4 5
v	I believe in the afterlife	1 2 3 4 5
vi	I believe in free will	1 2 3 4 5
vii	I believe in predestination	1 2 3 4 5
viii	Public/shared worship is part of my life	1 2 3 4 5
ix	Prayer is part of my life	1 2 3 4 5
x	Meditative practice is part of my life	1 2 3 4 5
xi	I have felt divine intervention	1 2 3 4 5
xii	I have felt oneness with the universe	1 2 3 4 5
xiii	I have felt completion	1 2 3 4 5
xiv	I have received communication from a higher power	1 2 3 4 5
xv	I have been consoled by spiritual writings or practices	1 2 3 4 5
xvi	My religious faith gives me strength to get through challenging experiences	1 2 3 4 5

xvii	I derive no strength from religious faith	1 2 3 4 5
xviii	My faith in humanity gives me strength to get through challenging experiences	1 2 3 4 5
xix	I derive no strength from a faith in humanity	1 2 3 4 5
xx	When I suffer, I think that I'm being punished by a higher power	1 2 3 4 5
xxi	When I suffer, I think that it is part of a greater plan	1 2 3 4 5
xxii	When I suffer, I think that I'm unlucky	1 2 3 4 5
xxiii	Suffering is an inevitable part of human existence that can't be avoided	1 2 3 4 5
xxiv	I believe there is a great deal of love in the world	1 2 3 4 5
xxv	I believe there is a great deal of sadness in the world	1 2 3 4 5
xxvi	I believe the world is an indifferent place	1 2 3 4 5
xxvii	Part of why we are here is to search for meaning	1 2 3 4 5
xxviii	I don't believe there is any greater meaning to existence	1 2 3 4 5
xxix	I believe prayer is pointless	1 2 3 4 5
xxx	I believe meditation is pointless	1 2 3 4 5
xxxi	I find religious practice boring	1 2 3 4 5
xxxii	I have a sense of purpose in life	1 2 3 4 5
xxxiii	While carrying out mundane activities I feel guided by a higher power	1 2 3 4 5
xxxiv	When events come to pass as predicted I feel comforted	1 2 3 4 5
xxxv	When events come to pass as predicted I feel powerless	1 2 3 4 5
xxxvi	When events come to pass as predicted I feel nothing	1 2 3 4 5

xxxvii	If there were a higher power that loved us we'd be free to make different futures	1 2 3 4 5
xxxviii	If there were a higher power that loved us our efforts would be rewarded	1 2 3 4 5
xxxix	Acausal matter and acausal information is proof of a higher power	1 2 3 4 5
xl	Time travel deepened my religious faith	1 2 3 4 5
xli	Time travel lessened my religious faith	1 2 3 4 5
xlii	Time travel made no difference to my religious faith	1 2 3 4 5
xliii	Time travel makes me a more moral person	1 2 3 4 5
xliv	Time travel brings me into contact with the divine	1 2 3 4 5
xlv	Time travellers don't need to abide by normal moral rules	1 2 3 4 5
xlvi	Time travellers are like gods	1 2 3 4 5

Reference: Stephens, T. (April 2020). 'The relationship between field experience and time travellers' spiritual beliefs.' *Journal of Psychology and Religious Practice*. 16 (1). 203–208.

Locus of Control Scale for Time Travellers (LoCSTT)

Indicate your agreement using the following scale:

1 = strongly disagree, 2 = disagree, 3 = neither agree nor disagree, 4 = agree, 5 = strongly agree

i	I have a great deal of influence over the direction of my life	1 2 3 4 5
ii	I have very little influence over the direction of my life	1 2 3 4 5
iii	I have a great deal of influence over the behaviour of other people	1 2 3 4 5
iv	I have very little influence over the behaviour of other people	1 2 3 4 5
v	We are fated to succeed or to fail	1 2 3 4 5
vi	We are in charge of our own destiny	1 2 3 4 5
vii	Self-determination is not equally available to everyone	1 2 3 4 5
viii	Self-determination is possible for everyone who works hard enough	1 2 3 4 5
ix	Ordinary people are at the whims of people in power	1 2 3 4 5
x	Ordinary people can take power by working together	1 2 3 4 5
xi	All of us are at the whim of forces we can't understand	1 2 3 4 5

xii	All of us have to power to change things for the better	1 2 3 4 5
xiii	I secured my post at the Conclave because I was the most skilled candidate	1 2 3 4 5
xiv	I secured my post at the Conclave because other candidates had fewer advantages	1 2 3 4 5
xv	I secured my post at the Conclave because it was predestined	1 2 3 4 5
xvi	I secured my post at the Conclave through luck	1 2 3 4 5
xvii	Time travellers deserve their high commissions because they work hard	1 2 3 4 5
xviii	Poverty is the fault of lazy individuals	1 2 3 4 5
xix	You can't do anything to prevent poverty	1 2 3 4 5
xx	Whether we're rich or poor is predestined and can't be changed	1 2 3 4 5
xxi	To receive financial rewards I must do as my employers demand	1 2 3 4 5
xxii	To receive financial rewards I must play the system	1 2 3 4 5
xxiii	There is nothing I can do to change the value people place on my work	1 2 3 4 5
xxiv	Genetics determine my health – whatever choices I might make	1 2 3 4 5
xxv	The environment determines my health – whatever choices I might make	1 2 3 4 5
xxvi	Fate determines my health – whatever choices I might make	1 2 3 4 5
xxvii	My lifestyle choices determine my health, even if I know the future	1 2 3 4 5
xxviii	Regular medical check-ups are the best way to avoid illness	1 2 3 4 5

xxiv	If I do what the doctor tells me, I'll have the best health possible	1 2 3 4 5
xxx	By giving my children the right care I'll make sure they're well adjusted	1 2 3 4 5
xxxi	How well adjusted my children are is a matter of fate	1 2 3 4 5
xxxii	Having foresight into my child's issues will give me more control as a parent	1 2 3 4 5
xxxiii	Having foresight into my child's issues will lessen my control as a parent	1 2 3 4 5
xxxiv	Having foresight into my child's issues will not influence my control as a parent	1 2 3 4 5
xxxv	Most problems will resolve themselves if you just leave them alone	1 2 3 4 5
xxxvi	Most problems need active intervention to be resolved	1 2 3 4 5
xxxvii	The way things turn out for people directly reflects the effort they've made	1 2 3 4 5
xxxviii	The way things turn out for people just happens, no matter what they do	1 2 3 4 5
xxlx	Nobody else governs my behaviour	1 2 3 4 5
xl	I have to change my behaviour to meet others' expectations	1 2 3 4 5
xli	I can use the things I see while time travelling to improve my life	1 2 3 4 5
xlii	Seeing the future sometimes leads me into bad decisions	1 2 3 4 5
xliii	Seeing aspects of my future gives me no extra influence over my life	1 2 3 4 5
xlvi	The things I see in my past show me where I could have made better choices	1 2 3 4 5

xlv	The things I see in my past show me my decisions were irrelevant to the outcome	1 2 3 4 5
xlvi	As a time traveller I have more control over my life than an ordinary person	1 2 3 4 5
xlvii	As a time traveller I have no more control over my life than an ordinary person	1 2 3 4 5

Reference: Joyce, S. (March 2020). 'Does an external locus of control predict adjustment to job role in time travel recruitment?' *Annals of Occupational Psychology*. 2 (1). 12–208.

Sexual and Relationship Health Scale for Time Travellers (SRCHS – TT)

Indicate your agreement using the following scale:

1 = untrue, 2 = slightly true, 3 = somewhat true, 4 = mostly true, 5 = completely true

	Satisfaction with primary relationship (if applicable)	
i	Foreknowledge has made my primary relationship more stable	1 2 3 4 5
ii	An imbalance in foreknowledge has had adverse effects on my primary relationship	1 2 3 4 5
iii	It is difficult to resolve conflicts when my partner and I have different chronologies	1 2 3 4 5
iv	It is easier to resolve conflicts when my partner and I know what the outcome will be	1 2 3 4 5
v	My primary relationship is a source of continuity for me	1 2 3 4 5
vi	I feel like my partner is the only person for me	1 2 3 4 5
vii	Knowing how my primary relationship will end has a negative effect on the health my relationship	1 2 3 4 5
viii	Knowing how my primary relationship will end has a positive effect on the health of my relationship	1 2 3 4 5
ix	My primary partner and I agree on how I should spend money in other time periods	1 2 3 4 5
x	My primary partner and I agree on whether I should have secondary sexual partners in other time periods	1 2 3 4 5
xi	My primary partner and I agree on how much foreknowledge I should disclose	1 2 3 4 5

xii	My primary romantic relationship has met my original expectations	1 2 3 4 5
xiii	I enjoy the company of my primary partner	1 2 3 4 5
xiv	I am happy with my primary relationship	1 2 3 4 5
xv	I am satisfied with my primary relationship	1 2 3 4 5

Changes in sexual behaviour, since entry to the profession

xvi	Talking through sexual issues with my older selves has improved my sexual confidence	1 2 3 4 5
xvii	Talking through sexual issues with my older selves has made no difference to my sexual confidence	1 2 3 4 5
xviii	Talking through sexual issues with my older selves has worsened my sexual confidence	1 2 3 4 5
xix	I don't talk to my older selves about sex	1 2 3 4 5
xx	Seeing my other selves has made me happier with my physical appearance	1 2 3 4 5
xxi	Seeing my other selves has made me more anxious about my physical appearance	1 2 3 4 5
xxii	Seeing my other selves has made no difference to how I feel about my physical appearance	1 2 3 4 5
xxiii	Exposure to sexual mores in other periods has positively affected my attitudes to sex	1 2 3 4 5
xxiv	Exposure to sexual mores in other periods has negatively affected my attitudes to sex	1 2 3 4 5
xxv	Exposure to sexual mores in other periods has made no difference to my attitudes to sex	1 2 3 4 5
xxvi	I am exclusively attracted to people from a specific time period	1 2 3 4 5
xxvii	I am exclusively attracted to inanimate objects from a specific time period	1 2 3 4 5
xxviii	I am exclusively attracted to my alternate selves	1 2 3 4 5

xxix	I am exclusively attracted to my descendants	1 2 3 4 5
xxx	I am exclusively attracted to acausal people	1 2 3 4 5
xxxi	I am exclusively attracted to acausal objects	1 2 3 4 5
xxxii	I am aroused by the smell of atroposium	1 2 3 4 5
xxxiii	I am aroused by being in time machines	1 2 3 4 5
xxxiv	I am only aroused in specific time periods	1 2 3 4 5
xxxv	I am only attracted to my long-term partner in specific time periods	1 2 3 4 5
xxxvi	I only feel sexually uninhibited in specific time periods	1 2 3 4 5
xxxvii	I feel freer to practise illegal sexual practices in time periods other than my home timeline	1 2 3 4 5
xxxviii	I feel freer to practise stigmatised sexual practices in time periods other than my home timeline	1 2 3 4 5
Experience of unwanted sexual contact, since entry to the profession		
xxxix	I have been the victim of sexual harassment in the course of my work	1 2 3 4 5
xl	I have been the victim of unwanted sexual contact in the course of my work	1 2 3 4 5
xli	In some time periods, I worry more about the risk of unwanted sexual contact	1 2 3 4 5
xlii	I avoid some time periods because I worry about the risk of unwanted sexual contact	1 2 3 4 5

Reference: Smolenski, W. (June 2020). 'Measuring relationship satisfaction in couples with asynchronous partnerships.' *Journal of Chronostudies.* 5 (2). 43–47.

Obsessive-Compulsive Scale for Time Travellers (OCScaTT)

Indicate your level of distress, over the past month, using the following scale: 1 = none, and 10 = very high

i	During time travel, I can't stop myself thinking things that scare me	1 2 3 4 5 6 7 8 9 10
ii	After time travelling, I can't stop myself thinking things that scare me	1 2 3 4 5 6 7 8 9 10
iii	I believe that germs from other time periods will contaminate me on a trip	1 2 3 4 5 6 7 8 9 10
iv	I believe that germs from the time machine will contaminate me	1 2 3 4 5 6 7 8 9 10
v	After using a time machine I obsessively repeat the Conclave's hygiene protocol	1 2 3 4 5 6 7 8 9 10
vi	I continually 'go over' events in the past to check I've done nothing wrong	1 2 3 4 5 6 7 8 9 10
vii	I continually 'go over' events in the future to check I've done nothing wrong	1 2 3 4 5 6 7 8 9 10
viii	I hoard things from the past	1 2 3 4 5 6 7 8 9 10
ix	I hoard things from the future	1 2 3 4 5 6 7 8 9 10
x	I repeatedly check that the time machine is secure, before or after use	1 2 3 4 5 6 7 8 9 10
xi	I repeatedly visit particular moments in the past to see I've done nothing wrong	1 2 3 4 5 6 7 8 9 10
xii	I repeatedly visit particular moments in the future to see I've done nothing wrong	1 2 3 4 5 6 7 8 9 10

xiii	I worry that I've left things I need in the past even when I know I haven't	1 2 3 4 5 6 7 8 9 10
xiv	I worry that I've left things I need in the future even when I know I haven't	1 2 3 4 5 6 7 8 9 10
xv	I get upset if my pre-time travel ritual is disturbed	1 2 3 4 5 6 7 8 9 10
xvi	I get upset if my post-time travel ritual is disturbed	1 2 3 4 5 6 7 8 9 10
xvii	I have thoughts that I'll harm somebody in the past even though I don't want to	1 2 3 4 5 6 7 8 9 10
xviii	I have thoughts that I'll harm somebody in the future even though I don't want to	1 2 3 4 5 6 7 8 9 10
xix	My preparations for time travel must be made in a specific order	1 2 3 4 5 6 7 8 9 10
xx	Every trip must be of a specific duration or I fear something bad will happen	1 2 3 4 5 6 7 8 9 10
xxi	I need to pray before each time travel trip or something bad will happen	1 2 3 4 5 6 7 8 9 10
xxii	I need to pray during each time travel trip or something bad will happen	1 2 3 4 5 6 7 8 9 10
xxiii	I need to pray after each time travel trip or something bad will happen	1 2 3 4 5 6 7 8 9 10
xxiv	I hate operating time machines because I worry I'll lose control of them	1 2 3 4 5 6 7 8 9 10
xxv	I am more concerned than I should be about safety issues relating to time travel	1 2 3 4 5 6 7 8 9 10
xxvi	I avoid touching objects that have come from particular time periods	1 2 3 4 5 6 7 8 9 10
xxvii	I worry about radioactivity in some time periods despite taking normal precautions	1 2 3 4 5 6 7 8 9 10

xxviii	I feel I can only visit years that fit a particular numeric pattern	1 2 3 4 5 6 7 8 9 10
xxix	I repeat time travel trips until they feel 'right' to me	1 2 3 4 5 6 7 8 9 10
xxx	It takes me longer than most people to prepare for time travel because of my rituals	1 2 3 4 5 6 7 8 9 10
xxxi	I only feel safe going to sleep in particular time periods	1 2 3 4 5 6 7 8 9 10
xxxii	After I've visited a particular era, I keep doubting that I really went there	1 2 3 4 5 6 7 8 9 10
xxxiii	I repeat certain phrases in my head to protect me before time travelling	1 2 3 4 5 6 7 8 9 10
xxxiv	I repeat certain phrases in my head to protect me during time travelling	1 2 3 4 5 6 7 8 9 10
xxxv	I repeat certain phrases in my head to protect me after time travelling	1 2 3 4 5 6 7 8 9 10
xxxvi	I frequently have unpleasant thoughts about time travelling that I can't control	1 2 3 4 5 6 7 8 9 10
xxxvii	I feel upset about periods where I'm 'missing' from the shared chronology	1 2 3 4 5 6 7 8 9 10
xxxviii	I believe there are good and bad years in the past based on their numerical value	1 2 3 4 5 6 7 8 9 10
xxxix	I believe there are good and bad years in the future based on their numerical value	1 2 3 4 5 6 7 8 9 10
xl	I have to wash the time machine before use to assuage my fears of contamination	1 2 3 4 5 6 7 8 9 10
xli	I have to wash the time machine after use to assuage my fears of contamination	1 2 3 4 5 6 7 8 9 10
xlii	I constantly worry I've harmed one of my ancestors while time travelling	1 2 3 4 5 6 7 8 9 10

xliii	Because I have these thoughts I worry I must want to harm my ancestors	1 2 3 4 5 6 7 8 9 10
xliv	I constantly worry I've harmed one of my descendants while time travelling	1 2 3 4 5 6 7 8 9 10
xlv	Because I have these thoughts I worry I must want to harm my descendants	1 2 3 4 5 6 7 8 9 10
xlvi	If I neglect my time travelling rituals, I'm being irresponsible	1 2 3 4 5 6 7 8 9 10

Reference: Joyce, S. (2020). 'A new scale for measuring obsessive-compulsive traits in workplaces requiring time travel'. *Psychometrics.* 1 (1), 115–120.

Eating Disorder Scale for Time Travellers (EDScaTT)

Indicate which of the following statements are true or untrue for you.

i	While I am in the past I am more likely to feel my eating is out of control	Yes / No / Don't recall
ii	While I am in the future I am more likely to feel my eating is out of control	Yes / No / Don't recall
iii	While I am in the present I am more likely to feel my eating is out of control	Yes / No / Don't recall
iv	I have made myself vomit in the past to prevent myself gaining weight	Yes / No / Don't recall
v	I have made myself vomit in the future to prevent myself gaining weight	Yes / No / Don't recall
vi	I have made myself vomit in the present to prevent myself gaining weight	Yes / No / Don't recall
vii	I have fasted in the past	Yes / No / Don't recall
viii	I have fasted in the future	Yes / No / Don't recall
ix	I have fasted in the present	Yes / No / Don't recall
x	I have exercised excessively in the past	Yes / No / Don't recall
xi	I have exercised excessively in the future	Yes / No / Don't recall
xii	I have exercised excessively in the present	Yes / No / Don't recall
xiii	I have used laxatives or diuretics in the past	Yes / No / Don't recall
xiv	I have used laxatives or diuretics in the future	Yes / No / Don't recall

xv	I have used laxatives or diuretics in the present	Yes / No / Don't recall
xvi	I only want to eat with other people in the past	Yes / No / Don't recall
xvii	I only want to eat with other people in the future	Yes / No / Don't recall
xviii	I only want to eat with other people in the present	Yes / No / Don't recall
xix	I only want to eat with other people at a specific point in time	Yes / No / Don't recall
xx	I only ever want to eat at a specific point in time	Yes / No / Don't recall
xxi	My eating habits influence my relationships with people in the past	Yes / No / Don't recall
xxii	My eating habits influence my relationships with people in the future	Yes / No / Don't recall
xxiii	My eating habits influence my relationships with people in the present	Yes / No / Don't recall
xxiv	In some time periods, I feel more pressure from friends to lose weight	Yes / No / Don't recall
xxv	In some time periods, I feel more pressure from my family to lose weight	Yes / No / Don't recall
xxvi	In some time periods, I feel more pressure from the media to lose weight	Yes / No / Don't recall
xxvii	In some time periods, I feel more pressure from my partner to lose weight	Yes / No / Don't recall
xxviii	I categorise food as 'good' or 'bad' depending on its year of origin	Yes / No / Don't recall
xxix	I fear eating food from some time periods	Yes / No / Don't recall
xxx	I fear I won't be able to eat in certain time periods	Yes / No / Don't recall

xxxi	I fear I won't be able to stop eating in certain time periods	Yes / No / Don't recall
xxxii	I need to eat a particular rate or chew a particular number of times	Yes / No / Don't recall
xxxiii	I can only eat portions of a specific size	Yes / No / Don't recall
xxxiv	I can only eat foods of a certain colour	Yes / No / Don't recall
xxxv	I hoard food from the past	Yes / No / Don't recall
xxxvi	I hoard food from the future	Yes / No / Don't recall
xxxvii	I collect recipes, photos and articles on food from the past	Yes / No / Don't recall
xxxviii	I collect recipes, photos and articles on food from the future	Yes / No / Don't recall
xxxix	I judge myself harshly	Yes / No / Don't recall
xl	I am motivated by wanting to be better than other people	Yes / No / Don't recall
xli	I often feel that my life circumstances are not in my control	Yes / No / Don't recall
xlii	I often feel that eating is the only aspect of my life that I can control	Yes / No / Don't recall
xliii	Time travelling has altered my feelings about my body in a negative way	Yes / No / Don't recall
xliv	Time travelling has altered my feelings about my body in a positive way	Yes / No / Don't recall
xlv	Time travelling has not made any difference to my feelings about my body	Yes / No / Don't recall
xlvi	I believe my eating habits are reasonable	Yes / No / Don't recall
xlvii	I would like to change my eating habits	Yes / No / Don't recall

Reference: Joyce, S. (2020). 'Detecting disordered eating among time travellers'. *The Psychology of Time Travel*. 60 (3), 7–13.

Time Travelling and Narcissistic Traits (TTaNT)

Indicate your agreement, where 1 = untrue, and 10 = completely true

i	I would like to use time travel for the purposes of influencing people	1 2 3 4 5 6 7 8 9 10
ii	I am drawn to time travel because it is an elite profession	1 2 3 4 5 6 7 8 9 10
iii	The thought of using time travel to influence how the world is run scares me	1 2 3 4 5 6 7 8 9 10
iv	I believe I blend into other time periods easily	1 2 3 4 5 6 7 8 9 10
v	Being a time traveller appeals because it often makes me the centre of attention	1 2 3 4 5 6 7 8 9 10
vi	I would like to use time travel for exercising authority over other people	1 2 3 4 5 6 7 8 9 10
vii	The thought of using time travel to manipulate people doesn't appeal to me	1 2 3 4 5 6 7 8 9 10
viii	Time travelling will mean I always know what I'm doing	1 2 3 4 5 6 7 8 9 10
ix	Time travelling shows we can't always live the way we plan	1 2 3 4 5 6 7 8 9 10
x	Controlling time is a skill deserving the respect of others	1 2 3 4 5 6 7 8 9 10
xi	Time travelling is a very humbling experience	1 2 3 4 5 6 7 8 9 10
xii	I am very good at understanding the motivations of people from other times	1 2 3 4 5 6 7 8 9 10

xiii	It is easy to underestimate how different people are in other time periods	1 2 3 4 5 6 7 8 9 10
xiv	Time travelling would demonstrate to the world I've made something of myself	1 2 3 4 5 6 7 8 9 10
xv	Time travelling would be its own reward	1 2 3 4 5 6 7 8 9 10
xvi	The Conclave succeeds through collective effort	1 2 3 4 5 6 7 8 9 10
xvii	The Conclave succeeds through strong leadership	1 2 3 4 5 6 7 8 9 10
xviii	By joining the Conclave, I am serving the public	1 2 3 4 5 6 7 8 9 10
xix	By joining the Conclave, I have become an important public figure	1 2 3 4 5 6 7 8 9 10
xx	When I travel back or forward in time, I feel that the eyes of everyone are on me	1 2 3 4 5 6 7 8 9 10
xxi	I have enough to do without worrying about people in destination timelines	1 2 3 4 5 6 7 8 9 10
xxii	I dislike time travelling unless I know I am going to be made welcome on arrival	1 2 3 4 5 6 7 8 9 10
xxiii	I believe I have much to teach people in other time periods	1 2 3 4 5 6 7 8 9 10
xxiv	Before time travelling I set myself significant goals	1 2 3 4 5 6 7 8 9 10
xxv	Time travelling is valuable to me because it gives me autonomy	1 2 3 4 5 6 7 8 9 10
xxvi	Time travelling disturbs me because I feel less autonomous	1 2 3 4 5 6 7 8 9 10
xxvii	My way of thinking is unconventional for my own time	1 2 3 4 5 6 7 8 9 10.
xxviii	No matter the time period, I express myself well	1 2 3 4 5 6 7 8 9 10

xxix	I have a great appreciation for the aesthetic	1 2 3 4 5 6 7 8 9 10
xxx	At times of frustration I persevere	1 2 3 4 5 6 7 8 9 10
xxxi	My leadership qualities make me an ideal time traveller	1 2 3 4 5 6 7 8 9 10
xxxii	People in other time periods are always happy to follow my lead	1 2 3 4 5 6 7 8 9 10
xxxiii	It would be terrible to have my authority undermined while time travelling	1 2 3 4 5 6 7 8 9 10
xxxiv	I would not return to a time period where I had been humiliated	1 2 3 4 5 6 7 8 9 10
xxxv	I enjoy the time periods most where my social status matches my self-image	1 2 3 4 5 6 7 8 9 10
xxxvi	I enjoy time periods that make me question my assumptions	1 2 3 4 5 6 7 8 9 10
xxxvii	It's not wise to share secrets while time travelling	1 2 3 4 5 6 7 8 9 10
xxxviii	The first priority in any period is to get important people on your side	1 2 3 4 5 6 7 8 9 10
xxxix	I protect my reputation in other time periods by not sharing much about myself	1 2 3 4 5 6 7 8 9 10
xl	It is important while time travelling to avoid dangerous situations	1 2 3 4 5 6 7 8 9 10
xli	Time travelling offers unrivalled opportunities for revenge	1 2 3 4 5 6 7 8 9 10
xlii	Most successful time travellers are moral people	1 2 3 4 5 6 7 8 9 10
xliii	I wait for the right time to get back at people	1 2 3 4 5 6 7 8 9 10
xliv	Most time travellers don't work hard unless they're made to	1 2 3 4 5 6 7 8 9 10

| xlv | Some people are just superior to others | 1 2 3 4 5 6 7 8 9 10 |
| xlvi | I get bored hanging round with ordinary people from my own time | 1 2 3 4 5 6 7 8 9 10 |

Reference: Joyce, S. (2020). 'Leadership qualities among time travel recruits'. *The Psychology of Time Travel*. 60 (3), 14–25.

Dream Symbol Inventory (DSI)

Indicate any symbols which were present in your dreams over the past week.

i	The dreamer confesses to murder and is unharmed by execution	Yes / No / Don't recall
ii	The dreamer hears a list of their sins on the radio	Yes / No / Don't recall
iii	The dreamer prevents their body from decomposing by reciting radio transmissions	Yes / No / Don't recall
iv	Unattended babies are found in a time machine	Yes / No / Don't recall
v	Corpses are found in a time machine	Yes / No / Don't recall
vi	God is found in a time machine	Yes / No / Don't recall
vii	The dreamer's teeth fall out in a new timeline	Yes / No / Don't recall
viii	The dreamer can't find lavatories in a new timeline	Yes / No / Don't recall
ix	The dreamer is suddenly naked in a new timeline	Yes / No / Don't recall
x	A time machine takes the dreamer to heaven	Yes / No / Don't recall
xi	A time machine takes the dreamer to hell	Yes / No / Don't recall
xii	A time machine takes the dreamer to the moon	Yes / No / Don't recall
xiii	A time machine takes the dreamer under the sea	Yes / No / Don't recall

xiv	A time machine takes the dreamer to the town of their childhood	Yes / No / Don't recall
xv	A time machine takes the dreamer to the suburbs	Yes / No / Don't recall
xvi	A time machine takes the dreamer to the forests	Yes / No / Don't recall
xvii	Doctors cut the dreamer open and find a time machine where their heart should be	Yes / No / Don't recall
xviii	Doctors cut the dreamer open and find a time machine where their brain should be	Yes / No / Don't recall
xix	Doctors cut the dreamer open and find a time machine where their womb should be	Yes / No / Don't recall
xx	Circles appear in the form of rings, wheels, cogs, crowns, suns, eyes, lassos, hoops, etc	Yes / No / Don't recall
xxi	Missiles appear in the form of arrows, spears, bullets, cannon balls, grenades and shells	Yes / No / Don't recall
xxii	Running water appears in the form of gushing taps, rainfall, canals, rivers and streams	Yes / No / Don't recall
xxiii	A time traveller is reformed by falling in love with a body of moving water	Yes / No / Don't recall
xxiv	A time traveller is reformed by falling in love with a newly found star	Yes / No / Don't recall
xxv	A time traveller is reformed by falling in love with an atroposium explosion	Yes / No / Don't recall
xxvi	A time traveller talks to their lover through a hole in the ground	Yes / No / Don't recall

xxvii	A time traveller talks to their lover through a hole in the air	Yes / No / Don't recall
xxviii	A time traveller talks to their lover through an electric socket	Yes / No / Don't recall
xxix	The dreamer uses time machines as shipping containers. Cargo is lost to the past	Yes / No / Don't recall
xxx	The dreamer uses time machines as rooms in a mansion. Guests are lost to the past	Yes / No / Don't recall
xxxi	The dreamer uses a time machine as a church. The congregation is lost to the past	Yes / No / Don't recall
xxxii	The time traveller sees a future city burning with all of its inhabitants	Yes / No / Don't recall
xxxiii	The time traveller sees the oceans boiling from the future country's coasts	Yes / No / Don't recall
xxxiv	The time traveller sees earth crack open from one future border to another	Yes / No / Don't recall
xxxv	The time traveller sees the future sky glow in neon greens and yellow and pink	Yes / No / Don't recall
xxxvi	The time traveller sees the world's animals perish, two by two	Yes / No / Don't recall
xxxvii	The time traveller sees birds fall dead from the sky	Yes / No / Don't recall
xxxviii	The time traveller sees buildings flee from cities, dragging foundations behind them	Yes / No / Don't recall
xxxix	The time traveller sees a god with eyes likes flames and feet in a burning furnace	Yes / No / Don't recall
xl	The time traveller sees a god with seven stars in his right hand	Yes / No / Don't recall

xli	The time traveller sees a god with a sharp two edged sword in his mouth	Yes / No / Don't recall
xlii	The time traveller sees a door into heaven and a god of jasper	Yes / No / Don't recall
xliii	The time traveller sees an emerald throne encircled by a rainbow	Yes / No / Don't recall
xliv	The time traveller sees a sea of glass and creatures full of eyes before and behind	Yes / No / Don't recall
xlv	The time traveller sees a lion, a calf, an eagle, and a creature with the face of a man	Yes / No / Don't recall
xlvi	The time traveller sees an angel clothed in clouds, his right foot on sea, his left on earth	Yes / No / Don't recall
xlvii	The time traveller hears a voice say that time will be no longer	Yes / No / Don't recall

Reference: Joyce, S. (August 2020). 'The development of a Dream Symbol Inventory (DSI) for time travellers.' *Freudian Journal of Time Travel*. 20 (2). 17–25.

Acknowledgements

During my research for the pioneers' world, two physics essays in particular were helpful: 'Cauchy Problem in Spacetimes with Closed Timelike Curves' (1990), by J. Friedman et al; and 'Physical Effects in Wormholes and Time Machines' (1993), by V. Frolov and I. Novikov.

The Society of Authors, as the Literary Representative of the Estate of John Masefield, granted permission to quote from *The Box of Delights*.

In 2015, when I was first tentatively developing the story of a time-travelling grandmother, I attended a taught retreat led by Shelley Harris and Stephanie Butland. They insisted the idea was worth pursuing. I also received helpful early feedback from my fellow retreaters – especially Allen Young, who beta-read the first draft.

Many people gave me invaluable moral support during redrafts. Richard Beard has been an ongoing source of professional advice; I appreciated his reassuring and authoritative replies to my emails. Writing a book involves quite a lot of grumpiness (at least the way I do it), and my friend Tracy King deserves special mention for listening to me complain. I also benefited from the encouragement of my family – Louise, Laurence, Sophie, Milo, William, Lynne, Dave, Charlotte and Gary. My mother Patricia and my cousin Alice were kind enough to answer my questions about Seychelles. And I am lucky to be married to Matthew, who provided emotional labour and plot solutions with aplomb.

Finally, thank you to Oli Munson at A. M. Heath, and Madeleine O'Shea at Head of Zeus, for supporting this book with such heart. My work has improved immeasurably in their hands.